The Sound of Drowning

KATHERINE FLEET

PAGE STREET
PUBLISHING CO.

PAGE STREET
PUBLISHING CO.

To Jacob, Liz, and Connor—
for supporting me, making me laugh,
and teaching me something new every day.

Chapter One

The sun hung low over the Pamlico Sound, a vivid smudge of orange against a watercolor sky. If I'd been a tourist, I'd have snapped a million pictures, seeking that perfect image to post on social media with some cheesy caption about the beauty of life.

Instead, I adjusted my earbuds and jammed my hands deep in the pockets of my hoodie. In early April, it should've been warmer, but even the local weatherman was stumped by this cold spell. With every exhale, my breath formed a small, wispy cloud, easily claimed by the wind. I leaned against the ferry railing and tried to ignore the chill worming its way through the denim of my jeans.

Watching the sunset over the sound—the wide expanse of

salt water separating my island from the North Carolina mainland—used to be my favorite thing. It made me feel like anything was possible.

Now, I just felt alone, bitter, cold.

It didn't make any sense. The ocean wasn't alive. It couldn't do anything to me personally, but that's how I felt. Like it had betrayed me.

If I had a choice, I'd steer clear of it for the rest of my life, but I lived on Ocracoke, one of the southernmost islands of the Outer Banks. Avoiding the ocean was like making a New Year's resolution to quit junk food and exercise every day. Eventually you found yourself back on the couch, eating Oreos and binge-watching TV shows.

A flock of seagulls screeched overhead. I twisted up the volume on my iPod until the husky voice of my favorite indie singer drowned out the ferry's engine and the constant roar of wind and waves.

Just a little while longer.

I inhaled, lifting my chin to the wind. The music may have blocked out the sound of the ocean, but nothing could block out the salty, tangy smell. Living on the Outer Banks, that smell permeated every part of my life—my clothes, my house, every good memory, and every bad one.

Under my feet, the engine vibrations changed. We were close to shore.

I left the railing and squeezed through a couple of parked cars, stopping next to my bright red scooter—a surprise birthday gift from my parents, from back when they still had a daughter they could be proud of.

Climbing on the seat, I rubbed life into my frozen fingers. Ahead, someone appeared between the vehicles. It was Henry—one of the few people in the world I liked. He'd worked as a deckhand on the Ocracoke-to-Hatteras ferry for as long as I could remember.

His weathered face lit up. "Mer." The wind lifted a patch of his gray hair and set it back out of place. Not that he seemed to care. "My favorite passenger."

"I'll bet you say that to all the girls."

"Nope. I just have a soft spot for the ones who scowl at everything for no reason."

A smile tugged at the corners of my lips. "Ah, Henry, you're such a charmer. How is it that some frisky lady at the seniors' home hasn't snapped you up yet?"

He winked. "Who's to say they haven't?"

"If you had a hot date, I want to hear all about it."

"I'll tell you what . . . " He shrugged inside his heavy jacket. At least he was smart enough to dress for the unseasonable weather. "I'll tell you, if you spill the name of the feller you've been meeting over on Hatteras."

Whoa. Conversation whiplash. I swallowed and looked away.

"There's no guy. Just a boring job at the arcade."

"Yeah, right. You get on this ferry at night, looking all flushed and dreamy." He rolled his eyes and made a pouty expression. "Never saw pinball games affect anyone that way."

"The fact you assume they're all pinball games shows your age, and I do not look like that." My eyes narrowed. "Not ever."

"Sure you do."

"The next time you go to the doctor, you need to get your vision checked."

"There's nothing wrong with my eyesight." He leaned against a nearby truck, his face turning serious. He squinted against the last of the daylight. "I just hope whoever you're seeing is good enough for you. Underneath all this"—he waved his hand in the general direction of my ripped jeans, black hoodie, and the purple streaks of hair mixed in with my own black strands—"there's a good girl. You need a boy with a big heart and a mind of his own, a boy who'll challenge you."

I snorted. "Even if a boy like that existed, I'm not sure I'd deserve him."

I said the words without thinking. They were true, but they hurtled forward, straight into a gaping void of awkward silence.

Damn.

Henry stared at me, his eyes almost lost in the folds of his weathered skin, but I still found the mixture of sadness and pity hiding there. I'd seen it so many times over the last few months, it was hard not to recognize. My fingers curled into fists, and I slowly exhaled. If I never saw that look again, it'd be too soon.

Henry straightened, looking uncomfortable. The Outer Banks bred tough old men who didn't express their feelings easily. "Mer, if there's anything I can do, you'd tell me, right?"

"I'm fine," I lied. "Everything's great."

"Well, good then." He rubbed one hand across his chin. "We're almost at Hatteras. Guess I'll be seeing you again later tonight?"

"Yeah. Later." I plucked my helmet from the back of the scooter, tugged it on, and fired up the engine, avoiding the lingering questions in his gaze.

My heel bounced as I waited for the ferry to finish docking. After a few minutes, Henry gave me the signal, and I drove straight off, passing the Hatteras terminal. Unlike the tiny landing on Ocracoke, this one had shops and stores, and people normally milled around. Tonight, though, it was strangely deserted. Everyone must've decided it was too damn cold to be out.

I worked the scooter up to the speed limit, fast enough for the brisk evening air to make my eyes water. The highway headed northeast, away from the last of the twilight sky. By the time I reached the small road leading to the right spot on the beach, it was fully night. The sky stretched from horizon to horizon, inky black and a perfect contrast to the brightness of the constellations. I knew many by heart: Cassiopeia, Cygnus, Orion, Ursa

Major, Ursa Minor. I'd learned most of them from my dad. On warm summer evenings, we'd float together on our windsurfing boards. He'd tell me stories about all the places he'd traveled before he met my mom, and I'd tell him about all the things I wanted to see and do when I grew up. My dad, the optimist, believed we could be that way again, but I knew it would never be the same.

I parked at the end of the road and climbed off, my backpack slung over one shoulder. On the edge of the dune, blocking out the stars, he waited for me.

Ben.

My bag slipped. I sprinted forward and crashed into his chest. His arms circled around me, steadying me. I pressed my face against his flannel jacket and inhaled his scent—warm, salty, familiar.

"You're late. I thought you weren't coming," he said, his low voice trailing past my ear.

My chest tightened. I leaned back, keeping my arms around him. "I promised, didn't I?"

He didn't respond, his expression hidden by the shadows of the night. I pulled his head down until our foreheads met.

"You still don't trust me?"

His shoulders stiffened. If he doubted my promise, it was my fault. I'd lied to him once—the kind of lie you couldn't recover from. Only somehow, he'd given me this second chance.

"You know I trust you." His breath fanned my face. "I wouldn't wait here on this freezing beach for you every night if I didn't, but I still worry when you're late."

"I'm sorry." I used to be a punctual person, but it seemed like I was always late these days, no matter how hard I tried. "I wouldn't blame you if you left, but you always wait."

"Only because I have nowhere better to be." His cool lips brushed my forehead, and I looked up at him. His eyes crinkled at the corners. "And maybe because I like you . . . a little."

"Hey." I smacked him on the chest, then tugged him closer, pushing my hips against his. I buried my fingertips in the dark hair at the base of his neck. "Just a little?"

"Okay, maybe a lot." He chuckled in my ear, opening his flannel jacket and scooping me inside. "I love you, Mer."

His words surrounded me, like the warmth of the jacket he'd wrapped us in. They anchored me, seeping into all the cold, dim places I tried to hide from him. "Me, too," I whispered.

But my feelings for him were so much bigger than words. People didn't understand. Because I was only seventeen and Ben was eighteen, they figured we couldn't possibly understand real love. Sure, we could feel love for family and friends, but somehow adults believed that true romantic love was reserved for them. That we needed to be able to legally vote or drink before we could understand what we felt. But Ben and I were different. We'd always been different.

My lips found his neck, then his jaw, working their way up. When I reached the corner of his mouth, he sighed and captured mine back. I closed my eyes and welcomed the heat of his kiss, sweet and familiar, like curling up in my favorite blanket on a cold night. It was amazing how one kiss could erase all my doubts and make everything feel right again.

We broke apart, and I tucked my face into his neck, letting his solid presence block the wind off the ocean.

He caught my hands against his chest. "You're freezing. Where are your gloves? Why aren't you wearing a jacket?"

I huddled closer. "It's a matter of principle. I shouldn't have to bundle up in April."

"So you're taking on the weather now?" He blew on my fingers, warming them up between his callused hands. "Like that time you took on Santa at the mall."

I pushed away from him and groaned. "That was ten years ago, and I was just trying to prove he wasn't the real Santa."

"By punching him in the gut?" He tugged my hair and grinned.

"To prove it was padding." I tried to catch his hand, but he was quicker. "How was I supposed to know that part wasn't fake?"

"You got us all kicked out of the mall. I never even got to sit on his knee. You still owe me for that."

"After ten years?" I cocked an eyebrow. "I think it's time to move on."

He suddenly crouched, an evil glint in his expression. I turned to run, but he lunged forward. His shoulder dug into my belly, and next thing, I was spinning in a circle, five feet off the ground.

"Ah!" I squealed and smacked his back, but he whirled me faster. "Enough. Stop."

He set me down on the sand, and I stumbled into him. "Okay," I said, panting, "we're even now."

He swooped up my backpack in one hand. "Maybe if you let me sit on your knee."

"Yeah, right." I jumped on his back, and he hooked his arms under my legs. "You'd crush me." I snuggled my cheek against the warm flannel of his jacket and hung on while his long strides carried us to our spot.

It was a small nook between the dunes that gave some shelter from the wind. We'd claimed it years earlier, back when we were still kids, burying each other in the sand and gorging on Twizzlers until we both got sick. It was partway between his house on Hatteras and my house on Ocracoke. We'd never gone to the same school, but our mothers had been best friends, so we'd always had the weekends together.

Now, they didn't even speak to each other.

I slid to the ground and tugged my backpack from his hand. "But if you're good, I'll sit on your knee."

He waggled his eyebrows. "I'll be so good. Scout's honor."

"That would mean more if you'd actually been a Scout."

I pulled out a battery-powered lantern and a blanket. Together, we shook it out and spread it across the sand. He stretched out, propped up on one elbow, and I sat cross-legged facing him, with the lantern between us. In the fluorescent glow, I cataloged his familiar features. If I stared long enough, I could still find the skinny, dark-haired kid who'd taught me how to tie my shoes. He'd filled out over the years, but his brown eyes still held the same solid goodness. They still lit up when he teased me out of a funk.

He grinned, his hair curling over his forehead. "Like what you see?"

"Yeah." I boldly met his stare, until he flushed and looked away. I smirked, loving that I could make him squirm.

"So, what do you have planned for us tonight?"

"Ugh. You make me sound like the activity coordinator on a cruise ship, but I did bring this." I reached into my backpack and pulled out a harmonica.

"Wait, you're learning a musical instrument?" He stretched out his hand, and I surrendered it for his inspection. "Did hell freeze over?"

"No. I just wanted to try something new." Something to occupy the long hours when I couldn't be with him.

He shot me a skeptical look and handed it back. "I'm just remembering that poor flute."

This time, I blushed. My mom forced me to take flute lessons in middle school, claiming that I needed to broaden my interests.

Since I spent so much time listening to music, she decided I'd like playing it, too. I told her classical flute wasn't my thing, but she signed me up for lessons anyway. So I threw the stupid instrument on the ground and rode over it with my bike . . . multiple times. When Mom found out, she threatened to ban me from the ocean for a full month, but Ben saw how upset I was and told my mom that he ran over it with his bike. My punishment was miraculously lifted.

Ben had always looked out for me like that, even when I didn't deserve it. Maybe that's why his mom started seeing me as a bad influence.

"Hey." Ben's voice recaptured my attention. "You okay?"

The seriousness in his gaze held me prisoner. The wind lifted the corners of the blanket and my breath caught. I used to see my future in his eyes. More than anything, I wanted to see that again, to know that despite everything that had happened, we still stood a chance.

I looked away, swallowing back my dark thoughts and spinning the harmonica in my hand. "Yeah."

"Good." He rolled onto his back, stretching his arms up and linking his fingers under his head. "Because I'm ready for my personal Meredith Hall concert now, and if I'm not impressed, I expect a full refund."

I gave Ben a small smile. He was trying to lighten my mood, but tonight my worries hovered like thick fog on the horizon, impossible for even Ben to fully dissipate it. So, I lifted my harmonica and started to play. Sad notes drifted across the beach, mingling with the sound of the waves. The light from our lantern gradually gave way to the inky darkness of the night. In front of me, Ben's lips went from a smile to a grimace, and he threw his hands against his ears.

I stopped playing. "What's wrong?"

"No offense, Mer, but that was terrible. Maybe you're holding it backward."

"Gee, thanks. I'm not a complete idiot." I glared at the instrument, then chucked it at my backpack. "Stupid thing."

Ben snorted. "Maybe you should run over it with your scooter."

I considered it, but instead I lay down in the curve of his arm. He pulled the edge of the blanket around us. My hand spread out across his chest, and I tapped my finger in time to his heartbeats—solid and reassuring.

"You seem gloomy." His words rumbled under my cheek.

"I'm always gloomy. It's because of that stupid rain cloud that follows me around."

Ben laughed. "More gloomy than usual then." He brushed the hair from my forehead, his touch as soft and tentative as his words. "It's grown out again. I like it."

I focused on the stars above us.

Four months ago, I'd stood in my bathroom and chopped at

my long hair until there was hardly anything left. That night, I jammed my hands in my mouth to keep from screaming. I buried my face in a towel, but the sobs still tore my chest apart. I wanted to rip the skin from my body, but instead I sneaked out and rode into the night. I ended up here on the beach, at our spot, lost in the darkest of thoughts. I wanted it all to end—the pain and guilt, the weight of everyone's disappointment.

That's when Ben found me—the boy who'd been my best friend since we'd both been in diapers, the boy who'd escorted me to my very first school dance, the boy I'd daydreamed about marrying one day, and the boy I'd broken with my lies. After everything I'd done to us, his presence was a miracle, my miracle. I didn't deserve him anymore, but I needed him anyway.

For months since he found me, we'd met in secret. He'd become my lifeline, and I liked to think that maybe I'd become his.

Now, my hair was long enough to brush the collar of my shirt, and I'd learned to breathe again. I'd started to feel.

Ben's hand stilled. "Tell me what's wrong."

I scraped my teeth across my lip, welcoming the momentary pain. I'd already learned the consequences of not trusting Ben. I'd learned that he'd always have my back, even when I didn't have his. So why was my belly tightened into a hard knot?

I just needed to get it over with.

"This." I pulled the folded paper from my pocket and slapped it against his chest. He grabbed at it, playing tug-of-war with the wind that was fighting to carry it into the night. I almost wished he'd lost.

He sat up and unfolded the letter, then leaned closer to the lantern and scanned the invitation. A year ago, getting that letter would have been the single most amazing thing for me. Now, it was just a cruel and ironic reminder of all the things I couldn't have.

His gaze lifted to meet mine. "Mer, this is amazing. They're going to sponsor you to compete in the PWA World Tour events in Europe this summer."

It was more than amazing. It represented all the things I'd dreamed of doing: professional windsurfing, competing, traveling.

I snatched the letter from his fingers and stuffed it back in my pocket.

Ben frowned. "Mer—"

"I'm not going." I folded my arms, afraid he'd notice how badly my hands shook.

"But this is your dream. You've talked about it for years. You have the event posters plastered all over your bedroom walls."

My gaze flickered across his face, before falling to my lap. "I had them on my wall, and now I don't." A fact he'd have known if things were different. "I'm not traveling halfway around the world to compete when I can't even climb on a board in my own backyard."

Somehow Ben's silence was more deafening than the roar of the waves.

He looped his hand around the drawstring of my hoodie. "Can't or won't?"

"Does it matter? The end result is the same."

His dark eyes glittered in the glow of the lantern. "Of course it matters. You love windsurfing. It makes you happy. I get that you're scared, but you can't just quit."

"Why not?" I swallowed back an unexpected bitter taste. If the situation were reversed, I had no doubt Ben would conquer his fears. "Maybe I'm okay with just pretending I never got this letter."

"What did your dad say?"

"I didn't tell him, and I'm not going to."

"Come on, Mer. This isn't right. Maybe if you talked about it, it would help."

My spine stiffened. Ben's words sounded too much like the therapist my parents had taken me to after the "incident" back in October. I was mostly fine now. I'd been mostly fine ever since I'd found Ben on the beach and he'd forgiven me. It was just this whole ocean thing that still tripped me up, but I figured lots of people lived with phobias and still had full and happy lives.

My gaze wandered over his shoulder. Just beyond the sand, the ocean pounded the shore—continuous, relentless, vast, cold. I managed to ride the ferry, ignoring the pit in my stomach and the taste in my mouth. I also tolerated the beach, but wading into the waves with no protection other than my wetsuit and my board wasn't something I could do. Not anymore. And if I was resigned to my new relationship with the ocean, everyone else needed to accept it, too.

"That's why you showed me the letter, right? So we could talk about it?"

"No. I showed you the letter because I don't want secrets between us anymore, and I was hoping you'd support my decision."

He grunted. "So you wanted me to blindly agree with you?"

"No." I stuffed my hands into the pockets of my hoodie. "I wanted you to be on my side."

"Mer, I'm always on your side. I always have been." He tugged on my drawstring, tipping me closer. "Is this because of us? Don't give up on your dreams because I can't go. We already talked about it. You can travel and compete, but then you'll come back here . . . to me."

I pulled away. How could he really not understand? "We talked about it before everything changed. But this is not about you. It's about me. If I want to quit windsurfing, it's my decision."

I sprang to my feet, yanked up my hood, and paced the beach, my sneakers sinking into the sand. I should have thrown the letter away.

"Hey." Ben caught my shoulders and spun me around. "What's going on?"

My thoughts and feelings were jumbled. Ben was supposed to make me feel anchored and safe. He brought out the good parts in me, not this anger and uncertainty. I struggled to calm my breathing. "I don't want to fight," I mumbled into the cold night air.

He folded his arms around me. "I'm sorry. I shouldn't have pushed."

I released my breath. This was Ben. My Ben.

The wind tugged at us, forcing us to sway in its cold embrace.

"I just want things to be different," Ben whispered. "If things could just go back to the way they were, I could really be there for you. You deserve more than this."

"You are here for me . . . right now." I clung to him, my hands tunneling under his shirt and stealing his warmth. "I was a wreck before you came back. You brought me back to life, so I'll take whatever you can give."

We stood like that for a long time, tangled in each other's arms, lost in each other's doubts and uncertainties. Finally, he lifted his head. He glanced at his watch and I knew.

"I have to go now. Will I see you tomorrow night?"

"I don't think so." My chest tightened at his disappointed look. "The forecast is calling for wind and rain again. Seems to be all we get lately. When's the sun going to show up?"

He nodded and his mouth tightened. "The day after, then?"

"Yes." I reached up on my toes and kissed him, breathing in his goodness and strength. Fighting with Ben scared me. I'd lost him once and discovered the awful reality: I didn't know how to be happy without him.

"Mer," he whispered against my lips, "I'll always like you best. You know that, right?"

He released me, and I nodded and sank back down on my heels. The cold immediately claimed all the places his touch had warmed.

I closed my eyes. I couldn't watch him walk away. If I did, I'd want to follow him, but this arrangement only worked if we both played by the rules. So I dug my heels into the sand and stayed put. I could do this. I could be alone until I saw him again.

When I opened my eyes, the beach was empty. I sat on the blanket and found my harmonica. Who cared if I was a sucky player? I played anyway, because there was no one listening.

Closing my eyes, I remembered the very first time Ben promised to always like me best.

Chapter Two

I pulled at a rock buried among the tall grass at the edge of our yard, the part my dad never mowed. It let go, and I fell back on my bum. Ben laughed, but I didn't care.

I leaned over the small dent in the earth and grinned. "Found three. I'm winning."

"No, you're not. You've found more in your yard, but I already had a bucketful from my house." Ben dropped to his knees next to me, and we carefully put the worms in the plastic container Aunt Lila had given him.

I called her Aunt Lila, even though she wasn't really my aunt. But Aunt Lila and my mom were best friends, so it seemed strange for me to call her Mrs. Collins. At least, that's what my mom told me.

Ben had punched holes in the container's cover so the worms

could breathe. Once we caught enough, we'd talk Uncle Al into taking us fishing.

We put the last worm in, and Ben screwed the cover on. I held up the container and stared at the squirming, wriggling bodies through the clear plastic. Touching them had been kind of gross, not that I'd ever tell Ben that. I didn't want him thinking I was a baby just because I was five and he was already six.

"Do we have enough yet?" I looked at Ben through the plastic and laughed. It made his face look big.

"Yeah, maybe. Let's swing."

"I'll race you." Holding the container tight to my chest, I ran to the other side of the yard where Dad had hung a rope hammock between two trees. Somehow, I beat Ben, even though he was a faster runner. I set the worms down on the grass and narrowed my eyes.

"Did you let me win?"

He flopped down on the hammock. "Nah. I just didn't want to race."

I jumped on next to him, and the hammock curled around us. For a minute, our arms and legs tangled. My elbow got him right in the eye.

"Ow."

"Sorry. Lay your head that way, and I'll go this way."

We settled with our heads on opposite ends, his tanned bare legs next to my arm. He let one foot dangle off, pushing us with his toes in the grass while he stared up at the clouds. For a while, we swung in silence. A butterfly landed on a leaf behind Ben's head, and I watched it.

"Hey, I know a secret."

I pushed to my elbows and stared at him. "What secret?"

"I don't know if I'm allowed to tell you."

I kicked his shoulder with my bare toes. "We're best friends. You've got to tell me."

"Okay, fine. I'll tell you, but you can't tell anyone else."

I drew two lines across my chest. "Cross my heart and hope to die."

He looked around the yard, like he was making sure we were alone. "My mom and dad are taking me to Disney World for a whole week. I think it's supposed to be a surprise, but I heard them talking."

Disney World. Shoot. I'd always wanted to go there. Something twisted in my belly. I was supposed to be happy for Ben, but I wanted to go, too.

"You don't believe me." He looked hurt.

"No. I believe you. That's so cool."

"Maybe you could come, too. You could ask your mom and dad."

I stared down at my hands. "We can't. Dad has to work all summer because that's when the tourists with the money come." At least, that's what he was always saying.

"Then I'll bring you back something."

"For real?"

He nodded.

"I'd like that." He was the best friend ever. "I have a secret, too, but you can't tell anyone."

Ben crossed his finger over his chest. "Promise."

"My mom's having a baby. I'm going to have a brother or sister."

Ben sat up. "Hey, that's way cooler than a trip to Disney World! I always wanted a brother or a sister."

Only it wasn't cooler than a trip to Disney World. A baby would change everything, the kids at school explained to me. A new baby meant my mom and dad wouldn't have time for me anymore. They'd only have time to take care of the baby because all they did was cry and poop and eat. My eyes burned, and I looked away. I couldn't let Ben see me crying.

Of course, he saw anyway. "What's wrong?"

I wiped at my eyes with the back of my hand. "What if they like this new baby more than me?"

"That's just stupid. Of course they'll still like you best. You were here first."

"But what if they don't?"

Ben held up his pinkie, and I hooked mine in his. Our eyes met. Mine were blue, but his were darker than the ground we'd just been digging in. "I promise that no matter what happens, I will always like you best."

Just like that, my fears disappeared.

My harmonica playing ended, but I kept my eyes closed, trying to hang on to that feeling of Ben's presence—the feeling of being with a person who somehow sees past all the bleak parts of you to find the tiny shards of light hiding underneath.

Cold water hit my face.

What the hell? My eyes snapped open.

A guy stood over me in the dark, a black wetsuit hugging his lean body and a kayak dragging behind him. He looked to be my age, maybe a little older. Wet hair hung over his eyes, and he brushed it aside, showering me with more of the ocean.

"Jesus, when I saw your lamp and heard that god-awful music, I thought this damn kayak thing had actually killed me." A twang accompanied his words, nothing like the Outer Banks brogue I was used to. "Now I see you sitting here, hot as hell, and I figure my mama was right when she told me I'd never make it into heaven."

I blinked. This guy couldn't be for real.

He stuck out his hand and more water dripped on me. His long fingers looked real enough. "I'm Wyatt Quinn."

Wyatt? His name belonged in some old-fashioned western.

I didn't move, and he eventually dropped his hand and shrugged. "Where I'm from in Texas, we shake hands when we introduce ourselves. Must be different up here."

His sarcasm blinked at me like a glaring neon sign.

I swallowed. "I'm Meredith . . . Meredith Hall."

"Ah, she speaks." He plopped down on the edge of my

blanket. "I don't mean to sound dramatic, but you just saved my life, Meredith."

"Mer." I pulled my legs up to my chest.

He looked over at me. "Huh?"

"I prefer Mer."

"The French word for the sea? Kind of appropriate, given the circumstances."

His face was lean, like his body. His cheekbones were sharp, and his eyes were light, the color hard to determine in the unnatural glow of the lamp—maybe green. His wet hair was longish and plastered to his skull. Maybe I should have been afraid, but he didn't look like an ax murderer, more like a whole boatload of cocky arrogance.

I pulled my scattered thoughts together. So far, I'd been sitting here like a bump on a log while his smart mouth danced circles around me. "How exactly did I save your life?"

He kicked the kayak, sending up a small spray of sand. "I decided to take this deathtrap for a spin, but then it got dark and this whole damn shoreline looked the same. I couldn't find the spot where I parked my truck. So I've been paddling back and forth, freezing my ass off and looking for signs of life. Then like a miracle from heaven, I saw your light and heard your playing. At first, I thought I was back in Texas, but the playing sounded more like a choir of dying cats. So then I got to thinking that maybe I was just plain dead."

I lifted an eyebrow and slipped the harmonica in my backpack. Ben was right—I needed to run over it with my scooter. "That's a little dramatic, isn't it?"

He shrugged and grinned. "Maybe, but it makes for one hell of a story, right? For years, I'll be able to tell people about the night the ocean almost claimed its next victim, but I was saved by a purple-haired girl with sketchy harmonica skills. I mean, I couldn't make this shit up if I tried."

Man, this guy was so full of bullshit, I was surprised he didn't sink the kayak. I pushed to my feet.

"Wait . . . " He stared up at me. "What'd I say?"

"If I have to explain it to you, it's a lost cause." I reached down and tugged on the blanket, but his corner wouldn't budge. "Get off."

He lifted one side of his butt, and the blanket sprang free. "Look, it seems we got off on the wrong foot. They say a horse needs time to get to know you before you try riding it. Maybe I rushed things."

My mouth fell open. "I am not a horse, and you will never get to . . . ride me."

"Wow." He whistled low under his breath. "There's no need to get all uppity. You're the one who refused to shake hands, and in Texas, a horse is a very valued thing. You should be flattered."

I threw my head back and glared at the stars. If this was some kind of cosmic joke, the universe had a piss-poor sense of humor.

I opened my mouth to tell him where he could stick his horse compliments, but he was talking again.

"Look, I'm kind of stuck here, and I need help. So as much as it pains me 'cause I'm feeling like the wronged party, I apologize for whatever I did or said that pissed you off."

It was the most roundabout, backward apology I'd ever heard, but the hint of desperation in his words made me stop and really look at him. His whole body was shaking like one of those vibrating massage chairs they sell at the mall. In the lamplight, his skin looked almost gray and his lips a definite shade of blue. My mouth tightened, and I swallowed back every snarky response clamoring to escape.

"Here." I dropped the blanket around his shoulders, and he clung to it, letting out a long, low sigh, interrupted by teeth chattering.

He closed his eyes, and I hovered, not liking the uncertainty flowing through my veins. What now? But I already knew. My parents had raised me to do better. This guy may have been an arrogant jerk, but he was clearly in need of help. I glanced around the empty beach, surprisingly glad that Ben was nowhere in sight.

"Look, you'll warm up faster if you pull off the wetsuit and just use the blanket."

"Sure thing." He opened his eyes, their color still a mystery, a hint of swagger in his expression. "I make it a rule to always strip whenever a girl is doing the asking."

"Really?" I ground my foot into the sand. "I'm trying to help you here."

"Just joking. Did you lose your sense of humor in the same place you lost your harmonica-playing abilities?"

He cocked an eyebrow, and I bit back a grin. I should have been offended, but as comebacks went, he deserved some credit. Still, I didn't feel inclined to stand around and be insulted.

"Strip, don't strip, freeze to death—I don't care. I'm done." I reached for my backpack.

"Wait. Don't go. The cold is just making me cranky. Please."

The "please" part sounded sincere, so I slowly exhaled. "Fine. I'll wait."

He released the edges of the blanket and reached back for the neoprene strap on his zipper. He pulled, but it didn't budge. I shifted my weight. He tugged again. He grunted and shot me an impatient look. "I know this is pushing my luck here, but—"

I huffed and knelt down. With a couple of yanks on the strap, the zipper gave way, revealing his pale back and shoulders.

He glanced around. "Thanks."

I searched for sarcasm in his expression but found only gratitude. "Yeah. Sure."

Wyatt wriggled out of the top part of his wetsuit, and I tried not to look, but his muscles flexed and bulged with every movement. He wasn't big and solid like Ben, but there wasn't an ounce of fat on him. With his chest bare, I could count every one of his ab muscles. Not that I wanted to. I looked away and wiped my palms against my thighs. A pang of guilt curled in my belly, but I let it go. It wasn't a crime to notice something so obvious. Besides, his personality was a giant freezing shower.

A gust of wind whipped up a mini-sandstorm. It pelted my legs, and Wyatt shielded his eyes. "Jesus, I don't think I've ever been so cold."

"You're lucky you don't have hypothermia."

He staggered to his feet, the blanket wrapped around his upper body. "Maybe I do. I can't stop my teeth from knocking together." His eyebrow arched. "Isn't hypothermia the one you cure with shared body warmth?"

I shook my head. "You can't turn it off, can you?"

He shot me a not-so-innocent grin.

Digging into my backpack, I pulled out my favorite black beanie, the one I'd expropriated from Ben during a bonfire on the beach. He'd complained at first, but then I'd pulled it on, and he'd told me it looked cuter on me than it ever looked on him. We'd started kissing, and he'd never asked for it again.

"Here. You can wear this, but it's just a loan." Without giving myself time for second thoughts, I jammed it on his head. He was only a few inches taller than me, so I didn't even need to reach up like I did with Ben.

He pulled it down around his ears and huddled deeper in the blanket. Only his face stood out against the night sky.

After a long, quiet moment, his shaking subsided. He grinned at me, and I suddenly understood that he was very used to charming people. "You've already been a lifesaver, but I don't suppose it's possible to get a ride back to my truck or just to civilization? I'm guessing you have some form of transportation."

I held the lantern up between us, and he smiled again, revealing straight white teeth. I gritted mine. "I can't leave you out here to freeze to death, so I don't have much of a choice."

He held my gaze. "See . . . I'm already growing on you. What about this?" He gave his kayak another kick.

"I'll get you to your truck, and then you can come back for it. It'll be fine here for now."

"I wouldn't even care if it disappeared by the time I got back. It wasn't half as much fun as I thought it would be. Plus, I think it's leaking."

"Sounds like it's not even yours." I spun on my heel and started toward the path.

He easily caught up, his strides matching mine. "Nah, it came with the new house. I found it abandoned in the toolshed."

I skidded to a halt. "You live here?"

He stopped, too, tugging the blanket around his shoulders and cocking his head to one side. "Not here on Hatteras Island, but here on Ocracoke. Only no one warned me it'd be cold as hell with the furnace out."

My mind struggled to process his words. This swaggering

stranger, who'd compared me to a horse, was a neighbor. It didn't matter where he lived on Ocracoke; the island was so small that he had to live close by.

I forced myself into action. "Look, you can stand around and talk about the weather if you want, but I have a ferry to catch. If you're coming with me, let's go."

He looked unfazed by my sharp words. "Are you always so bossy?"

"I don't know. I normally hang out with people who have more sense than to go wandering around at night in a kayak."

"Ouch. Tell it like it is, darlin'."

"Darlin'? Really?" I fake-hurled. I lived in the Carolinas, so I knew all about the "sugars" and the "honeys," but coming from Wyatt's lips, it rubbed me the wrong way. "Do girls in Texas actually fall for this?"

He grinned like a shark in a tank full of seals. "Well, I've never had any complaints."

"That's great for you, but for future reference"—I started walking again—"I'm not your darlin'."

"I'll keep that in mind . . . for the future."

I caught the quick chuckle he tossed in my direction. He was making fun of me. I lifted my chin and kept moving.

"So, Mer, what were you doing out here anyway? Were you meeting someone?"

"No." I picked up my pace. "Why would you say that?"

"I don't know. Maybe because you were sitting on a blanket on the beach under the stars, playing a harmonica. Seemed kind of romantic."

My heart pounded. No one could know about Ben and me, especially not our parents. "Don't take this the wrong way, but that's none of your business."

"Ouch. You're a prickly thing, aren't you?"

We followed the path between the dunes, and the road came into view. "No. Just a private person, and there's nothing wrong with that." I stopped in front of my scooter, expecting a quick comeback, but when I glanced back, Wyatt just stared, a horrified look on his face. "What's wrong?" I lifted the seat and stowed my bag and lantern in the storage compartment underneath. "You've never ridden on a motorcycle?"

"Darlin' . . . I mean Mer, that's no motorcycle. That's a bicycle with a hamster wheel under the hood. And I'm not afraid of driving a motorcycle. I'm just afraid of sitting on the back and trusting another driver with my life, no matter how pretty she is."

I tugged on my helmet and climbed on. "Well, first, a girl's looks have nothing to do with her driving abilities." I started it up. "And second, I'm not letting you drive Sally."

"Sally?" he yelled, still frowning.

"Yeah, Sally the Scooter. So you can either get on or walk to your truck, because I was supposed to make the eleven o'clock ferry. Now, we'll be lucky to make the midnight crossing."

He mumbled something and stumbled forward. Hiking the blanket up, he swung his leg over. His chest bumped against my back. His thighs pressed against mine. I scooted forward on the seat, but he was still there—right behind me, too close for comfort.

"There's nothing to hang on to," he shouted in my ear.

I tightened my grip on the handles, understanding exactly what he was asking. "You can hang on to me."

His arms came around my waist, and I tried to relax. Being this close to Wyatt was no big deal. I was only giving him a ride. I'd just pretend it was Ben. Only Wyatt's closeness felt nothing like the solid, comforting presence of Ben. Concentrating on the road, I drove back to the main highway and turned north, away from the ferry.

"How do you know where to find my truck?" Wyatt yelled.

Because over the years, I've explored every inch of Hatteras and Ocracoke with Ben and our families.

"Trust me," I shouted back.

In the glow from my headlamp, the yellow dotted line passed by, the road feeling desolate this late at night. The cold easily penetrated my hoodie. Wyatt's hands tightened on my waist. I hated to admit it, but his presence helped with both the temperature and the loneliness.

Eventually, I put on my signal and turned off the main highway. We drove for a short distance, stopping right in front of a late-model black pickup.

I turned off the engine, the sudden silence a shock to the system. Only it wasn't complete silence. Like usual, the waves roared in the distance, the constant soundtrack of my life.

Wyatt hopped off, and I held the scooter steady between my legs.

"How did you do that? You knew right where it would be."

I waved my hands in the air. "Magic."

"Must be." He held out one corner of the blanket. "Just a sec and I'll give this back."

He stooped to pull a magnetic key box from under the truck, then opened the door and started the engine. Half hidden by the driver's door, he tugged off the bottom half of his wetsuit and pulled on sweatpants and a sweater. Frowning, he picked up a cell phone.

He approached a moment later, holding out my blanket. "Sorry. It's a little wet."

"It's fine." I rolled it up and stuffed it in the storage compartment, trying not to notice that it now smelled a little like the ocean and a lot like Wyatt—fresh laundry and warm spring breezes. "I'll take my hat back, too."

His eyes widened, and his hand flew up to his head. "Sorry. I forgot I was wearing it." He pulled it off and passed it back. "So, I realize I haven't bowled you over with my usual charm, but I need another favor. My phone's dead, and Mom's going to kill me if I don't tell her what's going on."

For a second, I didn't answer. Wyatt seemed so larger than life that I forgot he might have something as mundane as a worried parent. "Yeah, sure." I gave him my phone and tried not to eavesdrop, but it was hard when he stood two feet away.

"Hey, Mom, it's me." He ran long fingers through his still-damp hair. "I'm fine. Just had a little trouble, so I'm going to be late."

He listened for a moment and then glanced down at me.

"Sorry for making your hair turn gray, but it worked out well for me." He stuffed one hand in the pocket of his sweatpants and held my gaze. "Yeah, 'cause I was rescued by this really cool girl." My cheeks burned. Had he really just said that to his mother? "Yup. Her name is Meredith Hall, but she goes by Mer, and I think she's one of those local people you're always going on about." He listened for another moment. "I don't know. Let me ask her." He leaned away from the phone and considered me. "Mom would like to know how old you are and what grade you are in."

I choked back a snort. Really? "Seventeen. Junior."

A slow smile spread across his face—nothing good could ever come from that look. "Hear that, Mom? She's in my grade. I have officially made a friend on the island. You can now stop nagging me."

He listened to whatever his mom was saying, while I grappled with the revelation that Wyatt would be going to my school. Who switched schools in April?

"I'll be home as soon as I can. Yup . . . love you, too."

He hung up and handed me the phone. I gawked, still recovering from the emotional roller coaster of that call.

"Hello?" He waved one hand in front of my face. "Earth to Mer. What now?"

"You moved schools in April?"

He shrugged, but I saw a familiar flash of pain in his expression. How could I not recognize the look? I'd seen it a million times in the mirror. That expression, that vulnerability, wormed its way under the wall I'd built around myself, creating an unexpected twinge of sympathy for the guy.

"Mom decided she wanted a change of scenery. She's always wanted to own a coffee shop, and she loves the Outer Banks. She came here on vacation when she was a kid. If she wants to make a go of it, she needs to be up and running for the tourist season. So here we are."

He didn't mention his dad, and I didn't ask.

"But how will you manage classes and exams?"

He shrugged inside his sweater, still looking cold. "I was supposed to graduate this year, but I ended up missing most of my classes. So I've got to repeat senior year. Even though it's almost the end of the semester, everyone thought it'd be best if I hung out with the junior class for the next few weeks so I'd be ready for September. It's fine."

Despite his assurances, I couldn't imagine what it felt like—being uprooted from everything you knew and having to start over in a new school in a new state. I'd never lived anywhere but Ocracoke.

I wanted to know more, I realized. Why had he missed so much school?

He shivered. "Look, I don't mind explaining my life to you more fully, but maybe it can wait until we're someplace warm. I'm freezing my ass off here."

"Sorry." I blinked, surprised that I'd let his story distract me. "You can follow me back to the kayak."

He nodded and headed over to his truck. Halfway there, he yelled out: "Hey!"

I glanced over at him.

"Be careful on that thing."

Our eyes met. I was expecting humor or sarcasm in his stare, but I saw only genuine concern, like he really cared what happened to me.

Chapter Three

I drove Sally back to the main road, accompanied by the constant beam of headlights from Wyatt's truck. I wondered if he listened to music while he drove and if it was stereotyping to assume it was country music just because he was from Texas. More important, why did I care?

Back at the original turnoff, I slowed and signaled. A few hours earlier, I'd turned down this same road, anxious to meet Ben at our special spot on the beach—the spot where we'd beach-combed as kids, the spot where he'd told me a ghost story that gave me bad dreams for a week, the spot where we'd spent more than a few hours making out. Now our spot was intertwined with a stranger who cared whether I stayed safe and called me pretty. My jaw clenched with resentment.

I parked at the end of the road, pulled off my helmet, and yanked on my beanie, thankful for the warmth.

Wyatt climbed out of his truck and strolled over. "Okay, I'd never have found my way back here. Every part of this island looks the same—sand, sand, and oh look, more sand."

"Let's just get the kayak. I don't want to miss the ferry." I headed toward the ocean, stomping along the trail and trying not to think about Ben or how Wyatt's presence might affect our secret meeting spot.

"Hey." He ran to catch up. "I pissed you off again, right? What'd I do this time?"

I glanced around, feeling grouchy. Ben had left already, but I still worried he could somehow see. "Nothing. I'm just cold and tired."

Not waiting for a response, I kept walking, only stopping when I reached one end of the kayak. I snuck a peek at Wyatt. In the moonlight, I could see the frown on his face as he stood there looking a little hurt. Guilt pulsed through me. Great. I didn't need anything else to feel guilty about.

Silently, we carried the kayak to his truck. He slid it in the back and tied it down as I stood around, feeling unhelpful and impatient.

"You don't need to wait." He straightened. "I don't want to hold you up."

I flinched at his cool tone. "It's fine."

"You could miss the ferry." His words were a challenge.

I tugged my hat down and frowned. I'd no interest in making friends with the cocky new boy who looked like he belonged in an "Abs, Abs, Abs" magazine and said inappropriate things, but I also wasn't a total asshole, or at least I never used to be.

"Look, I'm sorry. I just get cranky." I glanced at my watch. "We'll make the ferry. We have time."

I must have been forgiven, because the corners of his mouth quirked up. He jumped down from the tailgate, his movements fluid and easy, and I wondered if he was a jock. I'd never been one for team sports, but before the ocean betrayed me, I'd spent most of my time on the water. Now, I ran every day—rain, sleet, or shine—like the damn postal service. I liked routine, and when everything else in my life fell apart, I needed that constant, rhythmic pounding of my feet on asphalt.

"Mom tells me I can be too intense." Wyatt slammed the tail-gate shut, his hair falling over one eye. "She says it's like drinking from a fire hydrant."

I snorted. "She obviously knows you well."

"Not really." He grinned. "'Cause she doesn't realize that most girls find me charming and irresistible."

"They're just being polite."

"I don't think so."

"Well, when you're done explaining what a stud you are, maybe we can head to the ferry."

He puffed out his chest. "Darlin', I'm right behind you."

This time, I just rolled my eyes, started up Sally's engine, and held up one hand to my ear. "What was that? I couldn't hear you." I took off without waiting for his response, but in no time his headlights followed me again.

At the ferry terminal, we pulled into the lineup and shut down our engines. Wyatt jumped out of his truck. "I'll be right back."

"I wouldn't take long. The ferry's pulling in."

He nodded and sprinted toward the terminal building, getting back just in time to start his truck and follow me up the ramp onto the ferry. When he joined me on the deck, his arms were full. "I wasn't sure what you'd like, so I covered all the basic food groups—M&M's, Skittles, and salt and vinegar chips." He handed me a bottle of Coke and kept one for himself.

My stomach growled in appreciation. On the other side of the deck, Henry checked on vehicles, working his way in our direction. I grabbed Wyatt's sleeve and tugged. "Let's go upstairs. We can sit inside where it's warm." The last thing I needed was Henry asking questions about Wyatt or making assumptions about who he was.

Wyatt's expression lit up. "See, I told you that girls find me irresistible. It was inevitable that you'd fall for my charms."

"Yup." I gritted my teeth and climbed the metal stairs. "That's what it is."

I opened the door to the small passenger lounge and a blast of warm air hit my face.

Wyatt groaned. "Damn, this feels so good. It's April, and it's still freezing out there."

I shrugged, secretly thankful for the warmth, and headed for an empty corner. Dropping into a seat, I cracked open the Coke and took a long sip. "This is unusually cold, but it'll warm up soon enough, which will attract the tourists. In a few weeks, you'll be tripping over people on the beaches. The lineup for this ferry will be several hours long."

"Wow. That's something to look forward to." Wyatt took the seat right next to me, unloading his stash of food on the next seat over.

I toed off my sneakers and Wyatt snorted. "Cute socks, but they don't really go with the whole 'dark, tortured soul' thing you've got going on."

I glanced down at my pink pony socks. "I like fun socks. So sue me."

"Hmm . . . " He stared, a smirk on his lips. "I wonder what other fun pieces of clothes you're hiding."

I choked. "Seriously? Let's be clear—whatever fun clothes I may or may not be wearing are none of your business."

"All right, all right. So, what will it be, Mer?" He nodded at the junk-food pile. "Pick your poison."

I slowly released my breath. Being with Wyatt was giving me whiplash, and not in a good way. "Skittles."

"Good choice."

"Are you kidding?" I took the bag he offered. "It's the only choice. Except maybe for Twizzlers. They reign supreme." An image of Ben filled my head: the two of us fighting over the last red licorice and finally splitting it in half.

I pulled open the Skittles and dumped a small pile in my palm. Wyatt held out his hand, and I doled out a couple.

"Hey, don't be stingy."

I shrugged. "Eat your M&M's."

He shot me a hurt puppy-dog look before tossing back the candy. "So, you never did tell me. Why were you out on the beach by yourself, strangling a harmonica?"

"Funny, and I was there because it's a beautiful night, and it's a great spot to think." I popped a red Skittle in my mouth and sucked on the candy shell. Could he hear my heart thumping?

"But everywhere you turn on these islands, there's sand and ocean. Why would you come this far, just to sit alone on the beach?"

"I see what your mother means."

"Ah . . . was I being too nosy?"

I nodded, chewing on another candy. "I almost mistook you for a wooden puppet named Pinocchio."

"Ouch." He pulled open the bag of M&M's. "All right. Let's pick a safe topic. What kind of movies do you watch?"

I slouched back in my seat. "Cheesy action movies."

"You mean the ones where the hero has ten guys shooting at him with machine guns and somehow manages to take them all out with a single knife?"

"Yup. I especially love it when he falls from a ten-story building, totals three cars, a motorcycle, and a speeding train, and walks away with only a slight limp and the mandatory cut on the forehead."

"Yeah." The smile fell from his face. "Take it from me—if you total a bike, you're not walking away from it." His fingers dug into his knee.

"Is that what happened to school?"

He looked up and blinked, like he'd just been a million miles away. "Huh?"

I swallowed, regretting my question. Wyatt's life was none of my business. But he still stared at me, that expectant look on his face, and I had no clue how to politely back out. "Um . . . a motorcycle accident? Is that why you missed so much school?"

In the little time I'd known Wyatt, he'd only worn an open expression on his face, a look that invited you in, even when I was being crappy to him. Now, his features tightened, closing me out and leaving me to wonder what awful thing was hiding in there. Was that how I looked all the time?

"Forget it," I mumbled. "I shouldn't have asked. I was being nosy."

"Nah." He crumpled the bag of M&M's in his fist. "It's not a big secret or anything. I had an accident last year. Ended up screwing myself pretty good."

Awkward silence followed. My gaze bounced around the small

lounge like a Ping-Pong ball, landing everywhere but on Wyatt. If my mom were here, she'd know the exact right thing to say, some perfect words of support and positivity that were obviously drilled into her when she trained to become a teacher. But my brain went blank.

After a stupid amount of time passed, I cleared my throat. "That sucks."

Wyatt snorted and hitched one ankle over the other. "Yup, that pretty much sums it up. It sucked."

"So, are you okay now?"

He tapped his thumb against his knee. "Almost one hundred percent. Plus, I have metal pieces in my body that freak out the airport detectors."

"That's cool."

"Yeah . . . just like the Terminator."

The heat of the room had dried his hair, and I could finally make out its color—a bronzy hue, somewhere between blond and brown. His eyes were hazel, more green than brown. His skin was pale, like he'd spent too many hours inside. In the hospital?

"Wait!" I sat upright. "Did I give you some kind of post-traumatic stress by making you ride my scooter?"

He laughed out loud—a big, warm, infectious sound that filled the lounge and had me looking around to see who might be watching, but the room was surprisingly empty. Where was everyone?

"Are you asking if Sally traumatized me?"

"Maybe."

His voice dropped, and he leaned close enough for me to see that most girls would kill for his eyelashes. "Darlin', climbing on the back of that little contraption would be traumatizing even if I wasn't recovering from a life-threatening bike accident."

"Hey, watch it."

He chuckled again. "One day I'll take you for a ride on a real bike, and then you'll see the truth in my words."

His cockiness stole my breath away. He talked about our future bike ride together like it was inevitable. I jerked upright because somewhere along the way, I'd leaned my head closer to his. Damn. I took a long swig of Coke and stared out the window. We were almost at Ocracoke.

Screwing the top back on the bottle, I swung back around. "Look, I need to make something clear. Despite what happened tonight and despite this"—I waved my hand in the general direction of his body—"whole thing you've got going on, I'm not planning on going anywhere with you."

He tilted his head to one side, his hair brushing his collar. "And what exactly is this thing you think I've got going on?"

I huffed. "You know what I mean—this 'cocky, flirty, nothing bothers you' thing."

"Ah." He slapped his hand against his chest. "You've mortally wounded me. It took me years to develop and nurture this persona, and you just crushed it in a single blow."

I rolled my eyes. "I think you'll live."

"Such a callous heart you have. Is it because you ran out of Skittles? Next time I'll remember to buy two bags."

"There's not going to be a next time."

He blew out a breath. "So you keep telling me. But who's going to save me if I get lost at sea again?"

I slipped on my sneakers and stood up. "Don't be stupid and you won't need saving. Figure out the difference between the soundside and open ocean. Here's a hint: No matter where you go on these islands, the Atlantic is due east. The Pamlico Sound is west. So stick to the sound until you know what you're doing."

"Ah, that's so sweet. You're concerned about my safety."

I shook my head. His arrogance knew no bounds. Frowning, I squeezed past him. "We'll be docking soon. We should head downstairs."

He gave me a small salute. "Yes, ma'am. Anything you say."

He followed me to the door, and I pushed it open, wincing. The night had turned even colder, or maybe it was just the contrast to the warmth of the passenger lounge. I pulled up my hood and dug my hands in my pockets. Behind me, Wyatt muttered curses. We were halfway down the stairs when the ferry shuddered. I stumbled sideways and grabbed the railing. Black water glistened below us, both terrifying and mesmerizing.

"Be careful." Wyatt leaned past me to also stare over the railing. "I don't want to have to jump in after you." His gaze met mine, his face illuminated by the reddish glow from the security lighting. His voice lowered, his words teasing, but his expression remained serious. "You just rescued me. So I would definitely return the favor, but I think my ass has frozen enough for one night."

He grinned, and I shivered because it suddenly felt like I was drowning in his gaze, unable to pull in a full breath. My brain turned to mush, and my limbs felt frozen. Something skirted around my consciousness, something I was supposed to remember.

Ben.

An announcement made my head snap up. A crackling voice asked motorists to return to their vehicles. Wyatt shot me a half smile. "Sounds like we're supposed to get going, although driving that scooter only barely qualifies you as a motorist."

He continued down the stairs, and I could finally breathe again. What the hell was that?

I managed the rest of the stairs, careful not to look over the railing. Wyatt went straight to his truck and opened the door. Really? I climbed on my scooter. After all the attention he'd given me, he wasn't even saying goodbye. But a few seconds later, he emerged with a puffy black bomber jacket and headed in my direction.

"Here. You'll freeze on the drive home without a jacket."

I blinked up at him. "I can't take your jacket."

"I'm lending it."

"I still can't borrow it."

"Sure you can because it's just plain stupid not to." He swung it around my shoulders before I could come up with another argument. "See, it's black, so it even matches your whole dark and broody look."

It was so wrong to take it, but my body was a traitor. It loved the blissful warmth too much. "Fine, but I'll get it back to you as soon as I can." I slipped my arms in, and he reached down and zipped it up, like I was a little kid.

"No rush." He stomped his feet on the deck and looked longingly at the cab of his truck. "Look." He leaned against my handlebar. "All joking aside, I want to thank you for your help tonight. I'm not sure what I'd have done if I hadn't found you."

For some reason, these quiet, serious words were even more disconcerting than his larger-than-life flirtations. I ducked my chin inside the collar of his jacket, breathing in his fresh laundry scent. "It's nothing."

"It's not. I've been on this island for a week, and I swear I haven't seen a single other person my age. I'd given up on finding anyone I actually wanted to talk to."

I sighed. "As soon as spring break ends, you'll meet everyone at school."

"Still, I get that I'm pushing my luck here and you'll probably turn me down for some mysterious reason, but I was wondering if you wanted to hang out sometime. Maybe go for coffee or watch a movie."

Wait. Was he asking me out? The cocky look on his face disappeared and uncertainty replaced it. My mouth opened and closed. "Wyatt—"

"So you're the boy Mer's been sneaking off to meet every night?"

Shit. Henry stood to one side, sizing up Wyatt.

"No!" Both Wyatt and Henry stared at me. "I mean—that's not him." God, I'd never wanted to disappear this badly. Rushed words stumbled out of my mouth. "This is Wyatt. I just met him tonight. He got lost in his kayak." I pointed to the back of Wyatt's truck, like Henry couldn't see it for himself. "He just moved to Ocracoke, and I was helping him out. Since we're neighbors and all. You know, trying to be friendly."

"Oh." Henry rubbed at his jaw.

Beside him, Wyatt gawked at me like my head had just spun three hundred and sixty degrees on my shoulders.

"I saw you and this feller up in the lounge all cozy together, and I figured it had to be him."

"That's okay." I patted Henry's arm, anxious for the conversation to end. "It's an honest mistake."

"Yeah. Sorry about that." He stuck his hand out to Wyatt, and they shook. "Still, nice to meet you."

Wyatt smiled at Henry. "Nice meetin' you, too."

"Is that a Texas accent I hear?"

"Yes, sir."

"You're a long way from home."

"Yes, sir, but everyone here's been real friendly." His gaze slid to me, and I busied myself, pulling on my helmet and adjusting the strap.

Henry slapped him on the shoulder. "That's good to hear. I got to get back to work. Mer—" He glanced in my direction. "I'll see you later?"

I smiled and gave a noncommittal response. Henry left, but the awkwardness remained. I fidgeted on the seat, aware of Wyatt still standing over me. Finally, I looked up at his wry expression.

"I get it now. There's someone else."

My cheeks heated. I didn't need any rumors started. "It's complicated." Ben and I needed to remain a secret.

"Ah. It's also too bad."

"Why?"

He leaned closer and winked. "'Cause you're missing out on all this."

My mouth fell open. My brain scrambled for a comeback, but he was already circling his pickup and climbing in the driver's seat.

As soon as the ferry stopped, his engine started, and in minutes, we were both back on the highway.

This time, I followed his taillights, but I couldn't keep up. Eventually, the red glow from his truck disappeared over the horizon.

Chapter Four

I glared at the kids throwing a Frisbee in the surf and silently cursed my body. Why did I have to get my stupid period today? Of all days? The kids from Ben's middle school always threw a beach party after the last class of the year. Because I was finally old enough, Ben had invited me to come. I'd been looking forward to this party for ages, ever since Ben had shown me the pictures from last year. The girls looked so grown-up, with their cute bikinis, laughing faces, and their arms hooked around Ben.

Of course everyone loved Ben. He played on the basketball and football teams, while I'd never gotten the hang of team sports. My gym teacher always yelled at me to pass more, but I didn't like depending on others. That's why I loved windsurfing and kitesurfing. It was just me, my board, and my sail. The ocean understood me.

It didn't tell me that I wasn't smart enough or social enough, that I listened to the wrong kind of music or wore the wrong clothes, that I needed to work harder to make friends and be accepted.

The ocean liked me just for me.

But even if Ben was way more popular than me, he never left me out. He never forgot his promise to like me best. We hung out most weekends. When it was too cold to surf, I sat on the bleachers during his basketball practices and read.

If he made a great shot, he'd shout at me: "Did you see that one, Mer? Nothing but net."

I'd look up and grin, but most of the time, we both knew I'd missed it.

Now, I sat on the beach, sweating inside my thickest shorts and oversized T-shirt. I pulled my knees up to my chest. Hidden underneath was the bikini top I'd talked my mom into buying. Normally, I wore a tankini or a one-piece under my wetsuit. This new suit was purple with little ties that went around my neck and back, and showed off my waist.

Last night, I'd felt desperate enough to try a tampon. But after fifteen minutes of fumbling and poking, I'd given up, wiping away my tears before Mom found them and gifted me another talk about "just being myself." She never understood, because she was beautiful and everyone liked her. I only had Ben.

Now, he stood over me, blocking out the sun and wearing only his swim trunks, the newly formed biceps in his arms, and a huge grin. "Come on, Mer. Come play with us."

I bit my lip, and something fluttered in my belly. Ben used to be just Ben—my best friend. But lately, when I looked at him, something funny happened inside. I tugged on the end of my ponytail and glanced away. Of course, I knew what was happening. I had a stupid crush on my best friend, not that I'd ever say anything. Everyone knew that crushes ruined friendships. If I ignored it, it would go away. It had to.

"Can't. I'm reading." I clutched my tattered copy of Harry Potter and the Half-Blood Prince.

Ben plopped down on the sand next to me, and I leaned closer to his shoulder and breathed in. He smelled of coconuts, salt, and sweat. Ugh, did he notice I'd just done that?

He held out his hand for the book, and I surrendered it. He inspected the back cover. "You've read this one already."

I snatched it back. "I know, but it's my favorite."

He nudged his elbow into mine. "So, read it later. You've been talking about this day for ages."

I dug my toes into the sand until I found the cool dampness buried underneath. "I don't like Frisbee."

"Then swim with me. I'll race you out to the buoy."

"That wouldn't be a race; I'd easily beat you."

"Ha ha." He piled more sand on my feet, burying them. A friend called out to him, and he glanced up. Then he turned back to me, clearly torn. "Please come swimming. For me."

A big lump clogged my throat, and hot tears pricked my eyes. I looked away so he wouldn't see. This was stupid. I wanted to tell him the truth, but that would literally involve dying of embarrassment. So I shook my head instead.

Ben sighed. "I know you think that you don't fit in, but you could if you just let people see the real Mer. If they saw you on your board or heard you talking about music and movies, they'd see that you're amazing and fearless and way cooler than all of them put together. Plus, you're the only one who loves the ocean as much as me—not just hanging on the beach, but being out there."

Ben spent his free time on his dad's boat. He wanted to be a fisherman when he grew up, even though his teammates were always trying to talk him out of it. They thought it wasn't exciting or cool enough. They wanted to leave the islands as soon as they were old enough. I wanted to go places, too, but I always pictured myself right back here in the end. I loved living on this island with the ocean as my backyard.

Now, the sincerity in Ben's brown eyes made mine burn even more. Why couldn't the universe have given me this one perfect day? I let myself imagine it—pulling off my T-shirt and wiggling out of my shorts, the expression on Ben's face when he saw my new bikini. I'd walk to the edge of the beach, and all the other kids would stare, awestruck. Then I'd challenge them to a race and laugh as they all fell far behind. After, they'd crowd around me, wanting to know where I'd learned to swim so fast, but Ben would step in and tell them to give me space . . .

"Mer!" Ben waved his fingers in my face. "Hey."

I blinked. Heat crawled up my chest and neck, and into my cheeks. "Sorry."

"What were you thinking about?"

"Nothing," I mumbled.

Another friend called out to Ben, frowning in my direction. They tolerated Ben's friendship with me because they didn't have a choice. Somehow Ben had made them understand that we were a package deal, but it didn't mean they liked me.

"Go!" I gave him a gentle push. "I'm going to read anyway." Finding my bookmark, I flipped to the right page.

But before he stood up, he stretched out his hand and opened his fingers. In his palm lay a perfect sand dollar. "For your collection."

I gazed over at him, holding the shell between my fingers carefully so the fragile edges wouldn't break. "It's perfect."

He winked. "I know. When I saw it, I thought of you."

I wanted to ask him: Was it because he knew I collected them, or did he possibly think I was perfect, too?

Something brushed against my arm and my eyes flew open. Rachel's face lay inches from mine. My little sister smiled, her blond hair splayed out across the pillow, her blue eyes blinking at me. It was hard to believe she was already twelve, the same age

I was when I first started crushing on Ben.

"I woke you up. Sorry."

I tucked my cold hands under my cheek and yawned. "What time is it?"

"Eight."

She curled into me and I sighed—my own private heater. It seemed like I was always cold lately. I glanced over at my window. Raindrops obscured the glass, the cloudy sky making my room dark and gloomy. "Ugh. I hate running in the rain. What happened to the sun and spring? Did someone steal them while we weren't looking?"

"Maybe, but I think you should run anyway." Something in her voice made me turn back.

"Why? What's going on?"

She frowned, looking too serious for her pink flannel pajamas. "I overheard Mom and Dad talking last night. They thought I was in my room, but I'd come down to make popcorn."

I tensed. *Last night.* Ben's face appeared in my head, but so did Wyatt's. That wasn't right. It should have just been Ben's.

Rachel drew in a noisy breath. Whatever it was, it had to be bad.

"Just tell me."

"They know you haven't been working at the arcade on Hatteras. Mom ran into Mr. Flores at the grocery store last night after you left."

Great. Mr. Flores owned the arcade. He'd been my boss until

I quit and never told my parents. The no-longer-existent job had been the perfect excuse to keep meeting Ben in secret.

"They're pissed?"

She raised a pale eyebrow. "You could say that. Mom was yelling, and Dad was just quiet."

My parents had been in bed when I got in last night, which meant they'd decided to confront me this morning. I pushed the heels of my hands against my eye sockets and groaned.

"Mer?"

"Yeah."

"Are you drinking or doing drugs?"

"What?" I dropped my hands. "Where'd you hear that?"

"I overheard it from Mom. She's worried." She lifted her chin. "I am, too. I don't understand what's happening."

Her burst of determination dissolved in front of me. Tears welled in her eyes, and my breath caught. I wiped at the tears with my thumb.

"Nothing's happening. I'm fine. Mom's wrong."

"Don't do that. No one talks to me because y'all think I'm too young, but I'm a part of this family, too."

"Rachel . . . " My mouth fell open and snapped shut. There were too many things I couldn't tell her.

"We used to be happy. Mom and Aunt Lila used to talk all the time, and Ben was like my big brother. Now nothing is the same." A sob escaped between her heated words. "It's like everything is broken, and I don't know how to fix it."

My head pounded with guilt. "It's not your job to fix it. I'm so sorry." My apology was low, desperate. "I did this. I broke everything."

"Can't you make it better?" Her wide eyes pleaded with me.

"I don't know if I can."

We lay only inches apart, but I felt the distance between us grow. Over the past months, as my relationship with my parents crumbled, at least I'd still had Rachel. Some nights, when it had all felt bigger than my will to keep going, I'd climbed into her bed and curled around her. I'd matched my breathing to hers and finally found sleep.

"Mer, please tell me what happened between you and Ben. You were together all the time, and then he wouldn't even talk to you."

I winced at the seriousness in her tone. When had she grown up, and how had I missed it? I still remembered the first day I went to the hospital to see her. Dad had laid this little bundle in my arms. She'd been asleep, her blond hair so pale against her skin that you could barely see it. I thought I'd resent her, but instead I'd felt only love and a fierce protectiveness. As she'd grown, we could all see how much she was like Mom. Mom was from the Outer Banks but hated doing anything on the water. She actually got seasick. So Mom had Rachel, and Dad and I had the ocean. We were all okay with the arrangement, until I'd ruined everything.

My hand found hers, and I squeezed her fingers. "I can't tell you." My voice cracked. "Please don't ask me."

Anger flashed in her eyes. "You don't trust me."

"No. That's not it." I released her hand and pulled the quilt up over my chest. "It's because it's awful. If you knew the truth, you'd look at me differently. You'd maybe even hate me."

Rachel wrapped her arm around my shoulders and pulled my head down next to hers. "That's not true. No matter what it is, I'd always take your side."

"Then please don't ask me. Not now. Maybe someday."

She nodded and pulled away. "Mom and Dad are in the kitchen." Disappointment edged her tone. "I'll distract them and you can sneak out the front door."

I kissed her forehead. "You're the best and I don't deserve you."

"Yeah, yeah. But they'll still be waiting for you when you get back."

"I know." But at least I'd have a few hours to get my story straight.

Rachel slipped out of my bed, and I got dressed in my warmest running tights, sweatshirt, and sneakers. A bandana kept my bangs out of my eyes. I found a crumbled granola bar at the bottom of my backpack for breakfast and made a pit stop in the bathroom.

Dark shadows under my eyes made them look more purple than blue. Mom and Rachel shared the same dainty features, perfect complexion, and blond curly hair, but my nose was too big, and my lips were too wide. I was normally tanned from hours on the ocean. Only now I was pale, too—washed out, worn down, and tired. Ben always made me feel beautiful. I figured it was just the way he saw me, but last night, Wyatt had also called me pretty.

I tucked the knowledge away, swallowing back a smile, and tiptoed down our narrow stairs, the wooden steps warped from years of use. Ben had needed to duck at the bottom so he wouldn't crack his head on the sloped ceiling. Our house had belonged to my grandparents, and when they'd decided to retire to Florida, Mom and Dad had bought it. We'd updated it a bit, with brighter paint in the rooms and new countertops in the kitchen, but it still felt old and rambling and comfortable. When I neared the bottom of the stairs, I gripped the thick railing and used it to hold my weight while I skipped the second-to-last step. It always creaked the loudest.

By the front closet, I stopped and tugged on my running jacket. A gust of wind rattled the windows. Rachel talked in the kitchen, keeping up a steady stream of conversation. I reached for the doorknob.

"Going somewhere?"

"Jesus." I jumped and spun around. My mom stood right behind me. "You scared the crap out of me."

"Really?" She hugged her arms around her chest. "I know the feeling because you've been scaring the crap out of me for months." Her words were sharp, and her eyes were red rimmed.

"How? I'm fine. I'm just going for a run."

I reached for the door again, but my mom's words stopped me cold: "Meredith Hall, don't you dare take one step outside of this house. You march your butt into the kitchen right now."

I glanced over her shoulder. Dad and Rachel stood at the end of the hall. Dad should have looked angry, but somehow they both looked apologetic.

Mom stepped aside, and I walked past her to the kitchen. I slid into my usual spot at the thick wooden table—the chair against the wall, the chair I'd secretly carved my initials into when I was five, just in case my new baby sister decided to try and steal it.

"Rachel, could you please leave us alone while we talk to Mer?"

Rachel shot me a sad smile. *Sorry*, she mouthed.

I shrugged. She'd tried her best.

Dad silently went to the cupboard and pulled down my mug. He filled it with coffee and added two spoonfuls of sugar and a boatload of creamer. Then he set it in front of me and took the opposite chair.

"Thanks."

Mom always kept a vase of fresh flowers on the table, even during the winter. She said they made her smile every morning when she saw them. Most months, she picked them from the garden. When it was too cold, she bought them from the grocer. This morning, the blooms weren't tall enough to block my view of Dad's disappointment. I curled my hands around my coffee. The heat burned my palm, but I kept it there anyway.

Mom pulled a plate of pancakes from the oven and laid them next to my mug. That was my mom. Even while preparing to read me the riot act, she wanted to make sure I was fed, but I wasn't hungry. I couldn't eat when I knew what was coming.

Maybe the best defense was an offense. "I meant to tell you about the job, but . . . " What? *I was using it as a cover for my other secret activities.* I fell silent and looked over at my dad.

He sighed and lowered his head. My dad looked like a kinder, gentler Grizzly Adams, his dark beard blending in with his shaggy hair. All summer, he wore an endless supply of cargo shorts, T-shirts, and flip-flops. He always looked a little lost in winter, like he didn't know what he should be doing in his jeans and flannel shirts.

Mom sat up straighter and spread her palms flat on the table, as if she were lecturing her class of second graders. "Are you doing drugs?"

I knew it was coming, but my breath still caught at her matter-of-fact question. "No."

"Kids lie to their parents all the time." My mom clasped her hands together so tight, her knuckles turned white. "How do we know if you're telling the truth? Maybe we should give you a drug test."

"Jess!" My dad looked at her, disapproval on his face.

"What? She's been lying to us. We can't stick our heads in the sand anymore."

"If she says she's not using, I believe her."

I shot my dad a small smile, knowing how hard it was for him to take my side against Mom. She always insisted they present a united front.

Mom threw her hands up. "Fine, if you believe her, you figure out what she's been doing every night for the last few months."

Dad slid the vase to one side. "Maybe we should just ask her."

I saw the hope in my dad's eyes, the belief that despite everything that had happened, I was still the little girl who'd followed him to the ocean, hanging on to his every story, sharing his passion for the sport he'd dedicated his life to. My dad—the quiet optimist.

"I wasn't doing anything wrong. I wasn't using drugs or drinking or having sex."

My dad looked away, and my mom exhaled. "Meredith!"

"What? You obviously wanted a frank and 'real' conversation. You both know I'm not a virgin, so I'm just covering all the bases."

"Then what exactly have you been doing?"

I shrugged and focused on my untouched plate of pancakes. Maybe the simplest lie was the truth. "I go to the beach."

"All winter? Do you really expect us to believe that?"

"Yeah, Mom, because it's true. I go to the beach and sit there. I read, listen to music, and try not to think. It's not a crime, but I knew you wouldn't understand. You'd send me to that therapist again, but I don't want to talk about my feelings with strangers anymore. I just want to experience them. On my own. Without feeling like everything I'm doing is wrong. Like everyone has an opinion on what I'm supposed to be doing with my life."

My fist smacked the table, and we all jumped. Damn. My heart pounded like I'd been sprinting. Maybe there'd been a whole lot more truth in my confession than lies.

"Mer . . . " My mom frowned. "I know it's been tough for you since Ben—"

Tears clogged my throat. "Don't, Mom." I hated crying in front of people. "I just want to go running, okay?"

She lifted her chin and her mouth opened. She was preparing for her current favorite speech about how I was young and losing Ben wasn't the end of my world even if it sometimes felt like it, that I'd get over this if I only changed my attitude. But my dad stood and put a hand on her shoulder. She looked up at him, confused.

"She answered our questions, Jess. Let her go running."

Not waiting for Mom's response, I bolted from the table, stopping next to him. I stepped into his hug, and he kissed my forehead. "We both love you." His beard brushed my cheek. "That's all."

I nodded and pulled back, not looking at my mom. Maybe she was mad at my dad for cutting her off, or maybe she understood. Either way, I needed to get out of that kitchen.

I needed to feel my feet pounding the pavement, rain falling on my face, my lungs tightening and expanding with each breath. I needed to keep my shit together until I saw Ben again.

He'd tell me what to do. He'd know how to fix this.

Chapter Five

"Stop fussing with your hair, Meredith. It looks great."

"Are you nuts? It looks ridiculous. I'm not going."

My mom's face turned red. "I know you're nervous about your first middle school dance, but I just shelled out good money for that updo." She raised her hands. "Next you're going to tell me that you also hate the dress."

My fingers plucked at the pale blue satin. "It's just as stupid-looking as my hair."

"But you picked it out this morning." She planted both hands on her hips. "I swear you do this just to spite me. We finally had a good day together, and now you're acting so contrary."

But she didn't understand. When I asked her if we could go shopping, I'd wanted to be the girl who wore blue satin dresses, with curls piled on her head. I'd wanted to be the girl who went to her first dance looking like she belonged there. And secretly, I'd really wanted to be the girl who slow-danced with Ben in front of everyone. I'd invited him . . . just as friends, of course. I couldn't let my crush mess up our friendship, but this was a major milestone. I couldn't go without him.

My confidence lasted until I stood in front of the mirror in my bedroom with this stupid dress and huge hair. I felt like a caricature of myself. I wanted a hole to open in my bedroom floor and swallow me. There was no way I could show up at school looking like this. I didn't even like to dance. The whole thing was a huge mistake.

I wanted Mom to understand that.

I wanted her to tell me she loved me, no matter what girl I turned out to be. But instead she shook her head. "I give up. Go. Don't go. You're impossible to please."

She disappeared down the hall.

I blinked, refusing to cry. I yanked at the pins holding up my hair, but the lady at the salon had coated every inch with hairspray, so everything I touched clung to my fingertips. "Ah!" Half of the pins came out with my hair still attached.

"Let me help."

Rachel stood in my open doorway. I sniffed. "How?"

"I've done my dolls' hair a bunch of times. You have no experience." She climbed up on my bed, one hand on her hip and one hand pointing in front of her. "Sit here."

I flopped down in a poof of annoying, slippery satin. Rachel stood behind me and gently extracted each bobby pin. When she was done, she reached for a brush and untangled the worst of the curls, before finally pulling my hair into its usual ponytail.

For a moment, neither of us said anything. Then her fingers skimmed my shoulder. "Hey, Mer."

"Yeah?"

"I think you look really pretty just the way you are."

I found her blue-eyed gaze and swallowed back the lump in my throat. "Thanks, but I think you're the one who's beautiful and not just on the outside."

She giggled and helped me with the zipper. When I wriggled into my jeans and T-shirt, I could finally breathe again. Rachel picked up the dress, slung it over her arm, and headed for the door.

"Hey, where are you taking that?"

She grinned. "My closet, 'cause in five years, it's going to be my favorite dress." She stuck out her tongue, and I laughed.

But just when I thought the whole awful experience was over, Dad called me from the living room. I trudged down the steps to find Ben standing by the front door wearing dress pants and a button-down shirt. His dark hair was gelled into place, and he smelled like his dad's aftershave.

"Mer?" He frowned at my sour expression. "What happened? Are you sick?"

I looked at Dad, but he only smiled, squeezed my shoulder, and lumbered off in the direction of the kitchen. Basically, he was leaving me to clean up my own mess. Not that I blamed him.

"No . . . I mean, yeah, maybe." I glanced at Ben. A little lie wouldn't hurt, especially not since my head was still throbbing from all those pins.

But Ben's eyes just narrowed. "Come on, Mer, tell the truth. What's really going on?"

"You'll think I'm being stupid," I huffed.

"When did I ever think that?"

"I don't know. Never."

"So just tell me."

I stuffed my hands in my pockets and looked up at Ben. He'd grown so much taller and broader than me already, but he could never be intimidating. Even now, with his forehead creased from frowning, his dark eyes were soft with concern. "I bought a dress to wear to the dance, but it looks stupid. So I can't go because I have nothing to wear."

"Is that all? Jeez, Mer, I thought it was something serious."

"What's that supposed to mean?"

Ben shrugged. "I can't remember the last time I saw you in anything other than shorts, jeans, or a wetsuit. I already figured you'd be going casual."

"But you dressed up."

His cheeks turned red. "My mom kind of made me. If not, I'd be wearing jeans, too."

"So you think it's all right if I go like this?"

"Are you kidding? You invited me and I got all dressed up. You can't bail on me now."

His words eased the tightness I'd felt in my chest ever since I'd first looked in the mirror. "Really?"

"Yeah." He grinned, reaching out to tug at a curl mixed in with my ponytail. "Let's just go and have fun, okay?"

So I went to my first middle school dance wearing my favorite jeans and an "I'd Rather Be Windsurfing" T-shirt. I didn't even feel envious of the girls in their pretty dresses, because in the end, Ben still danced with me. It wasn't a slow dance, but laughing and jumping around the gym with him, I felt like the girl I was meant to be: Ben's best friend.

The sky above me remained gray, the rain tapering off to a drizzle. Cold water dripped off my jacket and soaked through my running tights. A brisk wind whipped at my cheeks, and I ran to the pace of the music blaring through my earbuds, right until my sneaker landed in a deep puddle. Shit. Water seeped through my already damp socks. I jumped the next puddle and picked up my pace.

My normal route always took me around the backside of the village and along the highway, but today, I headed toward the harbor. For a Saturday morning, the streets were empty, the rain and wind keeping the normal walkers, shoppers, and coffee seekers inside. The island had seemed deserted a lot lately.

Before I hit the harbor, I turned down a quieter street, running past the flower shop and a bakery. I slowed at the next house. A black pickup truck sat in the driveway. The FOR SALE sign that had resided in the front window was gone, replaced by one that said: OPENING SOON.

When Wyatt mentioned his mom was starting a coffee shop, I knew there weren't many places that would be suitable, but this property used to be a deli. The owners had lived in the attached house, until they'd decided to move back to Philly. I got it. The Outer Banks were a beautiful vacation spot, but living here wasn't for everyone, especially in the winter. Despite my current relationship with the ocean, I'd somehow never considered ending up anywhere else.

I jogged in place. Yeah, it didn't take a genius to find Wyatt's house, but why was I now standing in front of it? Why was I stopping altogether, leaning over, and rubbing my hands up and down my frozen thighs?

I knelt to retie my shoelace. Yup, that's why I stopped . . . because my lace had loosened. I could have tripped.

"Mornin', sugar."

My head snapped up so fast, I wobbled, almost falling right on my ass. "Um . . . hi." I stood and stepped back, making sure I was on the curb.

Wyatt's mom was unmistakable—a shorter, pretty version of

Wyatt, with bronze-colored hair, now held back in a messy bun on top of her head; hazel eyes; and that same Texas accent. She wore snug-fitting jeans and a thick sweater that glistened from the drizzle. Her cheeks were flushed. She looked too young to be Wyatt's mom, but maybe she was just one of those women who didn't show their age.

"Wyatt didn't lie. You are the cutest thing."

My eyes widened, and I glanced around, searching for the stray kitten or puppy that must have wandered up behind me.

She chuckled. "You're Meredith Hall, right? But you prefer to be called Mer."

I stared at her. How the heck did she know?

She touched her hair. "It's the purple. I figure there aren't too many teenage girls on this island with purple hair and amazing blue eyes."

"Oh." Apparently that was the best response I could come up with.

"You must be looking for Wyatt. He's not much of an early riser, unless I boot his sorry ass out of the bunk. But I'm sure I can get him up, if he knows you're here."

"No!" I lurched forward. I definitely wasn't here to see Wyatt. At least, I didn't think I was. She looked up at me. I wasn't tall, but this petite woman made me feel like a giant. "I'm not here for Wyatt . . . I mean, I was just out for a run, and I saw his truck, and he mentioned your coffee shop and . . . " I shrugged and made a zipper motion across my lips. "I'm going to stop babbling now."

"Aw, aren't you funny." Her warm tone made it sound like a compliment. "I'm Harley Wilson, by the way. I know my last name is different than Wyatt's, but when I fell in love with a man named Jimmy Quinn, I knew I was in trouble. Needless to say, I kept my maiden name, which turned out to be a convenient decision all around." She rolled her eyes and laughed while I caught up with her meaning.

"Oh . . . Harley Quinn." And a divorce? Which could explain why Wyatt never mentioned his dad.

"Yup. Nice to meet you." She stuck out her hand, her fingers bare of any rings. We shook hands, and she grabbed mine in both of hers. "Honey, you're freezing and wetter than a newborn kitten."

"It's fine." I pulled my hand free. "I just need to start running again before I cool down."

"Well, shoot, I was hoping you'd do me a big favor."

I stared at the second-floor windows. Somewhere up there, Wyatt was sprawled in a bed, sleeping. I needed to leave before he decided to wake up. "Ms. Wilson—"

"Harley, please, and it's just a small favor. I've been experimenting with my muffin recipes—you know, to go with the coffee—and I need a second opinion."

The storefront beckoned. The smell of fresh baked goods escaped through the half-open door, tempting me. I imagined the warmth inside and welcomed the chance to dry out before running all the way back home. If it weren't for the argument we'd just had, I'd have called my parents for a ride. I peeked back up at the second floor. It was still early, and Wyatt apparently loved the bunk. What could go wrong?

In an unusual bout of cautious optimism, I nodded at Harley. I'd warm up and be gone long before Wyatt made an appearance.

"Yay." Her face lit up. "My first customer."

She spun around to lead the way, but I stopped in the doorway. Wyatt and his mom couldn't have been in town long, but the transformation was amazing. The deli had dark walls, curtains in the windows, and vinyl booths. Now, even with the overcast sky, the space felt open and bright, like a breath of spring air. She'd pulled out the booths, whitewashed the floors, painted the walls a soft pastel, and removed the curtains from the gleaming windows. Brightly painted tables and carefully mismatched chairs occupied the front of the room. An open counter ran across the back, with a huge chalkboard wall behind it.

"You like it?" Harley called from the counter.

"I love it." I glanced down at my muddy running shoes. "I don't want to make it dirty."

"Are you kidding? It's made to be easily cleaned. I'm counting on lots of sand on these floors, although with this weather, it's more like mud. Isn't it supposed to be warm now?"

"Yup. It's like someone towed our island up north while we

weren't looking." Despite her reassurances, I pulled off my sneakers and padded across the wooden floors, my wet socks leaving a damp trail. I climbed up on a metal stool. "How did you do all this so fast?"

"I hired a contractor and Wyatt helped, but I've been designing this place in my mind for the last ten years. Coffee?"

"Cappuccino?"

She grinned. "A girl after my own heart, but first"—she lined up three muffins on the counter—"be brutally honest. I want my customers to love everything about this place."

I stared at her offerings, curling my toes around the legs of the stool, and my belly growled. From somewhere behind the counter, a country ballad played softly. For the first time this morning, I didn't feel at odds with the entire universe. I finally felt warm and at peace. Sitting here felt right.

Harley watched me, an anxious look on her face. I broke a piece off the first muffin—banana nut—and stuffed it in my mouth. A groan slipped out.

She gave me a cautious smile. "I take it that was a positive groan and not a disgusted one."

I nodded, my mouth too full to speak.

"Well, that's encouraging."

She busied herself behind a fancy chrome espresso machine. The machine hissed and let out steam, belching out a fragrant blast of coffee.

I sighed and took a bite from the second muffin—lemon poppy seed, one of my favorites. I wasn't disappointed. Like the first one, my teeth sank into the moist muffin and flavor burst in my mouth.

Harley set the cappuccino on the counter. "I'm really glad you stopped by, Mer, 'cause I wanted to thank you."

"For what?"

She tilted her head, looking a lot like Wyatt. "For helping my son, of course. I know you helped him find his truck and make it to the ferry, but it was more than that. You made him feel welcome on the island, which means a lot to me."

Guilt flashed through me. I had helped, but I'd done it grudgingly, and taking credit for making him feel welcome was a definite stretch. "It was nothing," I mumbled.

She motioned to the third muffin. "Try the last one. I want it to be my signature flavor. I'm gonna call it Texan Glory."

I took a bite—pumpkin and spice, and an explosion of dates and raisins and nuts. It tasted like heaven. I gave a thumbs-up, and Harley grinned.

"Not that people have made Wyatt feel unwelcome," she continued. "It's just that I know I'm asking a lot of him. He gave up his friends and . . . everything else. But I'm hoping it's easier for him here. Going back to his old school, knowing all his classmates have graduated, would've been difficult."

I gulped my coffee, not sure what to say. It felt wrong, sitting here with Wyatt's mom, talking about his personal life. Still, she looked like she needed reassurance. "Wyatt seems like a pretty confident person. I'm sure he'll make lots of friends here."

"Confident?" Harley snorted. "Honey, there's no need to sugarcoat it. Wyatt was born cocky, just like his daddy. I swear the two of them could strut sitting down. That cockiness will get him in a world of trouble if he isn't careful. It almost got him killed."

I leaned closer. "The bike accident?" I felt guilty about gossiping, but curiosity still got the best of me.

"Yeah." She shot me an odd look, before picking up a cloth and wiping the already clean counter, while I sipped my cappuccino. Wyatt's mom obviously liked to be busy; I recognized the trait from my own mom. She never just sat and relaxed. "Is that what Wyatt said, that he had a bike accident?"

I frowned and thought back. "I think so. He didn't?"

She chuckled, but it was a hollow sound. "Yeah, but I'd say it was more of a spectacular crash of earth-shattering proportions. It left him in a coma for a week. A full week, where I had no idea if he'd ever open his eyes and call me 'Mom' again. But maybe that was for the best 'cause if he'd been conscious, he'd have felt the pain from umpteen broken bones and a punctured lung."

Her words painted a bleak and desperate picture. These were things I understood: bleakness, desperation, lying awake in the darkest part of the night and wondering if your sun would ever rise again. She'd probably struggled to keep herself busy that week—hovering over his bed, straightening his sheet, trying not to disturb the machines keeping him alive, grilling his doctors and nurses. A different outcome, and I'd have never met Wyatt. I'd have come home from my time with Ben last night without being distracted by a boy I didn't need in my life. I had more than enough complications.

"I'm sorry." I struggled to find the right words. "That must have been awful."

Harley's eyes glistened. "It's something no mother should go through, and I swear I couldn't live through it again." She shook herself. "Enough of this depressing talk. So tell me—how were the muffins? Be honest."

"Amazing. I wouldn't change a thing."

"Are you just being polite? 'Cause you strike me as a very polite person."

Wow. It wasn't every day I was accused of being polite. "No, really. Everything about this place is perfect. Tourists are going to eat it up. The locals, too."

"Sugar, that's music to my ears."

"When are you opening?"

"If everything goes according to plan, next weekend. I just need to find some part-time employees and get them trained." She paused. "Hey, do you know anyone looking for work?"

I swallowed. For the last three summers, I'd worked at my dad's windsurfing business. He hadn't officially asked me yet, but

I'd already decided my answer. I couldn't work there. He'd expect me to be on the water, to take care of the equipment and instruct, but I just couldn't. Not yet. Maybe not ever.

I straightened and met her gaze. "Me."

"Oh . . . do you have any experience?"

"It's not a coffee shop, but every summer, I work at my dad's business. He owns a wind- and kitesurfing shop. I handle rentals, take care of the equipment, and give lessons. We sell snacks, so I work the cash as well. But I have to be honest—I have no idea how to operate that." I pointed to her shiny chrome coffee magician.

Her expression fell and she shifted her weight. "Well, honey, I'd really prefer to find someone with experience. Plus, I wouldn't want to make an enemy by stealing your dad's employee. I don't want to make a bad impression on the island before I even open." She laughed, but concern stiffened her features.

Disappointment flickered through me, and I glanced down at my empty cup. "I understand, but either way, I won't be working for my dad this summer."

"That sounds like a story in need of more coffee."

She reached for my cup, but I shook my head and slid off the stool. "No. I really should be going."

"Wait." Wyatt's mom came around the counter and stopped next to me. "Sorry, honey. I wasn't trying to be nosy. I'm just used to listening to people's problems. They say I'm a good listener . . .

in case you ever need someone to lend an ear."

"Thank you," I mumbled, glancing at the door, my heart suddenly pounding.

She jammed her hands in her back pocket and stuck out one hip. "I'm makin' a mess of this, aren't I? Look, I've been running around here trying to get everything done, and Wyatt's sick of my company, and I really do need some help. So, were you serious about the job?"

My gaze wandered upward. By deciding to work at this coffee shop, was I just replacing one problem with another? Still, if I planned to avoid working on the ocean, I needed another job. My parents would never let me spend the summer just hanging around, especially if they found out I was turning down the windsurfing endorsement.

I curled my fingertips into my palms. "Yeah, I'm serious."

"Well, honey . . . " Wyatt's mom chewed on her lip. "I can't make any promises, but why don't you come in for a trial run, maybe one afternoon this week? I can train you, and we can see if we like working together."

I released the breath I'd been holding. "Thanks. That's really great." Why was I so excited about a part-time job? "But I can't work late in the evening," I added. That was my time for Ben.

"No worries. I only plan to be open during the day to start with and on the weekends." She stuck out her hand. "So, it's a plan?"

"Yeah." I shook her hand. "It's a plan."

"What's a plan?"

I spun around.

Wyatt stood in the doorway. He wore sweatpants and a worn T-shirt, his voice gruff with sleep and his hair sticking out. He rubbed one hand across his eyes, causing his shirt to rise and his ab muscles to flex.

Oh, man. I swallowed. Just as impressive as I remembered.

He focused on me, the corners of his lips twitching. "Guess I was more charming than I thought. You just couldn't stay away."

His mom crossed the floor and smacked him on the arm. "Honestly, Wyatt. No one likes a braggart." She looked back at me and winked. "Besides, Mer didn't come here to see you. She came to apply for the job."

Wyatt perched on a stool, stretching his legs out in front of him. Even his stupid bare feet were cute. "You're going to work here, at my mom's coffee shop?"

I shrugged, inching toward the door. "We're planning a trial run."

He leaned forward and raised an eyebrow. "Well, you can be my barista anytime."

"Wyatt!" his mom shouted at him from behind the counter. "Last time I checked, you weren't raised in a barn. So stop acting like it."

Immediately, his shoulders drooped, and his expression turned sheepish.

When his mom turned away, I stuck out my tongue at him. His eyes widened, and he let out a snort of laughter.

The sound made me smile, but I swallowed it back, because I was suddenly too aware of the playful tension crackling between us. Sweat popped up on my forehead. What was I doing here?

I needed to be running, but I'd just made it to my wet sneakers when a gust of wind rattled the front window. Seconds later, rain pelted the glass, streaming down in wide rivulets. My heart sank. The run home was going to be miserable. I tugged up my hood and knelt down to put on my sneakers.

Wyatt's bare feet came into view. "You can't run home in that."

"I've run in worse."

"You'll freeze."

"I'm fine. I was born and raised here." I jammed my foot in, shivering when my socks sank into my wet insoles.

"What's that supposed to mean? You come out of the womb waterproof? Don't be stubborn. Let me drive you."

Before I could find the words to convince Wyatt why this was such a bad idea, he called out over his shoulder: "Mom, I have to grab my keys. Make sure she doesn't leave."

Harley winked at me. "I'll hog-tie her if necessary."

Wyatt fixed me with another long look. "She's only half joking, you know. I'll be right back."

So I waited, wondering what the hell just happened.

Wyatt Quinn was nothing but trouble. He'd inserted himself into my life for the second day in a row, and for some reason, I'd let it happen.

Chapter Six

Wyatt's truck smelled like cinnamon. I adjusted the vents, grateful for the warm air blasting on my body. I'd gotten soaked again just running from the coffee shop to the passenger door.

Wyatt drove with one hand on the wheel and one hand on his thigh, tapping to the beat of a country song playing on the radio. I'd guessed right on that one. Raindrops clung to his hair, like spring dew on grass, and the collar of his shirt was damp.

I gave him directions to my house, hoping the weather would keep my parents from noticing when I pulled up in a strange vehicle.

"So"—he glanced over at me—"you were out running this morning and just happened to run by my house."

I stared out the front windshield. "Yeah, something like that."

"Hmmm . . . vague answers." He paused and winked at me. "If you admit to being curious, I promise not to read too much into it."

Maybe a tiny part of me had been flattered by Wyatt's charm and good looks, but this time, his flirting attempts fell flat. It was fake, an act. Once school started on Monday, he'd have his choice of girls. He'd be shiny and exciting, and many would willingly throw themselves on his hook, happy to be reeled in. But I had no plans to be one of them. If the job at the coffee shop worked out, I'd be seeing Wyatt more often, so I needed to set the record straight.

I jammed my hands in my pockets and watched the familiar streets pass through the thin veil of rain. "Look, Wyatt, I get that you're flirty like this with all the girls." I lifted my chin, searching for the least offensive words, but who was I trying to kid? I was clearly going to offend him. "I try not to judge people because I don't want them judging me. But you make me uncomfortable, and I don't like it. I don't make friends easily, because I need genuine reasons to actually care about someone. Not some bullshit act that's supposed to turn me on."

My words lingered in the too-quiet cab. I meant what I'd said, but I still couldn't look at Wyatt. The windshield wipers slapped, and the song on the radio turned to something sad and depressing. *Perfect.* My fingernails dug into my palms, and the awkward meter skyrocketed. I finally turned to look at Wyatt.

His jaw worked back and forth, and both hands gripped the steering wheel. His expression reflected the angry gray skies hanging over the island.

"I should have warned you," I muttered. "People tell me I should filter more."

Ben understood when I was direct with him. Or at least I always hoped he had. Admittedly, he'd also encouraged me to try harder to fit in.

"No one will think less of you for saying something nice, even if you don't completely mean it."

"Then why say it?"

"I don't know—just to be nice."

Of course, that made me wonder why Ben even bothered with me. Even before I'd broken his trust and angered his mom, deep down I'd always worried that I wasn't good enough for him, that one day he'd move on to someone prettier, happier . . . nicer.

When Wyatt went to school on Monday, he'd understand that also.

"You said it because you meant it," Wyatt finally spoke, his tone cool. "At least you're being honest."

"Still . . . " Still, what? Why did I feel so guilty for telling him what I really felt?

He stomped on the brakes and the truck lurched to a stop at a street corner. No cars approached, but we sat there anyway, waiting.

"Look, I've always done this—flirted, come off like a cocky son of a bitch—because that's the only way I know how to be." He looked over at me, his brow furrowed. "Maybe I worry that if I stop, people will be bored or whatever. Without that part, I don't know if there's much else to like."

The raw emotion in his words grated across my skin, but I didn't want to be Wyatt Quinn's therapist. If I couldn't fix myself, I definitely couldn't fix him. I looked away, my fingers curling around my seat belt. "I'm not asking you to change for me."

When I glanced back, my breath caught. His expression was defiant and expectant and haunting—all at the same time. "I know. You don't want anything from me."

He turned away, and my lungs started to work again. The truck skidded forward onto the empty street, and I bit my lip until it hurt. I wouldn't let myself care about Wyatt or his fears. Soon enough, he'd have other friends to care about him, other kids who'd willingly fall for his charms and not make him question himself.

We drove the rest of the way in silence, the short ride feeling like an hour.

In my driveway, Wyatt stared out at my two-story clapboard house. I'd worried about my parent's potential questions for nothing. Our vehicle was gone, which meant the house was likely empty. Mom and Rachel were probably somewhere in town, and my dad had no doubt walked down to the beach. If you followed the driveway past my house for another couple hundred feet, you reached the ocean and my dad's shop. So close, but yet so far away.

Outside, the rain eased to a drizzle. *Just my luck.* A few minutes earlier and I wouldn't have been forced to accept Wyatt's ride. I sighed. "Wait here."

"Why?"

"Just wait." I pushed the door and it swung open.

Wyatt frowned but nodded. "Whatever."

Running up to the porch and slipping inside, I toed off my wet sneakers and laid them upside down on the radiator to dry. I climbed the stairs to my room and found Wyatt's jacket in my tiny, overflowing closet—it was in the same spot I'd stuffed it last night.

I made a quick stop in the kitchen, before pushing my feet in my rubber boots and heading back out to Wyatt's truck. He rolled down his window.

"Thanks for the loan last night and the drive today." I handed the jacket to him, stepping close enough to catch his clean scent. "Without it, I probably would have frozen."

He leaned an arm against the open window, his expression rigid. "It's okay, Mer. You don't need to treat me with kid gloves. You were honest. I can take it."

I stepped back and wrapped my arms around my belly. "So, maybe I'll see you around?"

"Sure." He threw the truck in reverse and backed out of my driveway.

I stood and watched until he disappeared down the street. Then I headed inside and fell on the couch, burying myself under the heavy quilt Mom always kept there. I'd accomplished exactly what I'd wanted to. Wyatt was no longer a complication in my life.

So why did I feel like I'd just drowned a bag full of puppies?

"What's wrong?" Ben whispered. We sat in the darkened theater, gunshots and explosions vibrating through my body. "You love cheesy action movies."

I leaned forward, looking past Ben to the row of sophomores. A pretty blonde sat on Ben's other side. Kayla something or other. I'd have to be comatose not to notice the way she kept offering him popcorn and whispering in his ear.

I slouched in my seat. "When you asked me to come tonight, I didn't know you were bringing your whole posse. I can barely hear the movie with all the racket they're making."

Ben leaned close, close enough that the sweet smell of Twizzlers on his breath made my mouth water. "What's the matter, Mer? Jealous?"

Jealous! I jumped and my forehead smacked into his nose. Popcorn flew over the man ahead of me. Ben grunted, and the man spun around to give me the stink eye. Great. Smooth move, Hall.

Everyone else in the row looked in our direction, including

Kayla. She snickered, looking smug and perfect.

Heat flashed up my cheeks. I jammed the bag of popcorn against Ben's chest. "Here. Enjoy the movie."

"Mer!"

I heard Ben's shout, but I didn't stop. I couldn't stop. I'd just made a total ass of myself. Kids would be talking about this for years to come. Storming past the concession stand, I jerked on the exit door three times before the PUSH sign registered. Fantastic.

Outside, I slouched against the cinema wall, my heart pounding.

I closed my eyes and banged my head back. I was stupid. All this just because Ben teased me about being jealous. This annoying crush was supposed to go away, but it had grown stronger instead. When I was with him, it hurt to look at him. I held on to his every word like an idiot. My hands shook whenever we touched.

So, I'd tried to stay away. It had been easier than I thought. We were in different high schools. He had football practice, and I had windsurfing. Just a few excuses, and a few weeks passed without seeing him. We still messaged and texted, but I could handle that without giving anything away.

Then he'd asked me to this movie, and I'd thought it would just be us. I'd said yes because I missed Ben and the idea of sitting next to him in the darkened theater for a couple of hours was too tempting. When Dad dropped me off, I'd found Ben inside, standing in the middle of his friends. They'd all been laughing at something he'd said. He looked like he belonged there, with them.

I kicked the wall behind me. I'd almost left, but he'd seen me first. His face had lit up, and he'd come over and taken my hand, tugging me to the counter to buy popcorn and candy.

"Mer?"

My eyes flew open.

Ben stood in front of me, the concern on his face clear in the glow from the streetlight. I knew every one of his expressions. How could I not? He was my best friend.

I groaned and ducked my chin. "Just go away. Go back inside and watch the movie."

"No. Tell me what happened."

I shrugged. Dark hair fell over his forehead, and my fingers itched to push it back in place. I jammed my hands behind me instead, holding them captive between the wall and my butt. "You saw. I made a complete fool of myself."

He rubbed one hand across the back of his neck and frowned down at me. "There was more. You were upset about Kayla. You were upset because I said you were jealous."

I bit the inside of my cheek and looked away. What was Ben doing? He'd crossed into dangerous territory. Despite everything, he'd been my friend first. We couldn't risk all that by saying things we couldn't take back. If he knew how I felt, everything would be ruined.

I straightened from the wall and shrugged. "I wasn't upset about Kayla or whatever her name was. I was just annoyed because they were talking and I was trying to pay attention and . . . and . . .

I'm on my period."

There. A surefire plan to distract Ben.

*I glanced up, expecting to see his usual discomfort when I men-
tioned my monthly visitor, but instead there was something else on
his face, an expression I'd never seen before: a mix of fear and determination. That look caught me in its grip and wouldn't let go.*

*"I think you're lying. I think you're afraid to tell me the truth
because you're scared that it'll ruin what we have." His hand curled
into a fist and his nostrils flared. "I know you're lying, because I've
had the same fear. I think about it every day. I tell myself that it's
just me, that I can't feel this way because I'm just being stupid and
you don't feel the same. But it's not going away."*

A buzzing sound hummed in my ears.

*"You've avoided me the last couple of weeks, Mer, and it's killing
me. I need to know." His hand was somehow in my hair, tugging
through the long strands. "Is there any chance you feel it, too?"*

*The buzzing grew louder. Tears burned in my eyes and my
knees shook. This couldn't be happening, but it was. I bit my lip
and nodded.*

*He closed his eyes and his shoulders sagged. His arms came
around me, and my heart slammed against my rib cage. Ben was
holding me! He'd hugged me before, but this was different. His face
buried in my hair. My hands clung to his back, and I swore I felt
his tears on my cheek.*

I'd never kissed a boy. How could I when it had always been Ben

I'd dreamed about kissing? But this nervous, crazy, delicious feeling jumping through my body was better than I'd ever imagined. I hugged him tighter while my head spun in the stars. He smelled like everything good in my life, like warm flannel and the ocean.

His lips found mine, the same lips I'd stared at for years, the same lips that had smiled at my stupid jokes and whispered reassurances when my world crashed out of control. I couldn't believe the universe was finally giving me this perfect moment.

"Mer," he sighed against my mouth, his forehead leaning against mine. "I promised that I'd always like you best. It's always been you."

I breathed in the sweet purity of his words. I let them heal all my uncertainties and fears. Then he kissed me, and that kiss filled up every lonely place in my heart.

Whatever happened in the future, Ben felt the same way I did.

He'd picked me.

Dad pushed my legs to one side and dropped down on the other end of the sofa.

"Looks like you've had a busy day." He glanced at the stray kernels left in the popcorn bowl, the pile of DVDs on the coffee table, and the half-empty Coke bottle in my lap.

I shrugged, but his words left shards of guilt lodged in my chest. He'd probably needed my help today. In the past, I'd been more than willing to give it. "It's the last day of spring break and the sky is gray. What can I say?"

He nodded slowly, stuck his feet on the coffee table, and reached for the nearest DVD case. "*Die Hard.* Decent choice. I figured you might call for a ride this morning. It was raining pretty hard."

I burrowed deeper in the quilt. "Calling wouldn't have done any good. Mom and Rachel took the car, and the truck is still in the shop."

"I could have driven Sally."

"And then we both would have been soaked. It's fine. I made it home in one piece." And managed to break the confidence of another boy. Maybe not break. That might be giving myself too much credit. Maybe I just dented it.

"So"—Dad dropped his head back against the cushion and glanced over at me—"despite this weather, the season will be starting soon. I get that it's your last day of vacation, but I could have used your help." He stopped and looked down at his hands, callused from years of gripping booms. I had the same calluses on mine. "More than that, I'd have liked the company."

Dad could have lectured me for a week and grounded me for a month, and it wouldn't have had nearly as great an impact as those last gruff words. He'd always been in my corner—quietly supporting me, letting me know that even if I was far from being the perfect daughter, I was the perfect daughter for him.

He understood my flaws and my quirks and my awkwardness, maybe because he shared them, too.

My eyes burned, and I blinked and looked away. Months ago, when I'd lied to Ben, I'd also broken my dad's heart. For once, I'd seen the same disappointment on his face that I'd seen on my mother's face a million times before. On her, it was expected. She loved us, but she also held her daughters to the highest standard. Most days, Rachel reached the bar, while I always slid under. But Dad? That look told me I'd ripped the sail from his hands and left him drifting.

It didn't help that my distrust of the water had taken away the things we had most in common: windsurfing and the ocean. Now, he was extending an olive branch, offering me the chance to come back to the shop and rebuild what my actions had broken. I should have jumped at it. I should have forgiven myself *and* the ocean, but some wounds ran too deep. So instead, I squeezed a fistful of quilt and prepared to break his heart again.

"I'm not going to work with you this summer . . . " My voice trailed off, so I sucked in a breath and tried again. "There's a new coffee shop in town. It's opening next week, and the owner offered me a job. I said yes."

Dad's shoulders slumped. "I stuck up for you, Mer. You can't lie to us again."

"I'm not lying." I pulled my knees to my chest. "Not this time. You can even talk to the owner. She's opened up next to the bakery downtown."

"The old deli?"

"Yeah. She and her son just moved here from Texas. Wyatt's starting in my class on Monday."

"I see." Dad dropped his feet to the floor and sat up. "And you'd rather pour coffee this summer than work with me?" Dad wasn't one to make a lot of eye contact, but this time he held my gaze.

"Dad, it's not that." My fingers found his.

His eyes widened. "Jeez, Mer, your hands are freezing."

"Sorry. Maybe you can't understand this, but I'd rather serve coffee than be on the ocean every day. I'm not ready yet. I don't know if I'll ever be."

For a long moment, he stared at our linked hands. "More than anything, I wish this could all be different, but I am trying to understand."

I nodded. It was all I could ask for.

Mom knocked on my door later that evening. When I didn't respond, she came in anyway. "Are you ready for school on Monday?"

I didn't look up from my book. "Yeah."

"Is all your homework done? I know you had assignments over the break."

I snapped the book shut and sighed. "You don't need to worry about it."

"Really? Because all I do these days is worry. You don't put effort into anything anymore, except maybe lying to us."

Wow. Low blow. "So, I'm not going to make the honor roll. At least I'm passing everything."

She rubbed one hand across her forehead, looking tired. "I just want you to try your hardest. Is that really so much to ask?"

Guilt twitched inside me, but I pushed it aside. "I'm not one of your students."

"That's right. You're my daughter."

"And a disappointment."

Mom crossed her arms. "I know you've had a few hard months, but that doesn't give you a pass from trying." She paused, the tension in the room knotting my stomach. "I lost something because of all this, too, you know. I lost my best friend."

Because of me. She didn't say it, but the blame seeped from her expression.

I stood and walked to my desk, picking up my math book and a history assignment. When I turned and pushed them into her hands, she frowned. "What's this?"

"My completed homework. Feel free to read it, grade it, whatever you want."

She huffed and dropped the assignments on my bed. "You don't want to work for your dad this summer. You spend all your time alone. I want to know what's going on."

I met her gaze. Her mouth was pinched into a tight line, her spine stiff with frustration. I also saw the concern lurking in her eyes, but there was nothing I could say. I couldn't tell her about the amazing windsurfing opportunity I was turning down, or how much it hurt to know I'd disappointed Dad, or how I wished I could meet new people like Wyatt and just feel comfortable in my own skin. Mom would judge me for any one of those confessions and find me lacking. Most of all, I could never tell her about Ben and how my nightly visits to the beach were the only time I felt really happy. She'd never understood how I could love him that much. She'd never support what we were doing now.

I sat down and opened my book. "There's nothing to tell."

"Mer!"

I stubbornly stared at the words swimming on the page until my bedroom door finally shut.

Chapter Seven

Living on Ocracoke, I was "lucky" enough to go to one of the smallest schools in the country. I'd started here in kindergarten and wouldn't escape the tiny campus until graduation. Mom taught primary, so that was another "plus." She knew more about my school life than should be legal.

There were only eleven students in my junior year, and I'd been with them since the first day of Mrs. Lester's kindergarten class. With so few kids, people assumed we must all be best friends. *Wrong. So wrong.* Teachers and parents praised smaller class sizes as the Holy Grail of academic success, but from a social standpoint, it sucked. Fewer students meant nowhere to hide. How do you blend into the background when everyone sees you? They see the ways you're the same and all the ways you're different. I'd always been jealous of Ben's larger school in Buxton. It wasn't huge, but his class had thirty-plus students.

Now, I yanked on my lock for the fifth time and cursed. Why the hell wouldn't my combination work? I turned up the volume on my music and wondered what else could go wrong.

I'd already woken up late, not moving fast enough to get out the door on time. Then I'd had to skirt buckets and plastic strewn around the school. Apparently the unseasonable weather had revealed a bunch of leaks. Even though the skies had finally cleared, water still dripped from the ceiling, making the school resemble a sinking ship. A locker that refused to open was icing on the proverbial cake.

Someone tapped my shoulder, and I turned around.

Kim bounced in front of me like her sneakers were attached to a pogo stick, her brown ponytail bobbing with her. I sighed and pulled out my earbuds.

"Oh my God, you'll never guess who's joining our class."

I shrugged. "Wyatt Quinn."

"Yeah." She deflated, but in true Kim fashion, it took only seconds for the bouncing to resume. "But do you know who he is?"

"A guy from Texas?"

"Not just any guy from Texas." She pushed up her glasses, whipped out her iPad, and stuck it in my face. "He is Wyatt Quinn, a legend in the world of motocross. His dad is Jimmy Quinn, the famous race car driver, who is now engaged to Melody Adams . . . *the* Melody Adams."

Okay. I may not have listened to country music, but even I'd heard of *the* Melody Adams. Beautiful, blonde, and perky, she'd been shooting up the charts. I brushed the bangs from my eyes and scrolled through the images. My mouth hung open. There was Wyatt, the same shivering guy who'd landed on my beach dragging a kayak behind him—only in these shots, he looked drop-dead sexy. In one, he leaned against a motorcycle, wearing only red-and-blue biker pants and his boots, his chest tanned and muscled and his bronze hair damp with sweat. In another, he jumped that same bike over dirt mounds, captured fifteen feet in the air, hanging off the handlebars with his legs extended in a kind of crazy-ass attack on the sky.

Another image caught him with his arm around his dad. They were laughing with their heads back and were surrounded by some seriously beautiful people. He looked like his dad—both of them confident, grinning, and insanely hot. I pushed the iPad back at Kim. I did not need Wyatt Quinn's hotness rubbed in my nose.

She took another look at the images and swooned. "Mrs. Prince told my mom that he was coming, and my brother almost had a heart attack. He has posters of him on his wall. Apparently he had this wild crash last fall, and everyone's waiting to see if he'll make a comeback."

The accident Wyatt and his mom talked about suddenly took on a new meaning. I yanked on my lock one more time. If I searched his crash, would I find it in full color, captured by some fan's cell phone? But I didn't want to see. Hearing about his pain from Harley had been bad enough.

"Mer, why are you trying to open Cora's locker? That's yours." Kim pointed to a locker four doors away. I tilted my head back and blinked at the number. What the hell? How had I mixed this up?

I stomped over to the right locker.

"I still can't believe it." Kim tugged on her thin gold necklace with one hand. "Wait . . . " She dropped the pendant and pinned me with a stare. "How did you know he was coming?"

I spun in my combination and debated my options. Before last fall and before the whole thing with Ben had made me *persona non grata*, Kim had been the closest thing I had to a friend in my class, not that we'd been super close or anything. She tended to gossip, which she'd inherited from her mom, but most of it was harmless.

I yanked on the lock and it sprang open. *Thank you!* "I ran into him this weekend."

"Really?" She hooked her arm through mine. "You need to tell me everything. What's he like? Is he as sexy as he looks in his pictures?"

Her grip clamped off the circulation in my arm. "Why don't you see for yourself?" I muttered between clenched teeth, nodding my head in the direction of the office.

Wyatt had just emerged, strolling in our direction. Like

almost everyone else in my class, he wore jeans, sneakers, and a long-sleeved T-shirt, but somehow he still managed to stand out as shiny and new. He'd pushed up the sleeves of his gray shirt, revealing the muscles in his forearms and a long silvery scar on the right side. How had I missed that earlier?

Kim's fingernails dug into my flesh, and I shook her off. "Get a grip," I hissed, "and not on me."

Wyatt stopped in front of us. His faded jeans sat low on his hips, but not too low. His black Vans were battered, like they'd seen years of use, and he'd sculpted his hair into a deliberate mess. I preferred the way it had glistened with rain, back when we were in his truck.

"Hey." He stared at me, a backpack slung over one shoulder. I considered his expression. I wasn't sure what I'd expected, but definitely not this cautious optimism. Honestly, I figured he'd do his best to avoid or ignore me—a difficult task considering how many classes we probably shared.

"Hi!" Kim flicked her ponytail over one shoulder and shot Wyatt her warmest smile. "Welcome to Ocracoke." Her hand shot out, like she was a campaigning politician. "I'm Kim."

Wyatt grinned and shook hands. "Wyatt. Nice to meet ya."

"Oh my God," she gushed. "I love your accent."

Wyatt kept hold of her hand and cocked up one eyebrow. "Well, darlin', some folks might say that you're the one with the accent."

I snorted and rolled my eyes. Kim didn't notice because she

was too busy blushing all the way up to her hairline. But Wyatt did. He fired a quick look in my direction, challenging me to do something about it. But like I'd told him, I didn't need Wyatt to change for me. He was free to act the way he wanted.

"I've got class." I pulled out my books. *Great.* Even my notebooks were wet, like there'd been a mini-flood inside my locker. I wiped them off with my sleeve and slammed my locker shut. "See you around." I spun on my heel and headed toward homeroom.

"Hey, wait up." Wyatt appeared in my peripheral vision, keeping pace. "I want to talk to you for a sec."

"Sure. Talk away."

He touched my arm, and I flinched. His hand immediately fell. "Sorry."

We'd stopped at the edge of the hallway. Students flowed past, everyone staring. I wasn't stupid. They were looking at Wyatt.

"You're wearing black again."

"What?"

He nodded at my sweater. "Every time I see you, you're wearing black."

"I like black." I hugged my books to my chest. "So sue me."

"Chill. It was an observation, not an accusation." He tugged a crinkled bag of Skittles from his pocket. "You left these in my jacket." He retrieved a second rumpled bag from his other pocket. "Two bags," he stated, like I couldn't see the obvious.

"Yeah. I know. I put them there." I tapped one finger against my temple. "Mind like a steel trap."

His gaze raked over my face, hot and flirty. "Doesn't look like any steel trap I've ever seen before."

I blinked. "You literally can't turn it off."

"Sorry." He looked sheepish. "Old habits die hard." His expression switched back to cautious optimism, and he shook the bags of candy in my face. "So, what gives?"

I swatted them away. "I gave ... because my mother says you should never borrow something and return it empty. Of course, she's probably talking about casserole dishes, but I figured the same rule could apply to jackets."

He frowned and fisted both bags in one hand. "That's it. That's the only reason."

"Yeah, what'd you think?" That it had anything to do with the guilt I'd felt over the way I'd talked to him. That maybe I'd felt like crap for calling him out on what appeared to be the heart of his personality.

He rubbed his free hand across the back of his neck. "I figured they were a sort of peace offering."

He leaned closer, propping one shoulder against the wall next to me. *Damn.* The fluorescent school lights left most of us looking sickly, but they just made his eyes greener. And what was with this fresh laundry smell? Did he rub himself with dryer sheets before he left the house?

I focused, trying to find the right comeback. "Did you want it to be a peace offering?" I'd learned this tactic years ago to fend off my mother's criticism: Put the questions back on her.

He laughed, a soft sound that only I heard. "Nice way to put the ball back in my court, Hall. Very smooth. Here's the thing: I thought a lot about what you said on Saturday, and you raised some valid points." He straightened and offered me one of the bags of Skittles. "I was wondering if maybe we could start over again. I could try to put the bullshit aside, and you could see if you like me . . . as a friend."

I froze. I wasn't expecting this direct honesty. Once again, he'd knocked me off balance.

Kim still stood by my locker, watching us. The bell rang, and the noise level in the hall rose by a gazillion decibels. More students streamed past us, but Wyatt just stepped closer, blocking out their prying stares.

"Why? Why is this so important to you? Take a look around. You are the most exciting thing to ever happen to this school. You shook Kim's hand and called her darlin', and she almost peed her pants. You can be friends with anyone in the school. Hell, you can be friends with all of them. So why does it matter what I think? I'm just one person, and trust me, in this school, my opinion doesn't matter."

Wyatt looked around, the hallway nearly empty now. His gaze fell back on me, and his head cocked to one side. "Because I've never met a purple-haired, harmonica-playing hottie before."

I shook my head and pushed past him. "Keep your Skittles, 'cause you're doing it again."

"No. Maybe. I mean, I'm trying to be honest."

He followed me into homeroom, but I stopped just inside the door. Mr. Kendall must have rearranged the classroom because nothing looked quite the same. I found an empty spot in the back row, and Wyatt slid into the seat right next to me. *Really?* The guy was determined. He dropped his backpack to the floor, and I slouched in my chair. From the front row, Kim gawked at us, genuine confusion on her face.

Wyatt angled his chair toward mine. "Look, you're different, but in a good way. You seem cool and I'm interested. Isn't that pretty much the reason why anyone becomes friends?"

I sighed and pulled out my notebook. Our homeroom teacher also taught us math, which we happened to have first period. I hated math. I did okay in it, but I never really got the point.

"Nothing?" Wyatt said. "No response?"

"I'm thinking."

"Wow." He planted his elbows on his desk. "Maybe I should be offended. I've never worked this hard to get anyone to like me." He glanced sideways at me. "Not even a horse . . . "

I slapped my books on my desk, loving the flicker of worry on Wyatt's face.

Mr. Kendall stood at the front of the class and started attendance, not that it took much effort to figure out if all eleven of us were here. Correction. I glanced at Wyatt. Twelve.

I ripped a blank sheet from my notebook. *There would have to be rules,* I wrote, slipping the sheet on his desk. What was I doing?

He read it and the ends of his lips curved upward. His pen

flew across the paper, and then it was back in front of me, his handwriting bold and fluid and surprisingly neater than mine.

Like what?

I chewed on the tip of my pen. Yeah, Ms. Smarty-Pants, like what?

Mr. Kendall called out Wyatt's name and motioned to him. "Welcome, Wyatt. It's not every day we get a new student at our school. Why don't you tell us a little about yourself?"

Some people might feel awkward or shy at being put on the spot, me included, but not Wyatt. He leaned back in his chair and flashed his pearly whites. "Well, as you might have already heard, I'm from Texas, where we've got a lot of horses."

Jerk. I furiously tapped my pen against the desk.

"Me and my mom moved here a few weeks ago. She's opening a coffee shop in town. I've already met a few people"—he nodded at Kim and winked—"and I'm looking forward to meeting the rest of you."

Mr. Kendall smiled. "Well, we're pleased to have you and your mom joining our community. We may be small, but we've got a lot going on. We're always looking for new members on the student council and yearbook committees. Just let us know where your interests lie."

George Rawley, who sat on Wyatt's other side, leaned over and whispered loudly, "Dirt bikes and hot girls, right?"

Wyatt grinned at him and bumped fists. "Always, bro."

My pen flew across the sheet—our list of rules. *No flirting or calling me darlin'.*

When Mr. Kendall started teaching, Wyatt reached out and took the sheet from my desk. He scanned the paper, wrote something, and handed it back.

Agreed.

Are you sure? I mouthed at him.

He traced an *X* across his chest with one finger and shot me the most innocent look.

A drip of cold water landed on my nose. I blinked and looked up. A small water stain appeared on the ceiling right above my head. It dripped again and I flinched. Without skipping a beat, Wyatt's hand shot out, and his fingers wrapped around my chair. He tugged my desk closer, out of the path of the leak intent on soaking me.

Mr. Kendall looked down at the noise, and I pointed to the ceiling. "Another leak."

"Sorry, Mer. Seems the school is no longer watertight. Hopefully, they can get the roof fixed soon."

"It's okay, sir," Wyatt spoke up. "She can just sit closer to me. I don't mind."

Before I could protest, he reached out and tugged me even closer, until our shoulders were almost touching. Mr. Kendall passed down a bucket, and I placed it under the leak, still wondering why I'd thought it was a good idea to negotiate a friendship with the sexy new guy who thought it was a compliment to compare me to a horse. Oh, while also trying not to drown in the middle of my classroom.

Mr. Kendall turned back to the board, and I wiggled my desk away from Wyatt's until a couple of inches separated us. He frowned at me, but I just wrote my next rule: *I like my space at school. Don't crowd me.*

When I dropped the note in front of Wyatt, he stared at it, chewing on his lip before furiously writing and handing it back.

You like to "nyzg race" at school? Don't crowd you? What kind of race is this? Some funky North Carolina thing?

I rolled my eyes. My writing did bear a striking resemblance to a toddler attempting hieroglyphics with finger paint. I'd read somewhere that girls tended to have neater handwriting than boys. Clearly, that biological distinction hadn't been pressed on me in elementary school.

Crossing out my first attempt, I wrote above it in capital letters: *MY SPACE.*

The relevance of this rule was highlighted when Wyatt hooked his feet around the front legs of his chair, bumping my knee in the process.

I handed the note back. Wyatt glanced over it and started writing again, his forehead creased in concentration. I tried to peek, but his other hand blocked the paper.

Mr. Kendall turned to ask a question, and Wyatt slipped the

note under his book until he returned to the board. After, Wyatt swiveled to face me, holding out the note, one eyebrow raised. A few classmates watched, more interested in our note passing than the lecture. One of them was Kim.

I snatched it out of his fingers, folded it in half, and stuck it between the pages of my textbook. For the next five minutes, I tapped my heel impatiently, waiting until everyone had stopped looking. Finally, I slipped it out.

Your writing is the worst and this is the oddest set of rules. Do we need sub-rules for this rule? For example, what constitutes crowding? Is it temporal or spatial or both?

Smart-ass.

I wrote, *Amendment to this rule: I'll tell you when and if you are crowding me, and you agree not to be offended. Also, last rule: I'll respect your privacy, and you respect mine.* I read through my rules one last time before passing the paper back across the border.

At the end of class, Wyatt laid the folded paper in front of me, scooped up his backpack, and headed out the door with only a quick backward glance.

I slowly unfolded it. He'd written: *Agreed, especially on the last one.*

On the bottom, he'd signed his full name and dated it, like it was an actual contract. Based on this, Wyatt and I were now officially friends.

I stopped by the garbage can on the way out, intending to throw the note away in case anyone else saw it, like Ben. My fingers curled around one corner, a millisecond away from crumpling our agreement into a tiny ball, but I stopped. Instead, I folded the paper into squares and tucked it inside a pocket of my backpack where no one but me would find it.

Chapter Eight

"Hey, am I doing this right?"

I leaned my boom toward the rear of my board, turning into the wind to come up behind Jason, a guy in the group of beginners Dad had me instructing. It was a family group—siblings and cousins ranging in age from ten to sixteen. Jason was the oldest, blond and very sweet. This was their third day of lessons, and he'd been helping me carry the boards and sails and wrangle the younger kids.

"Looking good. Get ready to tack."

Jason leaned his sail to the rear, forcing the board to pivot into the wind.

"That's great. Move around the front of the board. Good. Now cross your arms over and grab the boom with your right hand."

He grabbed for it. At the same time, the board wobbled, and he lost his footing. As far as falls went, it was pretty spectacular.

I ducked my face, but I still got showered. Blinking, I watched his grinning face pop back up. He grabbed the board and pulled himself up. Water streamed down his body, and his biceps flexed. He was tanned and from Charleston, and it made no sense to me, but I could have sworn he'd been flirting with me.

"How was that? Pretty awesome, right?" He sat on the board, legs dangling, and caught his breath.

"Yeah, I'd give it a two out of ten."

"Ouch." He pretended to die. "Shot down by the Russian judge."

I tacked back and forth, staying within hearing distance. Officially, the lesson was over. The younger kids were already congregated close to shore. Dad stood knee-deep in water and motioned to me.

I looked back at Jason. "Time's up, which means less talking and more surfing."

He sighed and scrambled to his feet. "So since the lesson is over, maybe you can show me some stuff on the way in. Sailing back and forth is fun, but I want to know what I'm working up to."

"Can't. We're supposed to head back." Dad needed me to get everything set up for the next lesson. He'd be disappointed if I stayed on the water, showing off.

"Come on," he pleaded. "I want to see what you can do."

Something warmed my insides besides the sun beating on my

shoulders. I wanted to show off. Ever since Ben had kissed me in the parking lot last spring, I'd felt different—more confident, less worried about fitting in. The amazing thing was, kids in my class were treating me different, too. They sat with me at lunch and included me in their jokes. They invited me and Ben to their parties. I still felt awkward when we hung out with Ben's friends, but it was bearable. It was doable.

The wind gusted and I tightened my grip on the boom. Farther out on the Pamlico Sound, colorful sails decorated the horizon like sprinkles on a cake. That's where the serious fun was happening. That's where I headed every afternoon when all the lessons were over—sometimes with Dad and sometimes alone. I'd been doing this so many years, even the hardened windsurfers respected my presence out there. They knew I belonged.

What the hell . . . life was too short to miss out on the opportunity to impress the cute guy trailing behind me. Adjusting my grip, I pumped the sail to get the board on the plane. It rocketed forward, skipping over the waves. I blinked against the glare off the water and leaned back, slipping my feet into the foot straps. Pulling the sail into position, I attacked the next wave, using my forward momentum to launch myself into the air. For a moment, I was weightless, free, kicking the board out to one side in a shameless act of showing off.

Behind me, I heard Jason hooting and hollering: "Yeah! Go!"

The board landed back on the ocean, my knees absorbing the impact. I let my speed build, leaning back so far, my hair practically trailed in the water. My board shot out a bubbling wake. I imagined how I looked in my bikini bottoms and my favorite rash guard—the one that fit me really tight and showed off my small waist. My body was lean and tanned from the months I'd already been on the water this season.

I pointed my board toward the sound, my back to the island and all my responsibilities. More than anything, I wanted to keep going. Nothing on land ever gave me this feeling, except maybe being with Ben. I was on fire, and even the cold spray off the ocean couldn't put it out.

For the next few minutes, I freestyled, maneuvering my rig into a series of twists and flips that made my arms ache and my heart pound. The board obeyed my every command. It was small and light, and a gift from my dad two years back. Mom and Rachel never understood my excitement, the way I'd screamed and launched myself at my dad, like he'd just given me a car.

Eventually, I jibed the board around, ducking under the sail and heading back to shore. There was no running from my responsibilities forever. I caught up with Jason, who was still making his way back.

"That was amazing," he called out, winking at me. "Where did you learn to do all that?"

My cheeks heated, and it wasn't just from exertion. "From my dad." When I was really small, I'd sit on the front of his board, and he'd take me around the sound. Mom never liked that. She worried I'd fall off or something, but I'd learned to swim almost before I could walk, and being on Dad's board had been as natural to me as breathing.

The water grew shallow under our feet, and we steered our boards right to the small sandy beach in front of the shop. If it weren't for the jumble of kids and boards and sails, I'd have sailed right to shore and stepped off, barely getting wet. Instead, we dropped our sails farther out and slid off our boards into the thigh-deep water.

Dad looked at me from across the gaggle of kids and shook his head, but I saw the smile he tried to hide. How could he blame me when he'd love to do the same thing? I knew it killed him—watching those sails flying across the water, while he rented equipment to tourists who only managed to wobble back and forth in front of our beach. Most ended up too far downwind to make it back alone. So we'd launch our little boat from the dock, and either Dad or I would drag them back.

Of course, as far as summer jobs went, this one was pretty sweet. At least I wasn't flipping burgers at the local grill or bagging groceries. Ben spent most of his summer on the water, too, crewing for his dad's boat. I'd talked to him about crewing on a tall ship for a year after I graduated. I'd let myself imagine it—long, balmy evenings under the stars, Ben and I sitting at a little café on a cobblestone street in a town whose name I couldn't pronounce—but he was reluctant to leave the Outer Banks. He liked quiet and steady more than unknown excitement. I wanted both, but I wanted Ben more.

"Mer!" My attention returned to the present and Dad's curious look. "Want to give me a hand with these boards?"

"Yeah." I detached the mast from the closest board.

"Let me help." Jason stepped closer, and together, we carried the boards up on shore and stacked them on the special racks I'd helped Dad build.

The kids in Jason's family came up to me, all of them in awe over my jumps, wondering how I'd done them and more importantly, when they could learn.

Over their heads, Jason grinned at me. "You were awesome," he said, just loud enough for me to hear. His parents called the younger kids over, helping them shower and change, and suddenly it was just Jason and me.

"I think that was your last lesson. I hope you liked them."

"Yeah." He stood half a head taller than me, his blond hair hanging over his blue eyes. "Especially the instructor."

Wait! He was definitely flirting with me. My head dropped, and I stared at my feet. I dug my toes into the hot sand, not sure what to say.

"Look, we only have one more weekend on the island, but I was wondering if you might like to go for a burger or something."

What? Besides Ben, no one had ever asked me out before, and definitely not any tall, cute boys. My mind went blank.

"*Mer.*" *An arm circled my shoulders, pulling me close. Ben.* "*There you are.*" *He planted a quick, hard kiss right on my lips, a kiss that left me shaking. Whoa! We never kissed if my dad was anywhere in viewing distance. I hooked my arm around his waist and leaned into him, my knees suddenly weak. Ben stuck his free hand out.* "*Hey, I'm Ben. Mer's boyfriend.*"

Jason's face turned red, and he quickly shook hands. "*Hey, man.*" *He looked at me.* "*Thanks for the lessons. I'd better get going.*"

"*You're welcome,*" *I mumbled.*

Jason walked away, and I tensed, afraid to look up at Ben. Was he pissed? It wasn't my fault the guy had asked me out, and if Ben had only arrived a few minutes later, I'd have already turned Jason down—awkward moment avoided.

Ben stayed silent, so I tilted my head back to meet his stare. "*Ben, that was nothing.*"

He traced one thumb across my forehead. "*I always knew this would happen—*"

"*Nothing happened.*"

"*I always knew that one day I'd have to fight the other guys off. They'd see how amazing and pretty and funny you are, and I'd have to stay on my toes.*"

His thumb traced down my cheek to the corner of my mouth, his words and his touch assaulting my heart.

"*That's crazy. Jason obviously had way too much sun and wasn't thinking right. Or maybe he normally wears glasses, but he broke them and couldn't see right the whole time he was here. That would actually explain a lot, like the way he kept steering his board—"*

Ben scooped me up and I squealed. He spun me around, and I leaned my head back, watching the clouds swirl above me, watching Ben's dark eyes fill with the promise of everything I ever wanted.

He slowed, his heart pounding under my cheek. He released me and I slid to the ground. We were both breathing hard, like we'd been running. The air turned heavy with all the things that had been building between us—the feelings when we kissed, the nights when we parked in the shadow of the lighthouse and made out in the back seat of his mom's car, until I couldn't tell where I ended and Ben began.

"I love you," I vowed.

His voice dropped to a whisper, his words carried by the familiar ocean breeze. "And I'll always like you best, Meredith Hall."

I took his words and locked them inside my heart. Then he kissed me, and I didn't care who watched, because in that moment, his kiss was the only thing that mattered in my world.

"So everyone's talking about how you and this new guy, Wyatt Quinn, are all buddy-buddy."

I looked up from my book. Rachel sat down on a rock next to me, looking bright as a flower in her yellow top, skinny jeans, and ballet flats. We were a contrast in almost every way. She'd clipped her blonde hair back on one side, and her lips shone with clear lip gloss. Mom wouldn't let her wear makeup yet, but I figured it wouldn't be long.

Closing my book, I sighed. Only hours had passed since Wyatt arrived at my school, and the gossip mill was already in full operation. I stretched my shoulders and lifted my face to the sun. Ugh. I'd been hunched over my book for almost the entire lunch period, tucked back in a quiet corner of the school property under some trees, where only Rachel would know where to find me. But while the sun had finally poked through the clouds, I still felt cold. I stretched the sleeves of my sweater down over my hands. Maybe I was coming down with something. That would explain why I felt off all morning—a much better explanation than admitting that Wyatt's presence at our school had gotten under my skin.

"Let me guess—you heard this from Kim."

Rachel nodded, opening her lunch bag. She pulled out a container of neatly sliced cheese and crackers, so different from the sandwich I'd slapped together. "Yup, I think she managed to reach the entire school before first break, except maybe the kids in first grade. She's probably lying in wait right now, ready to ambush their jungle gym time with the news."

I pulled an apple from my lunch bag. "But we have to give her full points for efficiency."

"True. So, is he really the son of some famous race car driver who is now engaged to Melody Adams?"

I munched on my apple and shrugged. In the three times I'd met him, the details of his family life had yet to come up. Most of what I knew—the fact that his parents were divorced—had come from his mother. "We haven't exactly been baring our souls to each other."

She carefully stacked a piece of cheese between two crackers. "But you have met and talked."

"Yeah." I stretched out my legs in the grass and dropped my head back against the tree. "We met at the beach, and I saw him again at his mom's coffee shop on Saturday morning. He drove me home because it was raining." I deliberately left out our "friendship contract."

"Oh." Bits of crackers flew out of her mouth and she blushed. "I overheard Mom and Dad last night. He said you were taking a job at a coffee shop for the summer. Is that the same one?"

I snorted. "Yeah, and I'm sure Mom had lots to say about that."

Rachel brushed cracker crumbs from her fingers and shot me a sympathetic look. She seemed so much older and wiser than I did at the same age. "Mom loves you. I know you don't click with her the same way you do with Dad, but I don't click with him, either. It doesn't mean he doesn't love me, right?"

A flicker of uncertainty hid under her bravado. Most people

would miss it, but I saw it. My elbow nudged hers. "Of course, he loves you. Everyone loves you."

She slowly exhaled, her spine straightening. "They love you, too. Mom is upset right now, but we'll find a way to make her understand. Maybe free coffee would help."

I laughed, respecting her optimism. That was Rachel— always searching for the light, while I'd grown too comfortable in the dark.

Movement on our side of the yard caught my attention. Wyatt. He strolled toward us, a bottle of Coke in one hand and a pair of sunglasses hanging from the other.

"That's him, right?" Rachel nudged my leg with her foot. "That's Wyatt Quinn."

"Yup." I snapped off another bite of my apple. "In the flesh."

"He looks like he's from Texas."

It didn't seem possible to tell where someone was from just by looking at them—but she was right. It was probably the swagger in his hips, the smooth, comfortable way he moved, like nothing took too much effort.

"Howdy."

I rolled my eyes. If he'd had a hat, he'd probably have tipped it at us, but I knew this exaggerated accent was an act. Still, Rachel giggled.

"Mind if I join you?" He directed his question at Rachel, but his gaze flicked to me.

Rachel nodded. "Sure."

He stared at me. "I just want to make sure I'm not crowding anyone."

Rachel's head whipped back and forth between us, clearly aware of the undercurrents, but miles away from understanding them. In answer, I pulled my legs up and waved at the patch of grass directly in front of us. Wyatt dropped down and sat cross-legged.

I turned to my sister. "Rachel, this is Wyatt. Wyatt, this is my sister, Rachel."

He grinned and stuck out his hand. "It's a pleasure."

Rachel sat up straighter, brushing her fingers off before shaking his hand.

Wyatt winked at her. "I can see the family resemblance. Beauty clearly runs deep in the Hall genes."

"*Rule number one*," I muttered under my breath.

"Hey." He cocked an eyebrow and gave me an innocent look. "I was just complimenting your sister. You never told me there were two of you."

Rachel rolled her eyes. "I should be offended by that, but I'm not. Mer is a very private person. Prying anything from her is like . . . like . . . "

"Puttin' socks on a rooster." Wyatt smirked.

Rachel snorted. Then she slapped her hand over her mouth, totally embarrassed. I shook my head, my lips curling up at the corners.

"Wait." Wyatt leaned forward, hooking his sunglasses on the collar of his shirt. "Did you actually smile? Did I actually make Meredith Hall smile?" He pulled out his phone and pointed it at me.

My hand shot out. "What are you doing?"

"Just recording this moment for future generations of disbelievers. But, folks, it's true. I, Wyatt Quinn"—he flipped his phone around so he was recording himself—"have just said something that made Meredith Hall smile. I wouldn't be so bold as to call it a laugh, but there was definitely some twitchin' happening at the corners of her lips."

By this point, Rachel was laughing so hard, she held her sides.

"Very funny." I grabbed for his phone, but he only turned it back on us and held it over his head.

"So, Rachel, is this something you've ever witnessed before?"

Rachel swallowed her laughter and smoothed her hair, smiling for the camera. "That's something you'll never know. The Hall sisters stick together. We don't share our secrets easily."

Rachel winked at me, and my smile turned genuine. Point scored for the Hall family.

"Well, it's a good thing I had a reason for tracking you down, other than discovering the Hall sister secrets." Wyatt tucked his phone away. "First of all, why didn't anyone warn me how tiny this school is? Hell, I could two-step around every square inch of it and still have half a song left."

The image made a full assault on my mind: Wyatt with a girl in his arms, swinging her around to some romantic country song.

Rachel giggled again. "Well, you'll never catch Mer doing a two-step. She doesn't like to dance."

"No?" He twisted the top off his Coke and took a sip.

"No." I wiped the image from my mind.

"That almost sounds like a challenge."

"Nope. Just stating a fact." I barely danced with Ben. There was no way Wyatt Quinn would ever succeed.

"Never say never."

I took a last bite out of my apple and tossed the core in the woods. "I don't get that saying. *Never* is a perfectly good word. I will never meet JFK. I will never study at Harvard. I will never become an astronaut. I'm not being a pessimist. Just being realistic." If only my mom could understand that.

"Never mind my sister," Rachel said. "I love her, but she could make the Energizer Bunny quit trying."

"Ha!" I twisted the top off my water bottle and somehow spilled it all over myself. *Damn.* Rachel handed me a napkin, and I wiped at the cold water now seeping into my jeans.

Wyatt shook his head. "You always seem to be getting soaked."

"I know." My cheeks burned. "Was there a reason you tracked me down?"

"Yup. I need your phone number."

Rachel's eyes widened. Maybe this was the way things

happened in Texas, but we weren't used to boys this bold on our island.

I coughed. *"Rule number two."* I coughed again. *"Rule number three."*

"It's not for me," he clarified. "It's for my mom. She just messaged me and asked 'cause she needs to be able to contact you about the job."

"Oh," I mumbled. That's what I got for making assumptions. I stuck out my palm and he handed his phone over. I quickly punched in my contact information and passed it back.

"Thanks." He pushed to his feet and slipped on his sunglasses. "Rachel, it was great meeting you. Mer, I'll see you around."

We both watched him stride back across the yard.

"So, that was Wyatt Quinn."

"Yup."

"I think life on this island just got a whole lot more interesting."

And that's exactly what I was afraid of.

Chapter Nine

Ben held my hand in the dark, his other hand clutching the steering wheel. *"Did you like the movie?"*

Ahead of us, the headlights illuminated insects in the air like snow. The road was practically deserted. "It was such a snooze. Only one car chase and barely any explosions. Still, it was better than some stupid rom-com."

Ben shook his head. "What's so wrong with romance and humor?"

"Nothing. That's why action movies need great one-liners."

"And the romance?"

I didn't answer right away. Instead, I slowly traced my thumb across his palm. It was callused from the hours he spent working on the boat. His breathing grew shallow, and he turned to stare at me.

"Keep your eyes on the road, Collins," I teased, then released his hand and dug out my iPod. *"I have a new song to play for you."*

Ben groaned. *"Is it some experimental thing?"*

"Don't be afraid." I laughed. *"I promise it won't hurt."* I linked my iPod to Ben's stereo and started scrolling through my playlist. I loved discovering new music, especially small indie bands. Ben was more classic rock in his tastes, and I'd made it my mission to expand his musical education.

I found the right song and rubbed at my bare arms. At least, I was slightly warmer now than I'd been in the air-conditioned theater.

Ben glanced at me and frowned. *"Why didn't you bring a sweater?"*

"I was trying to be optimistic."

"It's got nothing to do with optimism. Theaters are always cold."

He leaned sideways to adjust the temperature on the heater, but what I really wanted was for Ben to pull over and warm me up in another way. The song started, the haunting lyrics filling the darkened car.

Something on the road caught my eye.

A deer—frozen in the headlights.

"Ben!"

His head jerked up. The vehicle swerved.

My gaze locked on the deer. It passed down the side of the car, its head so close I could reach out and touch it.

The car snapped around, dancing across the pavement and whipping my head forward. Tires screeched and my hands slapped the dash.

I flew back.

My head smacked the headrest, and everything was suddenly still. The heater blew hot air on my face, and music came through the speakers, like we hadn't almost been killed.

I pulled on my seat belt, but its death grip on my shoulder wouldn't loosen. I yanked again, my fingers fumbling for the latch. The seat belt gave way and I fell forward.

Ben stared straight ahead, his fingers still wrapped around the steering wheel.

"Hey." I scrambled to my knees. "Are you okay?"

He looked dazed. "Yeah. I think so."

"How many fingers?" I stuck two up in front of his face.

He reached out and gripped my hand. "Two. Are you okay?"

I rolled my shoulders. I was going to hurt in the morning, but it could have been so much worse. "I'm fine." I glanced out the front windshield. The car had stopped on the wrong side of the road and was pointing in the opposite direction. "Jesus." I turned back to him. "That deer was so close, I could count the hairs on its ass."

Ben's eyes widened, and suddenly we were both laughing so hard, I was wheezing.

I climbed into his lap, and he caught my face between his hands. His dark eyes glittered. I buried my face in his neck, and *my laughter died, adrenaline and shock giving way to something different. I tasted his warm skin. My fingers clung to the collar of his shirt. He smelled like my ocean. Every part of our bodies pressed together, and it still wasn't enough. I lifted my head, and we kissed like our lives depended on it, and I still wanted more. I wanted everything.*

My butt landed on the horn, the sudden noise breaking us apart.

I panted and looked into Ben's eyes. The same need burned there. "We could have died tonight."

"I know." His heart raced under my palm—maybe it was from almost mowing down a deer or maybe it was from kissing me. It didn't matter.

"I don't want to wait anymore. Anything can happen. It can all come crashing down at any minute. If it does, I want to know that I loved you completely." I bit my lip. "You want it, too, right?" I knew what I was asking. If Ben said yes, if we had sex, he'd see all of me, including my flaws and fears and imperfections.

He blew out a quick breath. "God, yes."

"Good. How? When?"

He kissed me again, softly this time. "I'll figure it out. It has to be special. You deserve for it to be amazing."

I shivered, but it had nothing to do with the cold. After another long kiss, I slid off his lap and back into my seat. Ben took a deep breath, put the car in gear, and eased onto the highway. I wrapped my fingers around my seat belt. Anticipation curled inside me.

"Are you scared?" I whispered a few minutes later.

"A little. Are you?"

In the darkened car, I bit my lip and stared at his familiar profile illuminated by the dashboard lights. "Yeah, but it'll be perfect. I know it will be."

It would be perfect because it was with Ben.

After missing the ferry I'd hoped to catch, I still arrived at our meeting spot in time to watch the sunset erupt across the western sky, casting golden rays of light through the dunes and spilling over on the sand.

I spread out my blanket and sat down with my knees pulled up against my chest. A seagull screeched past, and I gave it the evil eye, always a little worried it might shit on me. Closing my eyes, I tried matching my breathing to the rhythm of the waves, a trick I'd learned from my dad when I was a kid. It used to calm me, but I hadn't done it in months, afraid to let the ocean back into my life.

After a few minutes, I gave up trying. Even this old habit couldn't settle my twisting stomach or racing thoughts. Being with Ben normally made me feel steady and safe, but tonight I was nervous he'd bring up the sponsorship offer again.

I wondered what Wyatt would say if he knew. He'd survived a traumatic crash. Did he still ride? He'd brushed off my questions the night we met, when I worried his ride on Sally might have traumatized him, but I still didn't know if the accident had left him scared, or if he'd had the courage to face his fears. Would he judge me for choosing to avoid the ocean?

I rested my chin on my knees and stared at the horizon. I shouldn't be thinking about Wyatt. Not here, and especially not when my thoughts only made my stomach twist even more. I didn't make friends easily. Ben would be happy if I made a new one, but would he be okay with the "contract" we'd negotiated or the tension that seemed to bubble to the surface whenever Wyatt and I were in the same room? But being aware of an attractive guy and acting on it were two different things, so no reason to feel guilty, right?

Lost in my thoughts, I never saw Ben coming. Hands landed on my shoulders, and I looked up to find him standing behind me.

"Hey."

"Hey, yourself."

He sat and stretched his long legs out on either side of me. I scooted backward, until I was cocooned against his broad chest, his arms around me. I lay back against his flannel jacket, pushing aside all my worries and doubts. They could wait until after. Right now, I just wanted to pretend everything was okay, and being in Ben's arms, I didn't find it so hard to convince myself.

We watched the sunset in silence until the last rays gave up their hold and the night swallowed them.

In the darkness, Ben dipped his face into the hollow of my neck. His mouth skimmed over my skin, pausing where my pulse pounded under his lips.

"I'm sorry about last time, Mer," he whispered against my ear, and heat rushed through my chest.

"I hate fighting with you. I just want things to stay the same."

His arms tightened around me. "I want that, too, but things are always changing. We both know that."

I nodded, wanting to deny the inevitable truth, wanting to go back to all those other nights on the beach when we'd pretended the rest of the world didn't exist, but things felt different now. It felt like we were running from something, a shadow over our shoulders that threatened to catch us if we didn't stay ahead of it, a shadow that arrived with Wyatt.

I squeezed his hand. "My parents found out I've been lying about the job at the arcade. They wanted to know what I've been doing all this time."

"What did you tell them?"

"That I've been coming to the beach to think."

Ben brushed my hair back. "Alone?"

I turned around and sat on my knees. The moon had risen so full in the night sky, I could see myself reflected in Ben's eyes. "Yeah."

"That's a lonely thought. They must have been worried."

"Probably, but my dad seemed to understand."

He chuckled, but there was no levity in the sound. "You and your dad have always understood each other."

"We used to."

He sighed, the sound so heavy I felt it all the way to my toes. "Meeting you here on the beach is the only thing I look forward to, but it's not fair to expect you to come here every night, especially if it's coming between you and your family."

"This is my choice." I leaned forward, sliding my hands under the collar of his jacket. "I want to do it, and if I hadn't lied to begin with, everything would've been different."

He rested his forehead against mine. "I'm not blameless. I pushed too hard. I could have been more understanding."

"And I made a choice that hurt you and your parents. The least I could have done was be honest about it."

"Maybe that's the answer now." He looked at me, his expression serious. "Maybe you should be honest with your parents. Tell them what's really going on."

I pulled back. "Why would you say that?" I pushed to my feet, swaying from the sudden head rush. "They wouldn't let me see you. They'd keep us apart."

Ben also climbed to his feet. He reached for me, hooking his fingers through mine, but I stubbornly kept my distance, letting only our linked hands touch. "Maybe, but can things really keep going like this?"

"You're not happy?" The question scratched at my throat. "Do you want to stop seeing me?"

"Don't be stupid." He tugged me closer. "You know I don't."

The tiniest bubble of panic tightened my chest, panic I didn't even understand. "So let's just keep it like this. If I tell my parents, maybe they'll understand, but if they don't . . . " My body shook. I couldn't let myself even imagine it.

"Shh. It's okay." He wrapped his arms around me, and I leaned into him. "We'll keep it a secret."

"Do you promise?" I whispered.

"Yeah, I promise."

I let my breathing slow. My stance eased and my heart stopped racing. What were we doing? I hadn't seen Ben in a couple of days. I'd missed him so much. It was a gorgeous night, and we had the beach all to ourselves. The moon continued to rise, casting silver ripples of light across the ocean. I hadn't even given him a proper greeting.

I shoved my fears to the farthest corners of my heart and lifted my face to his. "Hi."

His eyes widened and then crinkled in the corners. "Hi back."

"I missed you. You have no idea how much."

He hugged me, lifting my feet clear off the ground. "I think I do," he groaned into my ear.

When he set me back down, our lips found each other's in the dark. Like always, his kiss made me whole. It made the jumbled mess of my life snap back into place. I didn't want to be one of those girls who couldn't survive without a boy, but this was different. Being with Ben made me a better person—not because he was smarter, kinder, or braver than me, which he was, but because he made me happy. Rachel was right. I tended to look for the darkness in every situation, but "happy Mer" was a little less afraid to believe in the light.

So I pulled his head down and kept kissing him with everything I had.

"Wow," he whispered against my lips a few minutes later, running his hands up and down my arms. "Kissing you just keeps getting better."

I grinned and slid my hands under his shirt and across his belly, exploring the warm skin and smooth muscles hiding underneath. "Ditto."

He winced. "Your fingers are like ice."

I pressed my palms flat against his chest. "So warm them up for me."

I wanted to keep playing, but his hands stilled, and his expression turned serious. "What you said last time about doubting how I really feel, it bothered me. I trust you, Mer."

I breathed his assurances in, storing them away, remembering a time when I never thought I'd hear them again. "I don't know who I am without you."

"That's not true." He touched the ends of my short hair, and I wondered if he was remembering the night he found me on the beach. "You'd still be you."

But every part of my life had been linked with Ben's for so

long. Without him, I felt lost, like a ship without its engine or an anchor, with nothing to guide me or hold me in place, nothing to keep me from just floating away on a big, dark ocean. Ben still looked at me, and I didn't want to argue anymore. "Yeah, you're right," I lied. "I would still be me and right now, I'd like to get back to the kissing part."

For a few seconds, he said nothing. Then he lowered his head, blocking my view of the moon. "Yes, ma'am."

After, we stretched out on the blanket together, our heads so close I heard his every breath, despite the rush of the waves. He wrapped the edge of the blanket around us, and I snuggled against him.

"So, what's new at school? Anything exciting on the first day back from spring break?"

I thought about the contract that was hidden in the recesses of my backpack and the rules that proved Wyatt and I would just be friends, nothing more. "There's a new family on the island. A mother and son from Texas. The son is in my class."

"Wow, a new addition to the junior class? That's got to create a buzz. Kim's gossip radar must have been working overtime."

I chuckled. "It was a lot to cover in a short period, but she seemed to keep up."

"Ha! So, what's he like?"

I stared up at the moon—with all its craters now visible, it appeared so big in the sky that if I looked hard enough, I could probably find that American flag we'd planted up there all those years ago. "I don't know. He has an accent and he likes motorbikes." There was so much more I could say about Wyatt Quinn, but I didn't. "I'm taking a job at his mom's coffee shop for the summer."

"Wait." Ben rolled on his side and looked at me. "You're not working with your dad?"

I closed my eyes, blocking out the quiet speculation on his face.

"Mer?"

My eyes snapped open. "I'm doing the best I can. Please don't judge, okay?"

"Ah, Mer." He dropped a kiss on my forehead. "I'm not judging. I'm just worried. You still didn't tell your parents about the sponsorship offer?"

"No, and I'm not letting that stupid letter ruin another night with you." I hooked my leg over his and tugged him closer. "You don't need to worry 'cause I've got it all under control. Besides, I figure I'm going to learn to make a mean cup of coffee."

Ben sighed. "Does this woman know you're basically allergic to the kitchen?"

"Hey." I shrugged. "How hard can it be? If I could teach you to windsurf, I should be able to master an espresso machine."

"You know what they say about famous last words." He chuckled and sat up. I immediately missed his warmth.

"Where are you going?" I groaned and tugged on his arm.

"I want to do something."

"Lying here and staring at the stars is something."

"Don't be a stick-in-the-mud," he teased, easily resisting my efforts to make him lie back down. "It's a beautiful night and I want to do something."

"Fine." I jumped to my feet and offered him my hand. "I challenge you to a beach bowling rematch."

"Perfect, but be prepared, 'cause I'm going to beat you so bad."

"Yeah, yeah. That's some big talk there, Collins, but can you back it up?" I ran ahead of him to the beach, stopping short of the waves. There was a time when I would have kept running, but not now. Breathing in the ocean's tangy smell and tasting the salt on my lips was close enough.

For the next hour, we played three rounds of the game we'd invented as kids, which basically involved digging different-sized holes in the sand and rolling smooth rocks at those holes. You had three chances to sink your rocks, and you earned more points if you managed to get your rocks in the smaller holes. It was actually nothing like bowling, but that was the name we'd come up with, and it stuck.

Laughing on the beach in the cool night air, competing with Ben, letting the breeze tug at my bangs, I almost felt normal again. Running back and forth to collect our rocks, I wasn't even that cold. After two rounds, we were tied, but I managed to eke out a win in the final round.

"That's not fair." Ben frowned. "You kept distracting me before my shots."

"What?" I sent an innocent smile in his direction. "I was just stretching."

He choked back a snort and caught me around the waist. "They didn't look like any stretches I've ever done."

I grinned up at him. "So what do I win?"

"Nothing, because you cheated." He lowered his head, and his cool lips skimmed mine.

"I guess you'll just have to challenge me to a rematch tomorrow night."

"You are so on."

But a comeback was impossible because his mouth had claimed mine fully. Eventually, we'd have to say goodbye again, but not yet. I rose up on the balls of my feet and tightened my grip on him.

Yeah. Everything else would just have to wait.

Chapter Ten

I pulled back my hand as the stupid machine continued to hiss at me like some angry cat with hot, spitting claws.

Harley leaned over my shoulder. "You all right, sugar?"

"Yeah." But the red patch of skin throbbed from the steam.

She moved to the sink and returned with a cold cloth that she wrapped around my hand. I sighed as the cold numbed my skin and took away the worst of the pain. Harley finished making an espresso for the man at the counter, then turned to me. "Let me see."

"It's fine."

But she stood in front of me, waiting, until I surrendered my hand for her examination. She gently unwrapped the cloth and held the spot up to the light. It was still red, but there was no sign of blistering. She wrapped it back up and looked at me.

"Honey, maybe we need to face facts here. It's been three shifts, and you're still no closer to mastering this thing."

My heart sank. It had only been a week, but I liked working with Harley. She was funny and sweet, and she made me feel . . . comfortable.

"God bless your little heart for trying so hard, but it just doesn't like you."

Ugh. She was right. I couldn't manage any part of the process—not the tamping, the frothing, or the pouring. Who couldn't even manage pouring? Me. On more than one occasion while a customer waited with impatience, she'd had to basically push me aside and finish the order. She normally followed up each embarrassing debacle with words of encouragement, but her patience had clearly reached its end.

"I'm sorry. I just want you to know that I really loved working here." I used my good hand to untie the straps of my pastel apron with the name of the coffee shop printed on it: *Yellow Rose Café*. It matched the one she wore. Pulling it off, I laid it on the counter.

Her eyes widened. "Honey, what are you doing?"

"You fired me, right? I'm turning in my . . . apron."

She laughed and gave me a quick, tight hug. "Aren't you the cutest thing? I'm not firing you. Just moving you over to the cash. When you're not taking orders, you can also clean tables."

"Really?" God, this was a roller coaster of a conversation. "I'm not fired? Wouldn't you prefer someone working at your coffee shop who can actually serve coffee?"

"Nah." Customers occupied her tables and chairs, filling the room with the constant buzz of chatter. "This place is a hit and the tourists haven't even shown up yet. I figure that I'll need to hire someone else anyway. I'll just make sure they're an experienced barista."

She swooped up my apron and dropped it back in my hands.

"You're sure?"

"Sugar, I've seen what a hard worker you are. So why would I possibly want to fire you? Besides"—she winked at me, loading some empty mugs in the dishwasher and pushing it closed—"if I fired you, I'd never get Wyatt to help me out. At least this way, I'm guaranteed a few hours of free work from him. It's like having two employees for the price of one."

My cheeks flushed, and I glanced around to locate Wyatt, praying he wasn't within earshot. Thankfully, he was clearing one of the tables near the front window. Outside, the cold weather had returned, and the sky was gray again. Although for now, the rain held off.

"We're just friends," I muttered. My hand already felt better, so I grabbed a cloth and wiped down the counter.

"I know." Harley stepped out of my way. "Wyatt told me the same thing."

"Then why are you looking at me like that?"

"'Cause you might be as bright as a new penny, but, honey, neither one of you can see what's right in front of your noses."

I balled up the rag in my fist, and my gaze drifted back to Wyatt. Today, he wore khaki cargo pants and a slim-fitting faded T-shirt with the Texas star on the chest. A pastel apron, with the café's name on it, circled his lean waist.

I'd brushed by him earlier when we'd both been behind the counter, close enough to feel the dampness from his recent shower. "Sorry," he'd said, immediately backing up and smelling like fresh laundry *and* mint toothpaste. "Don't want to violate rule number two." I'd clamped my mouth shut and finished making tea for an elderly couple. At least I could make tea without embarrassing myself.

Now, Wyatt caught me staring. He raised an eyebrow, a question in his gaze.

I looked back at Harley. She stood silently, no doubt watching our exchange. So I chose my words carefully. "Even if there was the . . . potential for something between us, it can't happen. My heart belongs to someone else. Wyatt knows that."

She leaned back against the counter. "Honey, you're awfully young to be permanently giving your heart to anyone. This is the time when you need to be young and carefree."

Many months ago, my mom had given me the same advice, but coming from Harley, it didn't sound half as judgmental. It also didn't apply anymore, because I hadn't felt young and carefree in almost a year. Sometimes you make choices. Things happen that force you to grow up, and once you've crossed over that line, you can't go back, no matter how much you want to. "I'm sorry. I know you're my boss, but I don't want to talk about this," I mumbled, aware that I was in tricky territory. I was basically telling my new boss to butt out and mind her own business.

"Mom!" Wyatt appeared on the other side of the counter. "What are you doing?"

Harley huffed. "Obviously, I'm being too nosy for my own good. My apologies, Mer." She disappeared into the kitchen, leaving me to face Wyatt.

He set down a tray of dishes. "What was that about?"

"It was nothing." I reached for the cups and began stacking them in the dishwasher. "She was just asking about . . . us."

He groaned and propped one elbow on the counter. "I never said anything to her. I swear. She just gets these ideas in her head, and then she's a force to be reckoned with. Take this business. She's never worked at a coffee shop, let alone owned one. But she made up her mind that this is what she wanted, and then she moved us halfway across the country to make it happen."

"She's determined and gutsy."

"Stubborn and crazy's more like it—two pickles short of a barrel, if you ask me."

I finished loading the dishes and stared at him. "Where do you get them?"

"Get what?"

"This endless supply of sayings. I swear it's like you and your mom are talking a completely different language."

Wyatt laughed. "You've never met my grandmother. That woman could talk the legs off a chair."

I slapped my hand against my forehead. "Of course she could."

A family with two small kids walked in, setting the bell above the door jingling. I moved to my new position behind the cash, and Wyatt stared. With a little help from Harley, I rang up their orders and served juices and cookies for the kids, while she handled the coffee.

"So, no more coffee duty," he said after they moved away.

"You don't sound surprised."

"We all have our talents." Wyatt shrugged. "Clearly, yours do not include fancy-ass Italian coffee machines. It's no big deal."

The thing was, I knew Wyatt meant it. As much as I'd judged him and his behavior, he never seemed to judge me. "Thanks. I have to admit that my pride took a little beating."

"It shouldn't. My mom wouldn't keep you on, unless you deserve to work here."

"Not even because we're friends?"

He shook his head. "Not even for that. Trust me. She won't let anything stand in the way of this coffee shop succeeding."

I started to respond, but the bell above the door rang again. When I looked over, my mom and Rachel stood just inside the shop, taking it all in. Under other circumstances, I might have thought my mom was here to drink coffee and support a new local business, but the determined, cautious look on her face revealed her true purpose: She was here to verify my story. She didn't trust that I'd been telling the truth.

Rachel headed straight for me, her eyes round. "This place is awesome. So cute." She climbed on a stool and spun around.

Wyatt grinned at her. "Rachel—the other Hall sister. Welcome to the Yellow Rose Café."

My mom stepped up next to Rachel and laid her purse down on an empty stool.

"Hey, Mom." My fingers curled around the edge of the counter. "What are you guys doing here?"

"What do you think? I came to check out the island's newest business."

Behind me, Harley emerged from the kitchen with a fresh batch of brownies artfully stacked on a glass plate. "Hello." She smiled at Rachel and my mom. "And welcome."

Wyatt glanced at my hands that were still gripping the counter. I let go and stuffed them in the pocket of my apron instead. "Mom, this is Harley Wilson, and this is her son, Wyatt Quinn. This is my mom, Jess, and my sister, Rachel."

Wyatt tipped his head at my mom. "It's nice to meet you, ma'am."

My mother nodded, but anything she'd been planning to say was interrupted by Harley's gasp of glee.

"Well, this is wonderful." She set down the plate of brownies and rushed around the counter to greet my family. She stopped in front of Rachel first. "I can't believe it—two beautiful Hall sisters. Honey, you're as pretty as a picture." Her gaze took in my sister's flowered blouse and jeans. "Like a real yellow rose. I might have to keep you around here for decoration." She reached out and pulled my sister into a quick hug. Rachel's face split into a huge smile.

During this exchange, my mom stood, her spine stiff, her hands clinging to the strap on her purse. My mom had friends. People liked and respected her, but she wasn't warm and expressive like Harley. She was reserved with her feelings, preferring to focus on the practical.

So when Harley turned her Texan charms on my mother, I stiffened, watching and feeling wary. Harley grasped my mother's hand in hers. "It's so wonderful to meet you. Mer has been a godsend."

"Really?" Mom stared at me and I shrugged. "That's good to hear."

"Ah." Harley's head whipped back and forth, taking in the silent exchange between us. "I've always found that our kids put a better foot forward when they're outside the house. Wyatt seems to save his best manners for complete strangers. Not that those strangers don't deserve some good manners, but it would be great if he saved some for me." She cocked her head toward Wyatt, still holding my mother's hand captive. "Isn't that right, darlin'?"

"Yes, ma'am. Whatever you say. By the way, maybe you could give Mrs. Hall back her hand."

"See." Her attention returned to my mom. "He saves all the sass for me, and I will give back your hand as soon as I thank you for letting Mer work here for the summer."

My mom's gaze skittered across to mine, her lips pulled into a thin line. "It was up to her. She's free to work where she wants." Harley released her hand, but I suspected my mom had pulled it free.

"Yes, but I understand that she normally works for your husband."

Mom sighed. "As I said, Meredith does her own thing."

I glanced at Wyatt. Was I the only one who picked up on the bitterness in her voice? Maybe he heard it, too, because he walked around the corner and slung one arm around his mom's shoulders. "Maybe we should see what Rachel and her mom would like. I'm sure they came in here hoping for coffee."

Mom stared at Wyatt, her expression unreadable.

"Wyatt's right," Harley said. "What can I get you? On the house."

"That's very nice of you, but I'd prefer to pay. Rachel, sweetheart, what would you like?"

Rachel stared at the plate of brownies. "One of these, please, and a chai tea latte."

I shook my head. My twelve-year-old sister had fancier taste in drinks than I did. Harley and I got their order ready, then I rang up the items and took Mom's money. Harley frowned but didn't stop me.

After, they sat at a table by the window, and Wyatt stepped behind the counter. "Well that was . . . awkward."

"Yup." I finished loading the dishwasher and turned it on.

"Don't you get along with your mom?"

I thought about his question, about how there was no easy answer. "As well as I ever have."

He silently nodded, leaning against the counter. "Sorry. My mom can be so pushy sometimes."

"Don't apologize. Your mom is amazing. You're lucky to have her."

He turned and our gazes hooked together. "I know."

He didn't offer anymore, but I knew he'd left a lot unsaid.

I waved goodbye to Ben and slipped into the house, quietly toeing off my sneakers. It was past curfew, but I didn't care. I was on a high from my date, floating on air.

"You're late."

I jumped and swung around, my heart accelerating. Mom was waiting for me in the living room with a cup of tea on the coffee table next to an open magazine.

"You scared me."

"And you're still late."

But even my mom's anger couldn't kill my good mood. I fell back in the chair and stretched. "I was with Ben. We missed the ferry and had to get the next one. I texted you."

"I know you did, but we set a curfew for a reason. We expect you to follow it."

"You mean you expect me to follow it. I don't see Dad waiting up to give me a lecture."

Mom frowned. "That's not the point, Mer."

"It is the point." I sat up. "I'm really happy for the first time in my life, but of course, there's still something you don't approve of."

"That's not fair. I'm just worried about how much time you're spending with Ben."

"So, now you don't approve of Ben?"

She sighed. "You know that's not it. Ben's a great person, but you're still young. It's not right for you to be so serious about any boy so soon, even Ben."

I sucked in a frustrated breath and buried my fist in a throw pillow. "Well, it's too late for that warning because I love him, and nothing's going to change that." It felt so good to declare it out loud.

She made a little sound of disbelief.

"You don't believe me?"

She leaned closer, tucking a stray strand of blond hair behind her ear. Even this late at night, she looked perfectly put together in her jeans and pale pink sweater. "You're barely sixteen, Meredith.

You may think you're in love, but you don't even know what that means. Being in love isn't just about kissing and staying out past curfew and being irresponsible."

"Wow. Thanks, Mom. Thanks for trying so hard to respect what I'm telling you."

"Respect is a two-way street. If you want me to treat you like a mature person, you need to start acting more responsible. Respect the rules we set."

"Why are you trying to ruin this?" I shook my head. "Ben makes me happy. He makes me feel confident, like I'm finally good enough. Why can't you just be happy for me?"

Her shoulders sagged. "Because you don't need a boy to make you happy. You could be happy on your own if you just tried harder, if you just worked on changing your attitude. There's more to life than windsurfing and Ben."

I stood, my hands shaking with bottled-up anger. "No, you just think I should be more like you."

"Really, Meredith, you make me sound like an awful parent just because I want the best for you. Is it so wrong of me to want you to live up to your full potential?"

"That's just it." I swung around, blinking back tears. Why did her disapproval always get to me? I stopped at the bottom step and looked back at her. "Ben loves me now, for me. He's not holding back his approval until I become this perfect person—a person I'll never be."

For the next week, I fell into a routine of work, school, and Ben, somehow managing to keep all the pieces separate. The rain returned, with more flooding at school. Some local roads washed out, and I started to worry that maybe our tiny island would disappear back into the ocean. I met Ben as much as possible, but the beach was cold and wet, which shortened our time together.

At school, Wyatt followed the rules. If you didn't see us together at the café, you'd think we were nothing more than casual acquaintances. At work, we joked and talked, and I let him see a little of the "me" I normally held inside, the side of me I normally reserved for Ben—not everything, but a little.

On Saturday morning, the weather finally cleared. I was just finishing my shift when Harley sent me to her family kitchen for a bag of sugar. It was my first time crossing the threshold between the business and Wyatt's home, and I paused just inside the door. Harley's decorating taste was evident everywhere. The living room had the same wooden floors and pastel colors as the shop, but here they'd been matched with an oversized couch and armchairs that looked more than comfortable enough for an afternoon nap.

I quietly crossed the floor, on the lookout for Wyatt.

I heard him before I saw him.

Low curses came from the direction of the kitchen, and something skidded across the floor, like someone had just kicked a chair. I stopped and looked back at the door to the shop.

Harley wanted sugar, but I'd no intention of intruding on an angry Wyatt.

"What are you doing here?"

Crap. His sharp words shot across the room, and I pivoted to find Wyatt standing in the kitchen doorway, a tablet gripped in his hand.

"Your mom sent me for sugar."

"How much did you hear?"

"Not much." I leaned my hip against the back of the couch and avoided his gaze. "Just some religious terms of endearment and something about familial connections to female dogs."

He snorted. "That's one way of putting it."

Silence descended on the room, and I fidgeted with the pen in my apron pocket. "So, do you want to talk about it?" He tossed his tablet across the room, and it landed on the couch in front of me. I winced. "Hope you went with the extended warranty."

Wyatt followed his tablet, landing on the cushions and looking up at me. "Dad was supposed to Skype with me. We planned it last weekend, and then he bailed at the last moment. We've hardly spoken since the accident. He knows nothing about my life now, and he doesn't seem to care."

I nodded, not sure what to say. The silence stretched out, and I felt the need to fill it. "So . . . uhhh . . . Kim told me that he's engaged to Melody Adams."

"So I've read." Tension tightened the muscles around his mouth, and I saw the hurt in his eyes.

My fingers curled into a fist. I wanted to soothe that pain away. I wanted to comfort him, but why did I care so much? *Because we were friends.* That's all. "You don't know whether they're engaged?"

"Apparently I no longer warrant his attention. But if the gossip rags say they're engaged, it must be true. We all know they only print the facts. Fuck it." He sprang up from the couch and ran a shaky hand through his already mussed-up hair. "I need to get off this island." He vaulted over the back of the sofa and landed a few inches away. "Come with me?"

I stepped back, but my gaze never left his. He was a vibrating mass of pent-up energy, and his determined stare made it impossible to look away. I swallowed. "Where?"

"For a ride on my bike. Your life will never be the same."

I glanced away, counting all the reasons why his suggestion was the worst idea ever. Top on the list was my boy—

"Don't overthink it, Mer." He leaned closer. "Just come with me. For one afternoon, let's just have fun and forget about all the other bullshit."

I hesitated, tempted by his words. He saw it on my face and pounced. He found my hand and tugged me toward the door.

"Wait. You want to go now?"

"Yes. Your shift is over, right?"

I nodded, my thoughts struggling to keep up. "Sugar . . . your mom sent me for sugar."

"Got it." He spun me around, and his hands pulled at the ties of my apron. He whipped it off, and I laughed—a light, breathless sound that I didn't recognize.

"Don't move." He pointed at me. "I'll be right back."

He sprinted for the kitchen and I heard a cupboard slam. He disappeared through the door of the coffee shop with my apron and a bag of sugar in his hands. Seconds later, he reappeared. "You're still coming, right?"

I nodded.

I wanted to go, I realized. I wanted to feel daring and adventurous and . . . alive.

So I followed Wyatt's cocky grin right out the door.

Chapter Eleven

We took the ferry to the mainland and drove the back roads of North Carolina with the windows down and his country music playing. He wore a straw cowboy hat low on his forehead and aviator sunglasses. On anyone else, the look would have been outlandish, but Wyatt owned it. He flaunted it, in his worn, butt-hugging jeans and T-shirt.

Despite our rules, my stupid hormones lapped up every dangerous and exhilarating part of him. He drove with one arm draped across the back of the bench seat, belting out the words of twangy songs I'd never heard before. I thought about connecting my iPod and introducing him to some real music, but he just seemed so happy.

With my sneakers off and my feet propped on the dash, I

slouched low in the seat and breathed in the scent of a long-over-due Carolina spring: fresh-cut grass and magnolias. The music and wind made talking hard, but I didn't mind because there was a lightness in my chest, something I hadn't felt in a long time. Part of me wanted to keep driving and never go back to Ocracoke, like I could escape every bad thing that had ever happened to me if I just kept driving these roads with Wyatt. But that made no sense—my family was back there, and Ben.

I glanced through the rear window at the dirt bike Wyatt had wheeled up a ramp and secured in his pickup. Back at his house, the process of getting the bike into his truck had looked complicated and overwhelming, but within minutes, he'd finished securing it and hopped down.

I'd gawked up at it. "That was fast."

Wyatt had only grinned and opened the passenger door for me. "This is not my first rodeo."

Now, we slowed, following direction commands from his phone. At the top of a dirt driveway, a billboard displayed a full-color photo of a guy and his dirt bike flying ten feet in the air. Wyatt signaled and turned in.

"You really used to do that?"

"Yup. My mom always hated it." We headed down a dirt lane, stopping beside a few other pickups, all parked next to a low building. "The doctor says if I break my bones again, they might be non-repairable. I could end up in a wheelchair for the rest of my life."

My head whipped around, and I glared at him. Damn. I didn't want to be personally responsible for Wyatt ending up in a wheelchair. "Tell me again what we're doing here."

"Relax." He slipped the truck into park, shut down the engine, and pointed back at the billboard. "He told me I can't do that. He never said I couldn't ride at all."

I stared out my window. A dirt track sprawled across the horizon, with an occasional bike flying over the small hills and mounds carved into the earth. Doubt replaced my earlier excitement. "So your mom knows where we are? She's okay with you being here?" I didn't want to get fired over this.

"Yup." He opened his door and slid to the ground. "Don't worry—you're not aiding and abetting some criminal act here. She knows there's no way to keep me off a bike completely. You may as well chop off my leg or something."

I pulled my feet off the dash, his words striking a jarring chord. That's what I'd done with windsurfing. I'd quit it cold turkey, even if it did feel like I'd hacked off a part of myself.

"Hey, what's wrong? Are you nervous about doing this?"

I glanced over at Wyatt. He stood on the driver's side, one arm propped against the door frame, his hazel eyes shadowed with concern.

"No." I sucked in a lungful of dusty air. My first instinct was to lie, to tell him nothing was wrong, but when I opened my mouth, the truth unexpectedly fell out. "You just reminded me of what it feels like to give up something I really loved doing."

For a moment, he said nothing.

I unsnapped my seat belt and shoved my feet in my sneakers, needing to keep busy, needing to hide the regret I felt over sharing something so personal.

"What did you love doing, Meredith Hall?"

His low, serious words had me spinning around. "Does it matter if I can't do it anymore?"

His eyes widened because my tone was harsher than I planned. Crap. I ducked my chin. He hadn't expected an attack, and why should he? He'd only asked about something that I brought up. I swallowed, ready to apologize, but he cut me off.

"Hell, yeah, it matters. Sometimes life hands you shitty cards. It takes away your dreams before you get a chance to make them happen. But those dreams were still a part of you. You can't just forget them. They still deserve recognition."

My lungs deflated, and my shoulders drooped. They had been a part of me, but Wyatt's words just made the guilt worse. My dreams were victims of my own self-destructive tendencies. I had no one to blame but me, myself, and I. The sponsorship letter hiding in my desk drawer proved that. I pushed open the door and looked at him. "What if I dealt myself the shitty cards?"

"I haven't known you very long, but I find that hard to believe."

I shook my head, swallowing back a bitter taste. "You don't know me at all."

"Let me tell you what I do know." He hiked one foot up on the truck's running board and threw his hat on the seat. "Besides the part about you being totally hot, which you believe is bullshit, I know that you're funny as hell and you're a straight shooter."

"Great." I snorted. "I have the same positive attributes as a freaking rodeo clown."

"See, a classic example of your sarcastic wit, but I didn't even get to the good part." Wyatt paused. The air around us turned thick and heavy, weighed down by the sudden seriousness in his expression. "I know you're a hard worker. You're creative and smart. You don't act like the world owes you something or that you're better than everyone else. Actually, you don't act at all. You don't pretend things that you don't feel. I like that. It's refreshing. I'd been seeing the world through this tinted glass of fake bullshit for so long that I thought it was real. But you make me see things clearly. It's a little shocking at first, but I like it . . . I like you."

Breathe. I needed air. I dug through the recesses of my mind, trying to remember how my lungs worked. *Inhale. Exhale.* At some point during his speech, our gazes had collided. They remained tangled together, in a wreck of mammoth proportions. It took the Jaws of Life to finally pry my stare away from the intensity in those green eyes. "I'm not perfect," I mumbled. "I've made mistakes. Big ones."

"I know." He slowly grinned. "Like turning down a date with me."

I groaned. "I'm serious."

"So am I. My mom says that making mistakes is what keeps us grounded. It's what makes us real—our mistakes and imperfections. And you don't argue with Harley Wilson."

I rubbed at my damp forehead. He didn't understand. There were mistakes and then there were disasters—the ones that affected not only your happiness but the happiness of the people around you. "You have a medically legitimate excuse that's keeping you from your dreams. I was given the chance to make my dream happen, and I turned it down, all because of my own stupid fear."

"Bullshit. I know you well enough to know that you, Meredith Hall, are no coward. So if your fear is keeping you from your dream, there's a good reason for it. You need to give yourself a break. Find a new dream. Hell"—he pointed to the track— "maybe this will be it."

I looked out the window and breathed in the rich, earthy scent of the track, so different from the smell of the ocean. I let his words sink in. I let myself believe them, if only for one afternoon. For the first time since the letter arrived, it wasn't an anchor around my neck, pulling me under. For the first time in forever, I felt weightless, like I could finally breathe.

I turned back to Wyatt and let the words spill out. "My dream . . . I wanted to be a professional windsurfer. I wanted to spend every day on the ocean, traveling and competing and being the best in the world."

His gaze danced across my face. "That's an amazing dream, definitely worthy of recognition. I can see you now—flying over the waves, defying gravity. So, we'll just have to find you another dream. One that's equally worthy."

"Just like that?" My parents had clearly wasted money on a therapist. Apparently all I needed was one afternoon with Wyatt Quinn. "Are you a dream whisperer or something?"

He patted his back pocket. "Shit. I left my Rolodex of ready-made dreams in my other jeans."

"Yeah, yeah." I cocked my head at him, my thoughts tumbling. Somehow, I'd told Wyatt about turning down the sponsorship offer, and he hadn't made me feel like a quitter. He'd made me feel like that choice didn't define me—that I could still choose my own future. "Are we going to talk all day, or are you actually going to take me for a ride on your overgrown motorcycle."

His eyes narrowed, and he pointed at me. "Hey, watch it, Hall. Don't be crapping on my bike."

"Ha. As your mom pointed out, no one likes a braggart, Quinn."

Wyatt grinned and slammed the door. He pulled a duffel bag with his riding gear from the back of the truck and headed for the building. I followed, reveling in the nervous energy pumping through my veins. When was the last time I'd felt truly excited about something? As I trailed behind Wyatt, I also tried not to notice how good his butt looked in his jeans . . . and failed miserably.

Once inside, he dropped his duffel bag and dinged a small bell on the service counter. A fan whirred overhead, competing with a local radio station that piped in through some invisible speakers. I leaned next to him, staring at the posters and motocross gear lining the walls.

An older man emerged from an office door. "Can I help you?"

"Yeah," Wyatt said, "I'd like to use the track for a few hours and rent some gear and a helmet for my friend."

The man looked from Wyatt to me and back to Wyatt. His eyes widened. "Wait, you're Wyatt Quinn, right?"

"Yes, sir."

The man extended his hand and they shook. "It's a pleasure to meet you, son. I'm a huge fan. So, you looking to start competing again?"

Wyatt tensed and then exhaled, rolling his shoulders. Despite our earlier talk, Wyatt obviously still felt raw over the loss of this particular dream. "Not today. Just here for some fun."

"You've come to the right place. You're gonna love this track. I'm Lou, by the way. Just let me know if there's anything you need."

"Thanks."

Lou held up his phone. "Hey, do you mind?"

"Nah." Wyatt posed for a quick selfie while I stared. Wyatt's status in the motocross world was obviously bigger than I'd understood.

"I've got to post this right away. People will freak out when they find out Wyatt Quinn is on our track today."

Wyatt frowned and looked at me. "Maybe you can wait to post it until after we're done."

Lou followed Wyatt's gaze and grinned. "No problem, man."

I wandered to the vending machines and bought a couple of Cokes. When I got back, Wyatt handed me boots and a stack of riding clothes. "Change into these. When you're done, we'll fit you with a helmet."

Inside the bathroom, I wiggled into the black pants and zipped them up. They looked nothing like the riding gear I was expecting, with their red-and-white stripes down the side and built-in padding in the knees. I tugged on the boots and the tight-fitting jacket. The built-in rubber protective padding felt strange on my limbs, like I was swimming in Jell-O. I looked in the mirror. Not bad. The gear made me feel kind of badass, like a futuristic soldier ready to kick down some doors.

I returned to find Wyatt also dressed in his riding gear. Wow! And I thought his butt looked hot in jeans. His red-and-blue pants clung to his backside and hugged his lean hips, bagging a bit at the knees before tucking into his boots. A matching blue-and-red jersey stretched across his shoulders.

He whistled under his breath when he saw me, and my heart slammed against my rib cage. "Rule number one still applies," I said.

Wyatt stuck out a hip and grinned. "I was not flirting. I was just sharing a genuine male reaction to your . . . awesomeness."

"Ha."

He threw his arms out to both sides and tilted his head. "So, any comment on my . . . awesomeness?"

I leaned against the counter, pretending to concentrate on the lineup of full-face helmets, but my gaze kept drifting back to him. He was a sight to behold. "I don't think your ego needs any boosts."

He flattened his hand against his chest, his bicep flexing. "Hey, my ego is a fragile little thing that's constantly taking a bruising when I'm with you. Would it really kill you to be nice to it once in a while? Maybe give it a tiny bit of love and affection?"

I laughed and slapped my hand on top of his. "Baby, your ego is a fast-growing weed that will rapidly take over the entire garden if I don't keep hacking it back."

It was meant as teasing between friends, but his other hand landed on top of mine, trapping my fingers in his warm grasp. "Ouch, your heart is as cold as your hands." His gaze held mine, all glittery and enticing. "But you did just call me 'baby,' so you're forgiven."

I let my hand stay there a moment too long. I stood too close to him, inhaling the smell of Coke on his breath, staring at the angle of his jaw and the fullness of his bottom lip, caught in the magnetic pull of his personality. Shit. I blinked and snatched my hand back. What was I doing? I swung around to stare at the helmets, unexpected tears burning in my eyes. "So, which one is mine?"

He leaned closer and whispered, "Nice segue." He picked up the first one. "Let's see which one fits."

I pulled in a choppy breath and blinked a few times before turning back to stare at his chest. If Wyatt noticed, he said nothing. Instead, he helped me slide on the helmet and do up the strap.

"Too loose," he said, tugging on it. "We need it nice and snug. Safety first." I pulled it off, and Wyatt laughed. "Your hair's standing up."

We reached for the rebellious strands at the same time, and our fingers tangled. Wyatt stepped closer, trapping me between the counter and his body. Definitely a violation of rule number two.

"Let me fix it." His words were low, for my ears only.

I needed to protest, to shout all the reasons why this was such a bad idea, but my hand fell to my side. He cupped my scalp, his thumb brushing across my temple on its downward path. I shivered and looked away. His touch was not supposed to make me feel anything.

"There. It's perfect again." His voice was gruffer than normal. "Let's try the next one." He reached past me to retrieve the next helmet from the counter, and his warm breath fanned my cheek.

I slipped it on, the thick helmet muffling everything around me. Wyatt adjusted the strap and then yanked on the part of the helmet covering my chin. My body fell forward, and my hands landed on his shoulders. I closed my eyes, trying to slow my racing, guilty heart.

He tugged again and laughed, smacking his palm flat on the top of my helmet. "Perfect fit."

But I couldn't match the lightness in his tone. It wasn't fair. He seemed less affected by whatever just passed between us than I did. Maybe because he had nothing to feel guilty about.

He held up a pair of leather gloves. "Last step." I surrendered my hands and he stuffed them in, tightening the gloves at the wrists.

"Why am I wearing way more gear than you are?"

"I've got more, but you're not getting on my bike unless I can see that you're fully protected. I don't normally take people on it at all, so I'm making sure you get off in the same perfect condition that you get on."

The intense protectiveness in his voice curled around me, leaving me without a response. Fortunately, he spun on his heel, waved to Lou, and headed out the door. I followed at a distance, fighting with the strap under my chin. It finally loosened, and I yanked my helmet off, gulping in air. Wyatt and I were just friends. Nothing more. So why did my heart feel like it had just gone through a couple of rounds in a tumble dryer?

By the time I'd gathered my scattered feelings, Wyatt was back at his truck and had the ramp in place. In a few minutes, he'd completed the process of unloading his bike.

He quickly checked it over, pulled on his helmet and gloves, strapped on more gear, and swung a leg over. When he settled in the seat, he looked competent and in control, just like I knew he would. He clearly belonged there. He pointed to a small set of wooden bleachers perched on the side of the track. "Wait there while I do a few laps. I want to check out everything first."

I nodded and his bike sprang to life, loud and powerful. Yup, this angry-sounding beast was as far from my docile Sally as you could get.

Wyatt revved the engine and lifted his foot, and the bike shot forward. I walked to the bleachers and climbed to the top row, past a small group of kids around my sister's age. They all wore similar getups to Wyatt, but they'd pulled off their helmets and gloves and were now sipping on their sodas.

I stood and used one hand to block the sun, watching Wyatt speed around the course. He hugged the curves in the dirt track, leaning low in the turns and flying a couple feet in the air over the hills. On the sharp turns, he'd drop his foot and pivot around with ease, dirt spraying out from the knobby tires. He made it look effortless.

He was halfway around the track before I registered the conversation between the kids in front of me.

"I'm telling you that's him. It's Wyatt Quinn. I'm sure." A blond boy leaned forward on his knees, his expression adamant.

"No, it's not." A dark-haired boy slouched against the row

behind him, his booted feet stretched out. "Why would Wyatt Quinn be here? He lives in Texas. Besides, I read that he can't ride again after his accident. He broke, like, a hundred bones in his body."

The blond boy shook his head. "I don't care. I'm telling you that's him. Look at the white star on his jersey. I have his poster on my wall."

One of the other boys chimed in: "Man, did you see that crash? He was flying around like a rag doll, and then his bike landed right on top of him. Seriously epic moment. I watched it, like, ten times in a row."

Really? I pulled back my shoulders, ready to give the kid a piece of my mind. How could anyone enjoy seeing someone else get hurt? But then I thought of all the times I'd watched online videos of spectacular crashes and stunts gone wrong. This time was just different because it was Wyatt.

Someone called out my name, and I looked down. Wyatt was waiting on his bike right in front of the bleachers. He'd lifted his face shield and was grinning. He motioned me down with one hand, and I marched past the group of boys. When I was closest to the blond boy, I leaned over. "You were right. It is Wyatt Quinn."

The boy whooped and cheered while I walked over to the bike. Wyatt looked past my shoulder. "What's that about?" he shouted.

"Just a fan of yours."

He adjusted his helmet. "Cool. You ready to ride a real bike?"

God, he looked sexy, confident, and so dangerous. Every nerve in my body tingled. Yes. I nodded. I was ready. I slid on my helmet, and Wyatt reached out to make sure the chinstrap was tight.

"Looks good. Climb on."

I'd pictured myself gracefully sliding on the back. Instead, it was more of an embarrassing scramble.

Wyatt turned halfway around and laughed. "You okay there, Hall?"

The engine vibrated through the seat, and heat climbed up my neck. "Just perfect."

Wyatt wrapped my hand around his waist, holding it in place. "We're going to break your rules for a few minutes, but this is important," he shouted. "Stay tight to me. Keep both arms around my waist and lean when I lean. Don't fight it."

I nodded and wrapped my other arm around him. He checked my grip and gave me a "thumbs-up" signal.

Then the engine roared and we shot forward.

Damn. This really was nothing like my scooter. The bike slid and skidded in the dirt, but somehow Wyatt was always in control. I peeked around his shoulder, and we headed for the first turn.

I ducked my head and plastered myself to Wyatt's back like wallpaper, frightened I'd upset his balance if I messed up.

The bike leaned, and Wyatt and I went with it. I opened my

eyes and saw the ground rushing past. Then the engine surged, and before I knew it, we were coming out of the turn.

I released my breath and grinned. Wyatt gave me another "thumbs-up," and I squeezed his waist. Our first hill came next. He kept the speed low, but I still came off the seat a little when we popped over the top. The front of my helmet smacked against his back, but he didn't seem to mind.

I hung on, watching for the next turn. This time I was ready. I leaned with Wyatt, like we were one. I must have done something right because Wyatt gave the bike more gas, and soon we were whipping around the track. Dirt spattered my gear and my helmet, but I didn't care.

We hit a hill and the bike came off the ground. It was probably only a couple of inches, but it felt like five feet. I gasped and tightened my grip. Then we were landing in the dirt and shooting forward, and I was laughing inside.

When I windsurfed, it was equal parts strength, grace, speed, and subtlety. It felt like flying. Your mind wandered, seeking the beauty in the moment, a oneness with the wind and the waves. This was different—raw power and exhilaration and the smell of the earth. It was jarring and loud, and it forced you to hang on with every part of your body and mind. It forced you to work for it, not allowing your thoughts to go any further than the next turn, the next hill.

We finally stopped in front of the bleachers, and Wyatt

dropped the kickstand. I hopped off. My body pumped with adrenaline, and my breath came in pants. My legs still vibrated from the power of the engine.

I tugged off my helmet, my lips permanently curled in a stupid smile. "That was amazing."

Wyatt pulled off his gear and dismounted. His damp hair fell around his forehead, his cheeks were flushed, and his eyes glittered.

I bounced next to him—hot, dirty, and shaking with excitement.

Wyatt laughed and hugged me, leaning back and lifting me off my feet. I hugged him back, barely noticing when I came down to earth again. He was sweaty, grinning, and too close.

I stumbled back, and his eyes widened.

"Thank you." I swallowed. My pulse thrummed in my neck. "That was amazing."

"Yeah," he teased, "you mentioned that already."

Great. His bike had reduced me to a babbling fool. I tugged at the zipper on my jacket, desperate to let a little cool air inside. The blond boy from the bleachers appeared on my right side, a perfectly timed distraction.

Wyatt nodded at the kid. "Hey. How's it going?"

The boy held out his helmet and a Sharpie. "Could you sign this, please?" He stumbled over the words, his body quivering with excitement. Did I look the same?

"Sure." Wyatt went to work, signing the helmet and making the boy feel comfortable. He joked with him, learning his name and talking to him about racing. Soon, the other boys gathered around, and they all took selfies and talked over each other. I slowly backed up. These boys needed their moment with some-one they obviously looked up to.

I wandered back to Wyatt's truck, peeled off my jacket, and sat on the tailgate, my boots swinging under me.

Afternoon surrendered to early evening, and I shivered when the breeze hit my sweat-stained T-shirt, the smell of dirt sharp in my nose. My stomach rumbled. Man, I was starving. I was also happy. For a long time, I'd only been happy when I was with Ben. It was disorienting to discover that I could also feel this way without him, that I could feel this way with Wyatt.

As if my thoughts had summoned him, he appeared, stopping his bike in front of me in a little spray of gravel. He swung off and hopped up on the tailgate next to me, his hair and face still damp. He nudged me with his shoulder. "Sorry about that."

"About what?"

"The kids. Sorry it took so long."

I gripped the edge of the tailgate and leaned forward. "Are you kidding? You were really sweet with them."

"See . . . " He cocked an eyebrow and swiped the hair back from his forehead. "It's not just girls who find all this irresistible."

I choked back laughter. "Yeah, I'm amazed your boots are muddy, what with your ability to walk on water and all."

He swung his legs out straight. "Hmm . . . the mud does

taint my godly status." He smiled, but then uncertainty flickered across his face and I knew.

For him, this was so much more than a fun afternoon on the track and an unexpected moment with young fans. This was about all the things he'd never do again: racing, being a legend, being a hero to groups of new racers. He was eighteen years old, and his racing career was already over. He knew it, but like my sponsorship offer, this was a slap in the face—a painful and all-too-real reminder.

Wyatt's boots swung back down, and he slouched next to me.

My hand slid closer to his, close enough that our pinkies just touched. "Hey. This was an amazing dream." I carefully handed his earlier words back to him. "Those boys were giving it the recognition it clearly deserved."

He stared down at our hands, letting out a soft laugh. "Those words sounded really great when I said them earlier, but now I realize how useless they are. They don't take away the disappointment you feel in here"—he rubbed at his chest—"when you can no longer do the thing you wanted to do more than anything else in the world, the thing you believed you were born to do."

I tilted my head back, searching for the rain clouds that always seemed to follow me lately, but there were none. "I always look for the worse things in life. Maybe that's why I find them. Maybe I miss the good things—the opportunities and possibilities— because I never bother noticing them. Your words came from your optimism. You will find another dream because you're open to it. When you find it, you're going to grab it."

His pinkie brushed mine. "They say that acknowledging a problem is half the battle."

"Yeah?" I swallowed and looked across the dirt track, too aware of the tiny point of physical contact we still shared. "You think that one afternoon with you is going to turn me into an optimist—that I'll suddenly be seeing rainbows, roses, and pink ponies everywhere I look."

"Nah." He nudged my shoulder. "That would definitely take two afternoons. I'm not a miracle worker."

I shook my head and he hopped down from the truck, my eyes following his every move. He stood in front of me, golden rays of sun catching in his hair and reflecting in his eyes. He leaned against my knees—casually, like it was no big deal. "I never said it before, but today was my first time on my bike since the accident."

I froze, stunned by his confession. He'd seemed so confident and sure. If he'd been afraid, he'd hidden it well. "I didn't know."

"Because I didn't want you to know. I didn't want you to worry or be nervous."

Wait. He'd been worried about me.

"Anyway, I'm glad you were here. I know we're just friends. I respect that it can't be more, but sharing this day with you still felt right."

He looked at me, expecting a response, expecting my agreement about how perfect this day had been, but I couldn't find the words because my hand still itched to touch his. This was wrong. I wasn't supposed to feel anything more than friendship for Wyatt—definitely not this connection that kept tugging me toward him. I loved Ben.

I dropped my head and dug my fingers into the warm metal of the tailgate.

Eventually, Wyatt stepped back. "Well, I better get the bike loaded up."

He walked away, and I released my death grip on his truck. I rubbed my hands against my knees, but the memory of his touch remained.

What was I doing? None of this was Wyatt's fault.

"I'm glad I was here, too," I whispered, and lifted my head, but Wyatt was too far away to hear.

Chapter Twelve

Ben dropped his sail, our boards floating side by side. Water dripped off his hair and ran down his cheeks. He'd fallen at least ten times since we'd started windsurfing an hour ago. His face was red from the wind or the exertion or both, and he looked so frustrated and adorable, I could have sat watching him forever.

"Ugh. Enough, Mer. My arms are killing me. I'm going to have blisters."

"Poor baby." I lifted my feet and he scooped them into his lap, locking us together. Waves lapped at our boards, rocking us up and down.

"I get why you love this. I really do, but I'd take a boat with a motor any day."

I clucked at him, leaning back and soaking in the early spring sun. "Where's the fun in that?"

He held up one of my feet. "Your toes are so wrinkled."

"Yup." I stared at my shriveled fingers. "I hope I don't look like this when I'm old."

"We'll both have dentures and canes, and we'll walk like this." Ben hunched over and pulled his lips over his teeth, opening and closing his mouth.

"Hmm . . . That's a lot to look forward to."

"You know it, baby." He pulled me closer, until our boards were touching and our faces were inches apart. I crossed my feet behind his back, anchoring us. "You know I can see it—" He brushed a loose strand of hair from my cheek. "Growing old with you."

I slid my hands up his chest and around his neck, threading my fingers through his wet hair. "And how do you see this happening?"

"First, we both have to graduate."

"Yeah, and then we'll travel, right?"

He shook his head. "Only because you want to, but after, we'll come back here. I'll take over my dad's boat, and you can work with your dad."

I kissed him, tasting salt water on his lips. "When I'm not competing internationally."

"Exactly." His thumb stroked across my brow. "Your eyes are so blue. I wonder if our kids would have your eyes or mine."

"We could have one of each."

"Yeah." He pulled me closer, lifting me right off my board and fitting me snug against him. His board wobbled, and I clung to his shoulders, helping to balance us on top of my world. Above us, clouds drifted and changed shape in front of a clear blue sky.

I caught my lip between my teeth and stared at Ben. My fingertips followed the trail of water dripping from his hair and down his back. "Did you figure it out yet?"

Now that we'd decided to go all the way, I couldn't concentrate on anything else. I kept imagining it, wondering what it would be like. I'd even looked it up online, but Google could only tell me the mechanics of things. It couldn't tell me how I'd feel.

Ben laid his forehead against mine. "Mom and Dad are driving up to Kitty Hawk next Saturday and staying overnight for their anniversary. We'll have the house to ourselves."

"So I just need to convince my parents that I'm staying over at a friend's house." But who? It wasn't like I had any close friends besides Ben. I couldn't remember the last time I slept over at someone's house. But if this one lie was the only thing standing in the way of my perfect night with Ben, I'd figure it out. "What about, you know, protection?" Heat filled my cheeks.

"I drove all the way up to Roanoke Island last weekend to buy some. I didn't want anyone seeing me."

I giggled. "How did you choose which ones?"

Ben, my big, strong boyfriend, dropped his head and gulped. "I bought a variety and about twenty other things I didn't need."

I pictured him at the checkout of the drugstore with an assortment of condom boxes hidden among a bunch of random items.

I giggled again. "You're my hero."

He shot a palmful of water at me, and I squealed and ducked. "Next time you'll be in charge of the condom purchases."

"What next time? It sounds like you have enough condoms to last us for years."

"Yeah." Ben dropped a kiss on my temple. "I can't believe we're really doing this."

"I know. It's going to be perfect, right?" I whispered.

"Yeah." His voice lowered, and his fingers skimmed my waist, sending shivers across my skin. "It's going to be perfect."

In the cold evening air, Ben paced the beach, waiting for me. I stopped on the path and just watched him for a moment. He'd stuffed his hands in his pockets, and he was staring at the ground. I knew Ben well. He was worried or angry, or maybe both.

I hiked my backpack higher and started toward him. "Ben!"

He spun around, and I picked up my pace. He met me halfway, gripping my shoulders. His gaze roamed over me. "Are you okay? I've been worried sick."

I stepped inside of his grasp and hugged him. "I'm fine."

"You sure?" He squeezed me tight, but I didn't mind.

"Yeah." I almost wished I could blame my absence the previous night on some accident or injury. Instead, I'd made an impulsive decision to drive to the mainland with Wyatt. Even the awkward moment by the truck hadn't ruined things. Wyatt had finished loading the bike and then acted like nothing happened. He'd cracked jokes until it was impossible for me to stay in my funk. He'd even let me play some of my alternative music, although I was pretty sure he preferred his country tunes. We'd stopped for burgers and fries on the way home, and by the time we caught the ferry back to Ocracoke, it was dark and way too late to meet Ben.

I'd promised Ben I'd come, and I'd broken that promise.

"So, what happened?" Tension creased his forehead. "I waited here for hours."

Guilt churned in my belly. What was wrong with me? I'd been off having fun while Ben waited and worried. "I'm so sorry. You must hate me."

"Don't say that." Ben reached for my hand, but I pulled it back. "Just tell me what happened."

I walked to the top of the dune and sat down in a bare patch between the grass. It wasn't our normal spot. Tonight, I didn't feel worthy of it.

Ben followed, stopping a few feet away and facing the ocean, now mostly obscured by nightfall. "Did you forget?" His question was a whisper in the dark. "About me?"

"Yes . . . I mean, no." I sucked in a ragged breath. "It wasn't like that." I looked up at him. "I could never forget about you."

He stood with his feet apart, his arms folded across his chest.

When he stood like that, he looked like his dad. "So, what was it like?"

I couldn't lie to Ben. Not again. Even if the truth ruined everything we had, I wouldn't lie again. "I went to the mainland . . . with Wyatt."

"Wyatt?"

"The new kid in school from Texas. He's a motocross racer, or he used to be, and he asked me if I wanted to go riding with him."

Ben shifted his weight, staring down at me. "And you said yes."

I nodded.

For a moment, neither of us spoke. Ben's jaw worked back and forth. He was taking in my words, processing them. "Why?"

I sprang to my feet, leaving my backpack abandoned in the sand. "Because he asked me, and I wanted to do something exciting. Sometimes I feel trapped on these islands."

"Do you mean trapped here with me?"

"No." God, how could I explain this? "I wanted to take a risk and not worry about the consequences."

"Did you like it?"

I squeezed my eyes shut and remembered the feeling of hurtling around the track. "I loved it."

"Do you like him?"

My eyes flew open. Ben looked scared. "I love you."

"That's not what I asked."

"Yeah." I blinked. "I like him as a friend. Maybe it's because he doesn't know anything about . . . the past. He doesn't judge me." What was I saying? Why was I bringing this up now?

Ben pinched the bridge of his nose between his thumb and forefinger. "And I do?"

I wanted them to stop, but my words kept coming. "Maybe. You say you don't, but how do I really know? You'd have every right to. I messed everything up. I lied to you." I kicked at the sand, tired from the weight of my bottled-up feelings. "And when I'm with you, I'm constantly reminded of that. Every time I look at you, I remember what I did."

"I guess I finally know how you really feel." Ben looked like I'd punched him in the gut.

And I was the one responsible for hurting him. What was wrong with me? Why did I keep doing this to the first and last boy I would ever love? Sometimes I found it hard to remember how perfect it had been.

I hitched a ride to the ferry terminal, where Ben waited for me on the Hatteras side. He leaned against his mom's car, wearing a button-down shirt with his hair gelled back, like we were going on a formal date.

I slowed, staring down at my sneakers, denim shorts, and gauzy off-the-shoulder top. Damn. I'd underdressed. But at least I was wearing my best bra and panties, and I'd taken an extra-long time with my makeup. That gave me confidence, especially when Ben saw me and his lips curved into a broad smile. That smile made me feel like the most beautiful girl in the world.

We closed the distance, and I jumped into his arms. My legs wrapped around his waist, and my hair flew around his broad shoulders. He spun me, and our nervous laughter mixed with our kisses.

I felt grown-up and carefree at the same time. I wondered what we looked like to the tourists waiting around. Could they tell what we were about to do for the first time?

On the drive back to his house, my nerves set in. He turned the stereo up, maybe to cover our silence. We arrived at his empty house. I'd been here a million times, but this time, it felt different, like even the walls knew about our secret plans.

Ben held the door for me. "I ordered pizza. Should we eat first?" He looked as uncertain as I felt.

I chewed on my lip and smoothed back my hair. "Yeah. Pizza sounds great."

We ate at the dining room table, with a candle flickering between us. He even produced a bottle of wine and poured us each a glass. When I looked at him, he shrugged. "My parents have a big stash. They'll never miss one bottle."

I guzzled the whole glass. The alcohol warmed my body and took the edge off my nerves, but we both stopped after one glass. Neither one of us wanted to be drunk. Neither one of us wanted to miss anything that was about to happen.

After, we cleaned the dishes together, and then realized we'd run out of distractions. It was now or never.

I watched Ben's expression—the tense set of his jaw, the way he wouldn't look at me, the way he shifted his weight, rubbing the back of his neck with one hand. He was hesitant, and his uncertainty gave me confidence. This was Ben, my normally confident boyfriend who didn't know how to take the first step.

I caught his hand in mine. Our gazes met and I led him up the stairs. At the top, I slowed, unsure of where to head.

"My room." His low words filled the silence.

I nodded and pushed open the door.

What I saw there made me smile. He'd tidied up and made his bed. The room smelled like vanilla air freshener, and unlit candles lined the edge of his dresser. I released his hand and used the pack of matches to light them all.

When I finished and turned around, he stood with his back to the closed door, staring at me. His eyes were so dark, serious, trusting. I could lose myself in those eyes, but I couldn't take my clothes off under the harsh glare of his ceiling light.

"Turn off the light," I whispered.

He flipped the switch, and everything changed. The room filled with shadows, the streaming silver light of the moon, and the flickering glow of candles.

We met in the middle—our touches slow and fumbling at first. We bumped noses. He stepped on my toes. My hair tangled in his shirt buttons. But then somewhere along the way, we forgot to think about what we were doing. We forgot to feel nervous and unsure.

Our breathing sped up. We didn't have to stop this time. We didn't have to wonder what all these feelings led up to.

I slipped off my clothes and sat on the edge of his bed in my bra and panties. He pulled back his covers, and I lay on the bed and closed my eyes.

"Mer . . ."

My eyes flew open.

He knelt on the floor next to me, like he was still a kid saying his prayers at night—only tonight had nothing to do with praying. "Are you sure? We can stop if you want."

He'd taken off his shirt, and my gaze found the small scar on his shoulder where I'd accidentally caught him with my fishing hook when I was eight. He'd barely flinched, while I freaked out the entire fifteen-minute walk back to his house. Uncle Al had met us in the driveway and had fixed Ben up in no time flat.

"Mer?"

I rolled onto my hip, reaching for him, my fingertips brushing the small silver line. "I want my first time to be with someone special, someone I love. I can't imagine ever loving anyone else."

Ben caught my hand and kissed my palm. "You are the most beautiful girl I've ever met."

It wasn't true. I knew it wasn't, but it only mattered that Ben believed it, that it was how he saw me. I pulled him down, and his mouth dropped warm kisses on my neck, on my shoulder, on my bare belly.

"I want this," I whispered in his ear when he lay on top of me, nervous and excited about the feelings building inside me. "I want you."

So, in the dark, in his little twin bed, we went all the way for the first time, and it felt right. It felt as special as it was supposed to feel, because it was Ben.

I'd grown up with him. We'd shared every milestone, every significant event. Now we'd shared this together.

After, I curled against him, and he whispered against my temple, "Are you okay?"

"Yeah." I laid my palm flat on his chest. His heart still thundered, and his voice sounded hoarse. "Are you okay?"

"Never been better. I love you so much."

And as we would come to find out, nothing would ever be the same again.

Ben stared at me, the roar of the ocean not loud enough to obscure the pain in his words. "I guess there's nothing more to say."

He swung around, walking away, but I ran to block his path. "Stop!"

"What?" he yelled, sidestepping me. "We don't need to do this anymore. You clearly don't want to."

I blocked his path again, pushing on his shoulders. My chest ached with every breath, like I'd been sprinting for a mile in the cold. "Just stop. You need to hear the rest."

"What more can you possibly have to say?"

A tornado of anger, guilt, and fear whirled inside me—sucking up my thoughts and spitting them out in broken, jagged words.

I poked him in the chest with my finger. "Oh, I have plenty to say. Do I feel guilty when I'm with you? Yes. Do I wonder every day what life would have been like if I hadn't lied to you? Yes. But those are just tiny annoyances because I love you and that feeling is so much bigger than everything else." My eyes burned, and I squeezed my hands into fists, remembering the night Ben came back to me, the night he saved me. "I can't live without you, and that's not bullshit, because I know. I tried. So, I'm sorry that I promised to come last night and didn't, but I'm not sorry for being friends with Wyatt, and I'll never be sorry for being in love with you."

Ben stood rigid, frowning.

I held my breath, the truth of my words finally sinking in. Wyatt was a shiny new toy. I was attracted to the novelty of him, but Ben held my heart. I'd given it to him years ago, and no matter what happened between us, he still held it. No matter how much Wyatt distracted me, I'd always end up right back here, on the sand, waiting for Ben to make me feel whole again.

Ben's body collapsed in on itself, like a balloon deflating.

"God, I hate this." He groaned and looked up at the sky. "I just want things to go back to the way they were. I feel trapped, too, you know. We had plans. Things we were going to do together."

"I know." I collapsed against his chest, shivering, my tears wetting his shirt. "Just don't leave. Please."

He pulled me close, his words hollow and haunting. "I won't. I tried leaving you once before, too, but I didn't get very far."

Ben held me tight. I should have felt reassured, but the cold, dark shadow was back again—a sense that something bad waited for us and our time together couldn't last. I felt it creeping steadily closer.

While driving back to the ferry terminal that night, I found it on the side of the road. My headlight swept over its body as it lay there, twitching.

I slowed and stopped.

Freezing, I climbed off Sally and walked to the deer. It raised its head and stared at me, its eyes big and round and as velvety dark as the night sky. Blood stained the ground around it. I glanced up and down the deserted highway. A car must have hit it, but no one had stopped.

I crouched down, and its ears moved. It made a strangled sound.

It was dying, suffering. My throat tightened. I stretched out my shaking fingers and stroked the fur on its neck. The deer blinked, sagging back against the road.

As I stared into its eyes, I understood that it wanted me to help. It wanted me to ease its pain, but there was nothing I could do. It was dying, and I could only watch while it drew its final breath, powerless to change anything.

The darkness stretched around us, and suddenly it was me who couldn't breathe. I fell back on my bum and clawed at my hoodie. It was too tight around my neck, and my hands grasped for the zipper, yanking it down.

I dropped my head between my knees and willed my galloping heart to slow before it burst right out of my chest.

Long minutes later, the panic eased and I climbed to my feet.

I staggered to my scooter and climbed on.

I tried not to look at the deer as I drove past. Its death wasn't fair, but there was nothing I could do to change it.

Chapter Thirteen

On Monday morning, Wyatt leaned against my locker, checking something on his phone and clearly waiting for me. I slowed and considered my options.

I needed my books, but Wyatt's presence indicated our outing on the weekend had pushed us over some invisible line. His expectations of our friendship had changed, but I didn't want that. I'd confessed to Ben. I was confident in my love for him, but looking at Wyatt still made me feel guilty.

I lifted my chin and walked forward. In a school this size, I couldn't avoid Wyatt all day.

When I got closer, his face lit up. He straightened and smiled, showing off his perfect white teeth. "Hey, Mer."

"Hey." I reached for my combination lock, and he stepped

to one side, twisting so that his hip leaned on the locker next to mine, his face inches away.

"So, I just wanted to thank you again for coming on Saturday. I hope you weren't in too much pain after."

My hand shook. "What?"

"You know, I hope you weren't sore from the ride. If you're not used to it, it can be rough on the muscles."

"Oh, that." Damn. I'd messed up my combination. I spun the lock a few times and started over.

"Yeah, what did you think I meant?"

I twisted off the lock and swung open the door with too much force. It clanged and Wyatt jumped. I remembered the pain on Ben's face, the tightness in my own heart. I remembered the pain in the deer's eyes and the feeling that I couldn't breathe. "Heartburn. I figured you were talking about heartburn from the burgers."

Wyatt slowly nodded. "Ahh. Is this a problem you have on a regular basis?"

Great. Now I sounded like an old person. "No." I pulled out my books. "Look, I'm late. I've got to get to class." Spanish was the one class Wyatt and I were not taking together. He'd already finished AP Spanish, so he had study hall instead.

Wyatt frowned and took a step back. I was confusing him. I told Ben that I wanted to be friends with Wyatt, but last night, I'd finally understood that it wasn't just about what I wanted. I needed to keep my distance from Wyatt. I loved Ben, but somewhere deep inside, I also understood that being with Wyatt was a slippery slope to . . . something.

I swung away from him, but his hand landed on my arm. It was enough to bring me to a full stop. "Yeah?"

He hesitated and his hand fell. "Did I do something?"

"No." I hugged my books.

"I thought we were friends. I know about the rules, but I thought we had a good time on Saturday. I thought you had a good time. Was I wrong?"

I glanced around, feeling like a huge neon sign was hanging over our heads, but the hall was strangely empty. Had I already missed the bell? "Look, I did have a good time, but being friends with you is too complicated. We should just stick to seeing each other at work."

He rocked back on his heels, looking like I'd sucker punched him. For a moment, he said nothing, his jaw clenched. "Is this because of him—the guy you're seeing? Is he even real, because no one seems to know about him?"

"What are you talking about?" My heart thudded in my throat.

He ducked his head, his voice so low I had to strain to hear it. "I asked around about your boyfriend. People said you used to date someone, but you've been single for a while. So is this just some bullshit excuse you made up because you don't want to go out with me?"

I'd heard the expression before—about seeing red—but I

never knew it actually happened. Anger boiled up inside me, blurring my vision, tightening my limbs, and clogging my throat. "Stop. Right there."

My tone and expression must have scared him because he did a double take. "Mer—"

"Don't." Ice replaced the hot fury in my body. "Maybe you thought my rules were a joke, but I wasn't kidding about my privacy. If you want to gossip about someone, find a new friend."

"Hey!" he called out, but I spun around and charged down the hall.

I didn't stop at my classroom. How could I when all I felt was the overwhelming urge to scream or hit something? Reaching the front door, I shoved it open, stumbling out and sucking in fresh air. God, I was going to hurl.

Mom would throw a fit when she found out I was skipping class, and she would find out, but I didn't care. I walked to Sally, threw my books under the seat, and climbed on.

I was halfway to the ferry before I could even think straight.

Driving the length of Hatteras Island, I passed the spot on the road where I'd found the deer, but it was gone. Someone had probably removed its carcass. So why did it feel almost like a dream now?

I stopped for lunch and glanced at the many angry texts from my mom.

At least tell me you're okay. Please.

I texted back: *I'm fine. Don't worry. I'll be home later.* Then I shut off my phone.

I drove all the way to Nags Head, before turning around and heading back. When evening came, I parked my scooter at the beach, walked to our spot, and watched the rain clouds roll in.

Ben came with the rain and held me while it poured. Despite my soaked clothes and the chill in my bones, he gave me faith that everything would somehow be okay.

Wyatt and I avoided each other over the next couple of days. Mom grounded me for cutting class and disappearing for a whole day, confiscating the keys to Sally and not even letting me drive myself to school for the rest of the week. Fortunately, I'd already warned Ben that I'd probably be grounded. I'd offered to sneak out and meet him, but he didn't want me in more trouble. We'd reluctantly agreed that we'd survive a few nights without each other if we had to.

So except for work and school, I had nothing else now—not even Ben.

At the Yellow Rose Café, Wyatt and I maintained a pretense of polite civility for his mom's sake, but if anyone watched us carefully, they'd see how I moved in a coordinated dance of avoidance. When he waited on the tables, I stayed behind the counter. If he needed to drop off dishes or pick up an order, I found an excuse to head to the kitchen or take a bathroom break.

To Wyatt's credit, he'd tried to apologize twice during our first shift together. He sounded sincere, but I didn't want to hear it. Maybe I was clinging to his mistake as a shield against that spark I felt. If I hung on to this grudge with all my strength, I wouldn't have to think about the feelings Wyatt spurred in me.

On the third shift, Harley pulled me aside in the kitchen. Her expression warned me that she wanted to talk about Wyatt. "I know this is probably none of my business—"

"It's not."

She sighed. "Honey, I see you. I don't know what happened in the past that made you so afraid to show your feelings, but I know they're there. Wyatt obviously did something to hurt you." I huffed, but she held up one hand. "Look, I know my kid. He's rash and impulsive. He sometimes makes bad choices, but he has a good heart, and despite all that cockiness, he hurts, too. Whatever he did, maybe you could accept his apology and give him a second chance."

I wrapped my arms around my stomach and rolled my eyes upward. "Wyatt talked to you about this?"

She clasped her hands together and tightened her lips. "Wyatt won't tell me anything. He told me everything was fine and I should stay out of it."

I snorted but refrained from stating the obvious.

"I know, I know." She shrugged. "I am clearly not staying

out of this, but one day, when you have a kid of your own, you'll understand. As a mother, you'll do anything within your power to save your kid from even a minute of heartbreak. So, yes, this is me, standing here, not staying out of it."

I knew she meant well. I knew she could never understand how her words were slashing at my battered feelings like a million tiny knives. I struggled to control my aching heart and ragged breathing. *She doesn't know. She doesn't know.*

"I can't." My eyes burned, but there were no tears. Not anymore. "Not yet."

She swallowed and slowly nodded. "Okay."

"Do you still want me to work here?"

Her face softened. "Of course, honey. Whatever this is, I have faith that it'll work itself out. We'll just give it some time, like you said."

I nodded and turned away. Time healed all wounds. That's what they said, but whoever "they" were, they didn't know jackshit.

I texted Ben and told him to meet me at our spot at the beach—the place we'd discovered years ago, when we were still kids. I tried to calm my nerves, to plan out what I wanted to say, but all I wanted to do was throw up.

Ben called out to me, his voice reaching me above the roar of the surf. "Mer?" He stopped a few feet away, his face pale. "What is it?

What's wrong? You're totally freaking me out here."

"That's good." I laughed, but it sounded hysterical. "Because I'm already freaked out. No. I'm so far past freaked out that I'm somewhere in the range of losing my shit completely."

Ben grabbed my hands, and it was only then I realized I'd been pacing back and forth, my movements rapid and erratic. "Just tell me. Please."

I pulled my hands free and buried my face in them. But hiding didn't change the truth. Five different pregnancy tests didn't change the truth. It didn't matter how many times I'd cried alone in my bathroom and pleaded with God to please change the result on the next one. It didn't matter that I'd vowed to actually start going to church and never have sex again and never speak or think a single unkind word for the rest of my life. The stick had still shown the same stupid result each time.

So, I'd carefully hidden them all in a brown paper bag and thrown them in the outside trash can.

For two days, I'd done nothing. I'd told myself that if I just ignored it all, it would somehow go away, but then I'd woken up this morning and thrown up in the toilet. I'd stared at my face in the mirror and cursed everyone I could think of. Then I'd texted Ben.

Now, I lifted my head. "I'm pregnant."

If I thought Ben's face was pale before, I was wrong. He grayed like a corpse. "We used condoms." His statement sounded more like a question.

"Yes." I stabbed one hand into the air. "Maybe it's written in the fine print somewhere, but apparently condoms are not guaranteed to work."

"But we only did it four times."

"Again, apparently that's all it takes."

"Shit." He leaned over, his hands pressed against his thighs. "Shit. Shit. Shit. I think I'm going to be sick."

I slapped him on the back. "Join the club."

He knelt down and then sat, his head between his hands. I stood over him. I loved Ben. We were both responsible for making this baby that was apparently growing in my belly, but in that moment, I also felt the huge void between us.

I was the one who was pregnant. I was the one whose future would never be the same. I was the one who had to figure out what to tell my parents.

Ben was the father. He was also to blame, but he could walk away scot-free if he wanted. As I sank down beside him, the knowledge sat like a bitter pill in my mouth. I resented Ben.

His life wouldn't be ruined by this. Not the way mine would.

Chapter Fourteen

The rest of the week dragged by. On Friday afternoon, I met Mom and Rachel at the car in the school parking lot. My sister hooked her arm through mine. "We're going shopping in Buxton. Shopping and supper. Just the three of us."

I glared at my mom. "Just drop me off at home."

Rachel's grip on my arm tightened, and Mom's expression hardened. "You're coming, Meredith."

I huffed, but Rachel leaned closer. "Come on, Mer. It's going to be fun. A girls' night out."

Nothing about the night sounded fun, but my sister's expression silently begged me not to argue. So, I threw my backpack in the trunk and climbed in the back seat, leaving the front for Rachel.

The air in the car tasted stale. Mom started the engine, and I lowered the window, feeling like a prisoner being allowed their hour of fresh air a day. I poked my earbuds in and turned up my music. Mom frowned at me in the rearview mirror but said nothing. I knew she was picking her battles. She'd gotten me in the car with minimum fuss, so now she was giving me a little space.

Once we were on the ferry, we beelined our way to the railing. Rachel leaned over to watch for jellyfish, like she'd been doing since she was little. I stood a few feet away—with them, but always somehow apart.

Mom walked over and stood next to me. "I'm trying, but you have to meet me halfway."

"Why?"

"Because you're my daughter and I love you."

I gritted my teeth. "I'm a disappointment to you. If you can finally be honest about that, maybe we can be honest about other things."

Her nails dug into the railing. They were perfectly coated in a soft pink color, so different from my own black chipped nail polish. "Is that what you think?"

Clouds hovered on the horizon. They'd close in by evening. "It's what I know. When you think of your ideal daughter, it isn't me. Not even close. It's Rachel."

"This isn't about Rachel. It's about you and me. I don't understand how we got here. What did I do wrong?"

I scuffed the deck with the toe of my sneaker. "Maybe you didn't do anything wrong. You're my mom. I'm your kid. So nature or society tells us that we have to love each other. But I'm still me and you're still you." My heart raced, and I worked to steady my voice, but it still shook a little. "If we weren't related, we'd have nothing in common. The truth is that we wouldn't even like each other. So why can't we just admit it and stop trying so hard to have this 'special bond' that we can never have?"

Mom's face fell. "You don't really believe that."

I slouched against the railing. A jellyfish floated past, caught in the wake of the ferry, helpless to control its fate. "Give me a better explanation. What do you think is going on?"

But my mother stayed silent. I'd left her at a loss for words.

For the rest of the ferry ride, we didn't talk directly, using my sister as a buffer against the tension filling the space between us.

I followed Rachel and my mom around the small shop, trying hard for Rachel's sake to at least act interested. They stopped in front of an accessory rack to check out the two-for-one hair clips. I tapped my foot and struggled to not look impatient.

"Mer, which ones should I get?" Rachel held up four sets of barrettes, all of them with some combination of fake pearls and little glittery rhinestones. They all looked the same to me.

"Get the ones you like best."

"But that's the problem. I can't decide. You have to help me."

"Fine." I sighed. "Take these two." I pointed to the two closest to me.

She grinned. "That's exactly the two I was thinking about. Great minds think alike."

I shot her a quick smile and glanced over at my mom, who should have been heading for the cash. Instead, Mom stood deathly still, staring at something over my shoulder. Her face turned white and her nostrils flared.

I spun around. *Shit.*

Ben's parents stood a few feet away. Mom and Aunt Lila faced each other, frozen in disbelief like two garden gnomes. Aunt Lila emerged from her trance first. She shook herself and started to pivot away, but Mom stopped her.

"Lila, please. It's been months." Mom pressed her fist against her chest, like she was in physical pain. "I miss you."

Aunt Lila was a ghost of herself. She'd lost weight, and her cheekbones stood out. Wrinkles had sprouted up around her mouth and the corners of her eyes, and a few strands of dull gray hair mixed in with the brown around her temples. Guilt trapped me in place like wet cement.

Mom tried again. "If we could just talk. Tell me how you feel. We used to talk about everything."

Aunt Lila's inhale sounded more like a sob. Uncle Al reached for her, but she brushed him off. "I know what you want," she said, her voice surprisingly strong. "You want things to go back to the way they were, but I can't do it. I'm not ready."

Her cold stare landed on me like a bucket of ice water. The person who'd once been like a second mom to me now looked at me with hate. "I know it's not all your fault, Meredith. I know that in my head. But when I look at you, all I feel is anger in my heart. I know it's not fair, but it's how I feel."

Her attention shifted to Rachel. "I'm sorry, honey. You shouldn't have to hear this, but with Meredith as your sister, I suspect you've had to grow up too fast as well."

"Lila!" Mom gasped.

"What? You wanted to know how I feel. Now you know." She looked back at Uncle Al. "Please take me home."

Uncle Al nodded and took her arm, but he glanced back once. I wondered if we looked the same as we felt—like shell-shocked victims, still reeling from the attack. His gaze brushed over me, and I imagined he had something more he wanted to say, but he only bowed his head and kept walking.

It was Rachel who got us both to the parking lot, supporting my mom around the waist and leading me by the hand. When we reached the car, she pressed the keys into my palm. "You have to drive."

"I can't," I mumbled. Aunt Lila was right. I'd forced Rachel to grow up too soon.

"Mer! You have to drive because Mom can't."

My fingers curled around the keys, and I finally looked at my mom. Silent tears streamed down her cheeks and dripped off her chin. I'd never seen her look like this. Not even after all the things I'd done. It's like there'd been a thin, brittle shell holding her together all this time, and with Aunt Lila's words, that layer had cracked, splitting wide open and leaving behind nothing but a heap of broken pieces.

Rachel looked at me, real fear in her eyes. "We have to get her home to Dad. He'll know what to do. He'll know how to fix this."

"Don't worry." I hugged Rachel. "I'll get you both home," I said, reassuring her, but deep down, I doubted that even Dad had the power to make this right.

Ben finally looked at me. "This is a punch in the gut, but it's not the end of the world, Mer. We can do this."

My chin jerked up. "Do what?"

"Have a baby."

"WE are not having a baby. I am. It's inside of me."

"I know that, but I'm not going to run away from this." He straightened, his face still pale. "As soon as I graduate, I'll be working full time on Dad's boat. It's good pay, and we can live at my parents' place to save money. They have room. After you graduate, we can get married. It might take a little while, but we can save up for our own spot."

My head swam—a buzzing noise filled my ears, drowning out his speech. He was talking gibberish I couldn't understand, words that made it hard to think.

"Stop!" I jumped to my feet, sending sand flying. "What are you talking about?"

He looked up, his expression serious. "I'm talking about our future." Something flickered in his eyes. It looked dangerously like optimism, or even worse, enthusiasm.

"Are you high right now? Getting married as soon as I graduate? All of us living in your parents' house? What would I be doing all this time?"

"Mom could watch the baby while you finished high school. She loves babies. After that, you could do whatever you wanted."

"Really." I threw my head back and stared at the sky. "I want to windsurf. I want to travel the world. I want to experience all the things I've never gotten to do here. I'm sixteen. I don't want to get huge and push a baby out of me. I don't want to never have a moment of my life that's just for me ever again."

Ben stood. "I know you're upset, Mer, but it's what we both wanted eventually. It's just happening faster than either of us planned. But freaking out doesn't change the fact that it's still happening."

He reached for my hand, but I pulled away. Ever since I found out, I'd been counting on Ben to have the answers. I'd always counted on him to get me through the tough times. He was supposed to have a magical solution, but this was definitely not it. Not even close.

He was suggesting something I wasn't ready for. I loved Ben. Someday, I wanted to marry him. I couldn't imagine ever loving anyone more, but that didn't mean I wanted to be a mom at sixteen. I didn't want to be the girl who got knocked up and had to give up all her dreams because she sacrificed everything for her kid. Maybe I didn't have lofty aspirations—I didn't want to go to Harvard or cure cancer or become an astronaut or save the world—but I still wanted things that were important to me.

"I know it's happening, but I don't want this. I can't do it."

I walked to the water's edge. The waves tugged in and out, dictated by the tides and pull of the moon and all the other forces I didn't understand. I didn't want to be a wave. I wanted to decide what my own future looked like.

Ben appeared at my side. "What are you saying? Do you want to give the baby up for adoption?"

Maybe my thoughts made me a terrible person, but they were still there, screaming at me, too loud to ignore. Digging my foot in the sand, I watched the small depression fill with water. Ben said nothing, waiting. I couldn't look at him, so I lifted my head to stare at the distant waves instead.

"I want there not to be a baby. I want an abortion."

The wind whipped my soft words away, but I knew Ben heard them. Still, he said nothing. I finally looked at him.

Any other guy would've felt relief hearing these words. Any normal seventeen-year-old would want a Get Out of Jail Free *card from this whole situation, but Ben looked crushed. He shook his head and frowned, his dark eyes wide with disbelief.*

"How far along are you?"

"Why?" I whispered, the word sticking in my throat.

"Please, Mer..."

"I don't know, but my period is only a couple of weeks late."

"So, it's still early."

I wrapped my arms around my belly. "Yeah. So?"

Ben pulled my stiff body into his arms. His hands tangled in my hair, and I leaned into his chest. "So, we don't have to decide everything right now. We have time."

"Time won't make any difference," I mumbled against his T-shirt.

"You don't know that. You've always been the glass-half-empty person. My glass is half full. That's why we work so well together. We balance each other."

That was true, but there were some things that couldn't be solved by positive thinking.

"Just promise me you won't do anything until we've had time to talk more. I know we can figure something out, something that will work for all of us."

But I already had a solution that worked for me. "I don't know."

"I do." Ben stepped back and brushed my cheek with his thumb. "Do you love me?"

I nodded, tears clogging my throat.

"Then just give me a little time. Two weeks to show you that this could work."

I said nothing. I couldn't stand the hope in Ben's eyes.

"Please, Mer. Just promise me two weeks."

I slowly nodded, but two weeks felt like an eternity. Maybe he saw the uncertainty on my face.

His hands moved to my shoulders. His fingers bit into my skin. "I need you to say it out loud. Promise me."

I swallowed and clenched my teeth. Finally, I released my breath. "I promise."

Overhead, a gull screeched in disapproval, but in front of me, Ben's stance relaxed. His grip loosened. "Good. That's good."

I could feel his relief in the air. He trusted me. He had faith in my promise.

I ran to my room and slammed the door. Somewhere downstairs, my dad questioned Rachel, trying to figure out what had happened. He'd comfort Mom, try to make her feel better, but in the end, the situation wouldn't change. Aunt Lila still wouldn't talk to her best friend, because she couldn't look at me without feeling anger, hate, and blame.

I fell to my knees in front of my closet and burrowed my head in the darkest corner, reaching for the shoebox stacked under a pair of boots I never wore. I cradled the box in my hands and sat on my bum.

Mom's muffled tears reached me through the heating grate in the floor.

I pulled the top off and carefully lifted out the baby rattle. It was soft and plush—a yellow baby giraffe with green spots and a teething ring in its mouth. I shook it, listening to its soft rattles. Sometimes at night, I'd dream about the baby. I'd dream that I'd forgotten what I did with her. I'd run through my house, hearing her cry, but no matter how hard I searched, I couldn't find her.

After laying the rattle back inside, I returned the box to its home in the farthest corner of my closet and pulled out my running sneakers. Outside the window, dark clouds stretched down to the rooftops. I changed into my running gear.

I needed to forget the look on Aunt Lila's face and the sound of my mom crying. I needed space.

Chapter Fifteen

I waited until we were alone in the house. Rachel was at a friend's, and Dad was down at the shop. "Mom, I need to tell you something."

She stopped chopping vegetables and looked at me. "That sounds serious."

Without knowing it, she'd just delivered the understatement of the year. It was ironic. Even though I was closer to my dad, I couldn't bring myself to tell him, maybe because I knew how disappointed he'd be. I'd already let my mom down a million times, so what difference would one more time make?

Still, I jammed my hands in my pockets and stood, my cheeks turning hotter the longer she stared at me. She wiped her hands on a towel and stepped around the island. "What is it? You're scaring me."

"I . . . " I took a step back, fumbling for the words I'd already practiced, but somehow they'd disappeared. "I . . . " I wet my lips and swallowed, but then I realized, it didn't matter which words I used or how I tried to explain it. The end result wouldn't change. So I blurted it out: "I'm pregnant."

For a second, she froze, like one of those living statues, only her eyes blinking. I watched her trying to process my confession. I knew the exact moment it registered. Her spine collapsed forward, and she reached for the back of the chair, gripping it so hard the blood left her hand.

Her mouth opened and snapped shut, and then her eyes swept closed and she mumbled something under her breath. A prayer? She eased into the chair, the towel still hanging from one hand. Disappointment dripped from her face and my stomach sank.

"I don't understand. How could this happen?"

I shrugged, feeling defensive, embarrassed . . . scared. There were a million things I could have said, but like always, I chose wrong. "The usual way. I had sex."

Her head snapped up. "Really, Meredith. You're making jokes about this? Don't you understand how serious this is? I thought you were smarter than this. I expected more. I should have . . ." Her voice trailed off and she stared at her hands, like she couldn't even look at me anymore.

A bitter taste filled my mouth. I'd known how she'd react, but deep down, I'd hoped for something more. Deep down, I'd wanted

her to hug me and tell me that she still loved me, that I hadn't
messed up everything.

The weather matched my mood—wild and chaotic. I normally paced myself, but not now. I sprinted down deserted roads, barely outrunning the tsunami that had become my life. My breath wheezed in and out and my muscles burned, but I couldn't stop. I turned off the highway and ran past the airstrip. If I didn't live on an island, I'd have just kept running.

My sneakers kicked up little clouds of sand, and the wind whipped my breath away. I got a stitch in my side and slowed, but I still couldn't stop. The road stretched in front of me—a dark, endless stain on the horizon. Stupid tears burned my eyes, blurring my vision. Off to my right, the lighthouse flickered, refusing to get closer no matter how fast I ran. It taunted me—a reminder that I was standing still on this island, never moving ahead, still caught in the mire of my past mistakes.

My limbs protested. My feet tripped over each other and my ankle twisted. I stumbled and landed face-first.

Damn. I rolled over and sat on my bum, panting.

Blood welled on both knees and trickled to the edge of the tears in my leggings, soaking into the fabric. I brushed my hands together, wiping off the dirt and wincing at the scrapes on my palms. My iPod lay a few feet away, with its screen cracked.

I pictured my cell phone sitting back in my room. *Stupid.*

I bit my lip and swallowed. My ankle really hurt. My knees and hands throbbed. I looked up and down the deserted road. How long before someone else decided to drive out to the southern tip of the island?

It took about ten minutes for reality to sink in. I'd have to walk to find help.

Scooting my good foot close to my bum, I managed to stand without putting any weight on my bad ankle. For a long moment, I balanced on one foot, gathering my courage. The first step would be the worst. I put my bad foot on the ground and leaned on it. *Shit.* Pain vibrated through my leg, and tears streamed down my cheek.

I managed five pathetic steps before sinking to the ground and admitting defeat.

The wind gusted and the temperature dropped. Once again, the cold penetrated my life when it should have been balmy out. Running had kept me warm, but now my sweaty clothes clung to my skin. I shivered and pulled up my hood, then wrapped my arms around my knees and glanced at my watch.

Almost eight o'clock.

On a clear evening, there'd still be lingering daylight in the sky, but the dark clouds blocked out the last of the sun's glow. The road grew darker before my eyes, and too soon, I sat alone, even the lights from town not strong enough to penetrate the night and reach me.

I pictured Aunt Lila's face. Maybe the universe was dispensing the fate I deserved, punishment for everyone I'd hurt.

Time passed in a blur of pain and cold. I wondered if my mom and dad would even notice that I was missing. Then again, I'd been missing from my family so much over this past year, they'd probably stopped looking.

At some point, the real unease started. I tucked my face against my knees and tried to slow my stampeding heart. The wind howled, and I worried I'd die alone on the side of this road. No one would ever find me. It made no sense. I was cold and my ankle hurt, but someone would eventually come. So why did it feel like my entire life was racing toward some terrifying precipice?

I hummed to myself. I recited the capitals of all the states to keep the panic from spreading.

Then the sound of an engine overpowered the wail of the wind. I raised my head, squinting against the glare of approaching headlights. Rocks crunched under tires, and the vehicle stopped a few feet away.

The driver's door swung open, and I pulled back my hood.

"Mer!"

His voice broke through the cold and my fear. I should have known it would be him. Something kept bringing us together, throwing him into my path. I saw that now. No matter how much I fought it, Wyatt was destined to be a part of my life.

He knelt next to me, his headlights obscuring my view of him. "Are you okay? What happened?"

My numb lips tried to form words, but my body shook too hard.

Wyatt swore and unzipped his jacket, shrugging out of it. He dropped it around my shoulders, and I sobbed in relief. I breathed in its warmth and his familiar scent. I swear fresh laundry never smelled so good.

"Can you stand?"

I nodded, my teeth chattering together.

"I'll be right back." He ran to his truck and threw open the passenger door before heading back to me. Stooping, he wrapped an arm around my waist. "Are you ready?"

I nodded, and he surged to his feet, bringing me with him. I hissed. Every muscle in my body protested. They'd frozen into position and I stumbled again. My weight landed on my bad ankle.

The pain took my breath away, and my legs gave out.

I braced myself for another fall, but Wyatt was there, sweeping me off my feet and into his arms.

Relief flooded my body. I buried my face against his shoulder, and my muscles went limp. He did that for me. Even in my pain, I understood that he'd make sure I was okay. I'd been angry with him. I'd no intention of ever forgiving him, but in his arms, I felt safe.

His strides brought us to his truck, and he eased me into the passenger seat. Warm air blasted from the vents, but I missed the feel of his arms around me. He pulled an old blanket from behind the seat and tucked it around my shoulders.

In the glow of the dome light, I could finally see his face. It was pale and grim, and his mouth was set in a tight line. He was really worried about me. My hand rose. I reached for his face, but he caught it.

"Your hands are a mess. Did you fall?"

I nodded.

He brushed the hair from my face. "Mer, you need to tell me what hurts."

How often had Ben done the same thing? Brushed my hair aside? How often had his gentle touch left me shivering? Wyatt's touch was firmer, more assured, but my breath still caught.

I swallowed. "My left ankle."

"It's going to be okay. We just need to keep the swelling down until we can get you to the hospital." He closed my door and crossed to the driver's side. Climbing in, he reached down and gently lifted my leg. I groaned and his face twisted. "I'm so sorry. I'm being as gentle as I can."

"I know," I whispered. I knew.

Fortunately, his truck had a bench seat. I twisted until my back rested against the passenger door. He rolled part of the blanket under my foot to keep it elevated.

"Where's the closest hospital?"

I closed my eyes. "Nags Head. Anything closer is already closed for the night."

For a minute, he said nothing. The drive was almost two hours long and that didn't include the ferry ride. "Okay then. We'd better get going."

I smiled. He was actually willing to drive me that far. "Just take me home."

"Are you sure?"

I opened my eyes. The shaking had lessened. "Yeah. Our neighbor is a doctor. Dad will call him. It's probably just a sprain."

His jaw clenched. "Home it is." He turned off the dome light, and the cab became a warm, dark sanctuary. Wyatt drove slowly, trying to avoid the bumps, knowing each one caused me pain.

Outside, the wind gusted, but inside, I focused on his steady breathing. "Why did you find me?"

"What?"

"What made you drive down this road?" I huddled inside his jacket.

"Dad canceled on me again." His hands tightened on the wheel. "I wanted to drive all night, but there's only so far you can go before you run into water."

I tried to laugh, but the sound stuck in my throat. "But there's nothing out here."

"Yeah, I know. I guess I was driving without thinking."

But he'd chosen this road when I'd really needed him. We'd

met when I saved him, and now, he'd saved me. Maybe it was karma. Maybe the universe was trying to stay in balance—one act in exchange for another. I knew all about that.

"I'm really sorry about your dad, but thank you for rescuing me." Wyatt had saved me, but from what? It felt like I'd been in danger of so much more than just a sprained ankle and the cold.

"Seems only right, given the fact that you rescued me. And Mer"—his brow furrowed in the light from the dash—"I'm truly sorry for not respecting your privacy. I only did it because I was interested in you, and maybe in an 'us.'"

My heart stuttered. All the anger I'd been clinging to was gone. I couldn't find it now even if I tried. He'd made a mistake. He hadn't meant to hurt me. If I held that against him, I would be the biggest kind of hypocrite. "I have a tendency to overreact. Maybe that's why I don't have many friends."

He looked at me, his face all angles and shadows. "Or maybe you give up on people too soon."

"Maybe," I whispered.

A few minutes later, Wyatt pulled into my driveway. Lights blazed in the living room, and I wondered what we'd walk in on—my mom still in pieces, my dad trying to glue those fragments back together with hollow reassurances that Aunt Lila just needed time, that she'd eventually get past this, that I wasn't a complete disappointment to them, that maybe I'd eventually get my act together and become the daughter she'd hoped I could be.

I released a long, slow breath and pulled the blanket up to my chin. I didn't want to go in there yet. I didn't want to leave the dark, quiet warmth of Wyatt's truck.

"You okay?" Wyatt stared at me.

"Yeah." But I was lying to him, and I was suddenly tired of that. So, I tried the truth. "No. I'm not."

"It's going to be okay." His fingers curled around mine, warm and tempting. "You're going to be okay."

"How can you know that?" I stared at our joined hands. "I feel like I'm drowning, like I keep getting hit by wave after wave. Every time, it gets harder to surface, to take the next breath."

His thumb brushed the inside of my wrist, creating a trail of aching nerves. "I know it because I see how strong and amazing you are. And even if you get too tired to keep trying, I won't let you go under."

His words sank through the darkness and buoyed me up, but I knew the truth. They were a temporary life preserver only. I couldn't rely on Ben and Wyatt at the same time. They couldn't coexist in my heart without splitting it at the seams.

I pulled my hand free, refusing to acknowledge the disappointment on Wyatt's face.

In the end, my heart would always return to Ben. He'd been there first, and his hold on me was so much stronger than Wyatt's could ever be.

My mom met us at the door. "What happened?" Her face was pale, her eyes were puffy, and her voice sounded a little raspy. If you didn't know better, you might have thought she had a cold.

Wyatt shifted my weight in his arms, and I clung to his neck. "She fell and hurt her ankle."

Wyatt's words drew my mom's attention. Her bloodshot eyes widened slightly, like she'd only just realized he was there, standing on her doorstep and holding me high in his arms.

"Wyatt . . . how?" Her mouth fell open, her already shell-shocked brain seemingly failing to find the words.

Wyatt's arms tightened. I was probably getting heavy. "You can just put me down on the couch."

"Yup." He looked down at me and relief flooded his features. "Sounds good." He laid me gently on the cushions and stepped back.

Dad and Rachel arrived at the same time, and suddenly my family crowded around, asking questions, assessing my injuries. Dad sprang into action, coming back with a warm washcloth, the first aid kit, and some ice packs. Mom left to call the doctor. Rachel knelt on the floor next to me, asking what she could do to help.

Over their heads, I met Wyatt's gaze. From his perspective, we probably looked like a real family, with everyone worried about me and pitching in to help. The snapshot he was taking probably looked normal, but his lens filtered out all the blemishes and open sores.

"Thank you," I whispered.

"You're welcome." I was the only one to hear his words.

He wandered to the mantel over the fireplace. Family pictures in mismatched frames covered every square inch. He moved down the line, staring at each one. I knew them by heart: Mom and Dad on the beach on their wedding day, looking so young and happy; me and Dad on his surfboard when I was three; me in the hospital chair, holding Rachel on the day she was born; and Mom and Rachel on her first day of school. They kept going—a chronicle of our family, and like all families, it deliberately displayed only part of the story. Because that's what we're taught to do—to only capture the good times, the smiles, and the happiness. We don't take pictures of the tears or the fights, the losses and the loneliness, but why not? Why shouldn't they also be valued and remembered?

Wyatt paused near the end of the mantel and picked up a picture. Of course I'd known he'd stop there. It was an image of Ben and me, taken in my backyard on Rachel's birthday. Mom had taken it without us knowing, but it was perfect. It was before I found out about the baby, when we were still blissfully ignorant. We'd been swinging in the hammock together, the same hammock we'd shared for years. I lay in the crook of Ben's arm, my hair still long, both of us laughing at something. We were tanned and barefoot, and with our fingers linked, we looked ready to conquer the world.

I'd been surprised when Mom had enlarged and framed it. Maybe she'd done it because in that picture, I looked like the perfect happy daughter with her perfect happy boyfriend. In that moment, Ben's light had cast away all the darkness that lived inside of me, and Mom had immortalized it.

The picture probably haunted her now, like it haunted me—a constant reminder of all the things my lies had ruined. Wyatt stared at it a long time, before glancing over at me and setting the frame back on the mantel. I wondered what he saw in that picture. Did I look anything like the girl he knew now?

Dad loosened my shoelaces, and I hissed when he tugged off my sneaker. "Sorry, honey." My sock came off next, and we all stared at the swelling and discoloration. "It looks like a nasty sprain. Maybe a break. You're probably going to need an X-ray."

Wyatt leaned in for a closer look. He winced. "Looks painful."

Dad gently laid an ice pack over it, patted my knee, and stood up to face Wyatt. "I'm Steve Hall, Mer's dad."

Wyatt quickly extended his hand. "Wyatt Quinn, sir. It's nice to meet you." Dad towered over him, but Wyatt seemed confident. Apparently, even my dad's abundance of facial hair didn't intimidate him.

"I understand that you found Mer and brought her home."

"Yes, sir."

Dad slapped Wyatt on the shoulder, and Wyatt managed to only sway a little. "Then I'm very grateful. It's been a rough day for the Hall family. Thanks for getting her home safely."

"No thanks necessary. I'm just glad I was there to help." He looked past Dad to me. Under the bright ceiling light, his hair looked more gold than bronze, brushing the tops of his ears and hanging low over his forehead. His hazel eyes glowed with expectations and promises I wasn't ready for, but I was also tired of the effort it took to keep pushing him away. "I should probably be heading home. It looks like you're in good hands."

I nodded and motioned him closer. He dropped down on one knee, and I pulled off his jacket. "Thank you again. Sorry I'm returning it with empty pockets."

"You're forgiven," he teased, shrugging into it, "but I'm thinking you should try a less dangerous hobby."

"Like motocross."

"Exactly. I could teach you."

The tempting image filled my head, but I lowered my gaze. "Can you let your mom know I probably won't be at work for a few days?"

Wyatt laid his hand on my arm. His fingers slid down my bare skin, slowly turning my hand so my palm was up with all the scratches visible. The warm gentleness of his touch was almost enough to block out the throbbing in my bruised and battered body.

"Don't worry about anything but feeling better," he said, his voice lower and gruffer than usual. "All the other stuff, whatever it is, it can wait. Just take a break for a couple of days."

I bit my lip. He made it sound so easy. "I don't know if I can."

"Then call me. Anytime, day or night."

I laughed and looked down at my scraped knees. "You might regret saying that."

His fingers traced a line around the edge of my palm, carefully avoiding the abrasions in the middle. My breath caught.

"That's the thing, Mer. I don't think I will."

Chapter Sixteen

After Wyatt left, the doctor visited. He confirmed it was likely a sprain but recommended X-rays in the morning. He also gave me painkillers. Dad suggested I spend the night on the couch rather than tackle our narrow stairs. So Mom brought down every pillow and blanket from my bed, and Dad helped tuck them around me, propping my ankle up on a giant mound.

The pills, along with every other horrible part of this day, made me feel exhausted in a deep, sinking way—too tired to think anymore, too buzzed up on pain meds to feel.

Rachel kissed me good night, and Dad made his final check.

Then, I was alone in the room, with one small lamp glowing in the corner. Outside, the wind buffeted the windows, and I pulled the quilt up higher. My eyes closed and my breathing slowed.

Maybe I slept for a few minutes. Maybe longer. My eyes fluttered open.

Someone sat next to me.

The lamp silhouetted Mom's profile as she sat with her head bowed.

I licked my dry lips. "It's okay if you hate me," I said softly. Her face fell into her palms, her head shaking back and forth. "If I were you, I'd hate me, too. I ruined things with Aunt Lila. She can't even look at me."

Mom lifted her head and tears glistened in her eyes. She looked bone-tired, like me, too. "I don't know what I feel."

Her words hung there in the dark.

A voice inside me screamed, *You're my mother. You're supposed to have all the answers.* But that wasn't fair. I was almost a mother. That biological accident wouldn't have given me any answers.

She reached out and straightened my quilt, clenching the edge of it in her fist. "Before I had you, I was so scared I'd mess things up, that I wouldn't be a good mother—" Her voice choked up, and she wiped at her eyes. After a few seconds of silence, she cleared her throat. "But I was a teacher. I understood children and how to nurture them. So I figured I just had to do the same with you—set ground rules, be consistent, give praise and punishment fairly, and encourage you to grow and learn and be independent. I never once worried about the *love* part or even the *like* part. Of course we would love each other. Of course we would like each other. Of course I would be proud of whomever you chose to be."

The hollowness in her voice reached inside my chest and clawed at my heart. I didn't know that her opinion still mattered so much, that it still held the power to hurt me.

"I've watched you struggle your whole life—struggle to fit in, struggle to make friends, struggle to feel comfortable in your own skin. I wanted to step in and fix everything. I wanted to shake you and make you understand that you were creating your own struggles. If you only believed in yourself, you'd be happy. If you only decided to let people in, you'd have as many friends as you wanted. But it never worked that way. Even worse, as much as you struggled with everyone else, you also struggled with me. Everything between you and your dad is so easy, but before I talk to you, I go over every conversation a million times in my mind. I evaluate different approaches, come up with contingencies, and you still surprise me. Every time, you leave me feeling unprepared and unequipped. I feel like I fail far more times than I ever succeed."

Even the painkillers couldn't numb this ache in my chest, in my head, in my limbs. Maybe I'd always known it. I'd forced the same words on her earlier today on the edge of the ferry, overlooking the ocean that had once felt like home. So why did her acknowledgment of this truth still hurt so much?

"Stop." My throat protested. My whole body protested. "Please."

I needed her to leave me alone, but she stayed, her jaw working back and forth, like she had more to say, more words to break me even further.

"That's the thing. I can't. Because the one thing that has never changed is the love." She grasped my hand, squeezing so hard that I winced. "I need you to understand. Aunt Lila hurt me today, but I also realized something. I can live without her friendship. There's a space in my heart that belongs only to her, and right now, that spot is empty, but I can survive like this. I can learn to fill that emptiness with other things, but I cannot live without you. You're my daughter. Maybe we'll never be as close as you and your dad. Maybe we'll never really understand each other or be best friends. But you are not a spot inside my heart. You are a piece of me, and as much as I love Aunt Lila, I will choose that part of me over her every time. Do you understand that?"

I slowly nodded, and her grip on my fingers eased.

Maybe I should have said something, but as she'd pointed out, I'd only say the wrong thing. So we stayed like that, in the silence and the dark. Her words helped with some of the pain. Not all, but some.

Finally, she released my hand and kissed me on the forehead. "I love you, Mer. Never doubt that."

She started to leave, but I couldn't let her. I had to know the answer to the one question I'd been most afraid to ask. "Mom . . ."

"Yes."

I swallowed and stared over at the mantel. Somewhere in the shadows, a photo held a perfect image of me and Ben. "Was it wrong of me, to do what I did?"

She frowned and tugged a hand through her hair. "Aww, Mer, I wish I had an answer for you, but I don't. There's no instruction manual for finding out that your sixteen-year-old daughter is pregnant. All I could think about was how much I'd failed you. There were conversations we should have had. If we'd been closer, maybe you'd have confided in me about your plans with Ben. Maybe you wouldn't have gotten pregnant."

I thought back to that day in the kitchen when I first told her. All I'd seen was her disapproval and disappointment, but was it possible that they hadn't all been directed at me?

"In the end, it's not my opinion that counts. I see your choice weighing you down, sucking the joy out of your life. So many times, I've been tempted to tell you, 'Of course you made the right decision,' that you did nothing wrong. But I can't because I don't know. You were sixteen, still a kid, but those were grown-up decisions you made. And that's the thing about most grown-up decisions: They aren't black and white. They're complicated, and there are always consequences. In the end, you have to come to terms with your choice. You made it, and no amount of regret will change it. You have to find a way to live with it because if you don't, you'll never have a life at all."

This time when she stood up to leave, I didn't stop her. But her words remained.

Could I ever come to terms with the consequences of what I'd done?

I sat on the couch with a quilt wrapped around me, pretending to watch a movie on television. In reality, my mind battled with my jumbled stream of thoughts. They popped in and out, changing, shifting, never staying long enough for me to fully acknowledge or really understand. I'd tried to turn them off. The doctor told me to rest. I'd tried to sleep, but in the quiet, the thoughts only screamed at me louder. I sipped on a drink and ate popcorn because I needed something to keep me busy, even in the smallest ways.

Mom and Dad hovered periodically, still looking a little shell-shocked. They'd looked that way since Mom shared the news with Dad: Hey, our sixteen-year-old daughter went and did something really stupid, like getting herself pregnant. They'd shipped Rachel off to a friend's house for a few days so she wouldn't overhear any of the many conversations we'd had since my confession.

A knock sounded at the front door, but I ignored it. Someone knocked again, louder, and Dad appeared, wearing his now-familiar triple-D expression: a mix of disbelief, disappointment, and determination. It had taken me awhile to figure the last one out, but now I got it. He was determined to get us through this because he believed if we just made it through this hurdle, everything could return to the way it was.

He swung open the door and stiffened. "Ben."

No. I sat upright. I wasn't ready to see him yet. I needed more time.

"I came to see Mer. I tried calling, but she didn't answer. Is she here?"

Dad stepped aside, and suddenly Ben was standing right next to me. "What happened? Are you sick? Is something wrong with the baby?"

My mouth opened and closed, but no words came out. I looked for Dad, but he was still at the door because Aunt Lila and Uncle Al were also filing in. Shock entered my lungs and pushed out all the air.

Aunt Lila said something about us all needing to talk and make plans, since it affected everyone. My worst nightmare was coming to life. Actually, it was beyond my worst nightmare, because none of the possible scenarios I'd imagined included Ben's parents.

Ben moved, blocking my view of them. "Mer, are you okay? You're really pale." He sat and wrapped an arm around my shoulders, pulling me closer.

Somewhere in the distance, I heard my dad calling my mom, telling her that she needed to come now.

Ben kissed my forehead and spoke low in my ear: "I know my parents being here is a surprise, but I wanted you to hear directly from them so you'd believe me. They fully support us. I know you have doubts, but if you hear them out, you'll see that this can work."

I shook my head, but Ben didn't notice. He handed me a small gift bag. "I also got this for you. I know it's probably stupid and the wrong thing, but I wanted you to see that I'm committed. I'm not going to bail at the last minute and leave you alone."

He laid the bag on my lap, but I couldn't touch it. I recognized the logo on it—a store that sold baby things.

"Come on, Mer, open it up." He grinned, and it literally felt like I was dying. Finally, he huffed, still smiling. "Fine. I'll do it." He pulled at the tissue paper and something soft fell in my lap. He picked it up and shook it. It made the softest rattling sound. "The lady at the store said it was safe even for newborns, and I thought the giraffe was kind of cute."

He finally stopped talking, and I tried to move, but my limbs wouldn't cooperate.

"Don't you like it? What's wrong? Talk to me."

My hands shook. I looked up to find my mom standing over us. Her expression was grim, but her tone was calm and clear. "You need to tell him now. Right now."

Ben's gaze slipped back and forth between us. His body tensed. I watched fear and uncertainty work their way into his expression. "Tell me what?"

I lowered my head, staring down at the giraffe that had some-how ended up in my hands. My thumb moved over its soft velvet ear. "*There is no baby anymore.*"

"*What?*" *Ben leaned closer.*

I cleared my throat and looked up at him. "*There is no baby anymore.*"

His mother gasped, but Ben's mouth just snapped shut. I saw him figuring it out, working out what I'd done. "*Tell me you didn't.*"

I looked back at the giraffe.

"*Mer.*" *His fingers dug into my arm.* "*Look at me.*"

I owed him that much. So I did.

"*Why? You promised. You looked me in the eye, and you promised. We don't break promises to each other.*"

He was right. We never had before, but this was different. I just had to make him understand. "*I had to.*"

"*Why?*"

I pushed the blanket aside and stood. I couldn't look at Aunt Lila or Uncle Al. I could only focus on Ben. "*Because I thought about the life you said we could have. I tried to picture it.*" *I struggled to keep my voice calm, but it kept rising.* "*I thought about it over and over again, and there was not a single scenario where I ended up happy.*"

"*Maybe it wasn't all about you.*" *Ben stared up at me, bitterness creeping into his tone.*

"*You think I don't know that? That's why I had to act now because if I gave you time to keep talking, you'd convince me. You'd paint this rosy picture of the future. You'd look at it with all your naïve optimism, and you'd make me feel guilty. I'd end up doing it, but only for you, and then reality would happen. I'd become a teenage mom with a teenage husband, living in a house with your parents and a crying baby, and I'd start to resent you. I'd resent the baby, and eventually I'd hate you for forcing that life on me."*

"You don't know that."

I whirled around to confront everyone in the room—all the judging faces. "Yes, I do. Don't you see? I know exactly how I'd feel. You're the ones who refuse to see the truth."

Aunt Lila wrapped her hand around the strap of her purse, her eyes wide. "I can't believe you did this. It was selfish. Maybe I should have known. Your mother tried her hardest, but sometimes even a great mother can't turn out a great kid."

I flinched like she'd slapped me.

Mom inhaled. "Lila, don't. She made her decision."

"And you knew about this?" Aunt Lila swung around to face her.

Mom nodded. "We went with her."

Such a simple statement to sum up the hours we'd spent driving to the clinic, walking past the small group of protesters with their signs, waiting, filling out paperwork, blood work, and more tests, counseling, answering the questions of "Are you sure?" then lying on that narrow bed with my legs spread and Mom holding my hand, and finally, the long, silent drive back home.

Aunt Lila lifted her chin. "Did you know that Ben wanted her to keep the baby? That we'd worked out a plan for them? That he'd asked her to wait to decide? She promised him."

Dad stepped closer to Mom as we all suddenly realized that there was a new, unexpected consequence of my actions, something else I'd potentially ruined. "I knew, but it was Meredith's choice. I had to support that." She had to support me because I'd forced her into this corner. I'd been stupid, and now my mom was paying the price.

Aunt Lila's face reddened. She opened her mouth to speak, but Ben stood and cut her off.

"It doesn't matter anymore, Mom. It's done." He looked at me, his expression harder and colder than I'd ever seen it. "There's nothing we can do."

Uncle Al hadn't said a word the entire time. That wasn't surprising because he was a man of few words, but now he nodded at Ben. "I think we should go, Son."

"Yeah, I think we should." Ben's dark eyes raked over me one more time before he turned his back.

He made it halfway across the living room, following his parents toward the door before my voice returned. "Ben! Wait!"

Like a red light at an intersection, my words stopped the entire procession. They all turned in unison, but it was only Ben I cared about. I walked to him. My hands curled around the soft fabric of his shirt. "This doesn't change anything. I love you. Now things can go back to the way they were."

Ben's brow wrinkled, and he shook his head like I'd just tried to convince him the ocean was really the sky. "How can you possibly *believe that? This changes everything. You went behind my back and broke your promise, just to make things easier for you. You didn't care if your decision hurt me."*

I swallowed, fear numbing my cheeks. "You make it sound like you're the victim, and I was just being selfish. You think this was easy for me?"

"I know it wasn't, but you're acting like this decision had nothing to do with me. You say you love me, but do you even know what that means? When you love someone, you trust them. You don't go behind their backs. God, Mer."

Over Ben's shoulder, I saw Dad take a step forward, ready to intervene, but Ben and I weren't done yet. I still clung to his shirt, unable to let go or back down. Anger and pain churned inside me, my wounds too fresh to filter my harsh words. "Like your love is any better? I do one thing you don't approve of and now you're walking away. That's reassuring. You say that if I'd had this baby, you would have been there, but you'd probably have left the first time I messed up."

Ben stiffened. "Well, I guess we're finally being honest with each other. Maybe our love was never real. We were both stupid to believe it was something that could last."

"No…" My anger fled as quickly as it had arrived. He couldn't be right. We couldn't be over. Tears blurred my vision, the ones I'd stubbornly refused to cry even when I'd felt an emptiness after the abortion that I'd never expected to feel.

Ben pried my hands from his shirt. "I can't stay here."

No! My lungs constricted and my head throbbed.

He must have left with his parents, but I couldn't see because I'd slipped to my knees trying to find my heart. It was somewhere on the floor—pulled out of my chest, for everyone to see and stomp over. But instead of my heart, I found the giraffe, abandoned and alone. I picked it up and pressed it against my aching chest.

Dad's arms came round me. His hand brushed across my forehead. "Mer, sweetheart, it's going to be okay."

But he didn't understand. I'd just lost Ben, my best friend, the boy who'd promised to always like me best. Nothing would ever be okay again.

Chapter Seventeen

On Saturday, an X-ray confirmed that my ankle was only sprained and not broken. The clinic sent me home with an elastic bandage, crutches, and instructions to keep my foot elevated as much as possible. By Monday, I was bored stupid. Mom and Rachel were at school, and Dad was working, walking up from the shop every couple of hours to check on me, fix me snacks, and refill my water bottle.

"Is it still painful?" he asked around two o'clock, setting a glass of milk in front of me, along with a plate of Oreos. I felt like I was back in elementary school.

"Only when I try hobbling around. It's not too bad when it's elevated."

He sat in the puffy chair opposite the sofa. "Next time you

run, promise you'll take your cell phone."

"Trust me." I twisted an Oreo apart and licked off the frosting. "I've learned my lesson. Sitting on the side of the road in the dark will do it for you."

Dad nodded, his beard hiding most of his expression, but I could still read the concern in his eyes. "I'm sorry about what happened with Lila on Friday."

I stared down at my half-eaten cookie.

"She's wrong to blame you. It wasn't your fault. Your mom and I supported your decision. Maybe Ben would have been willing to accept it, too, if she hadn't held on to her anger. You may have been young, but it was your lives. It was your choice, not ours and not hers."

"It was a huge decision, and it affected both of us, but I chose to break my promise to Ben and go behind his back. What kind of person does that?"

Dad leaned forward on his elbows. "A sixteen-year-old girl who was suddenly faced with an impossible situation, a girl who was scared, but had the strength to make the choice she believed in. Don't do this to yourself anymore. Please."

"But I don't know how to stop," I whispered, swallowing back the lump in my throat. He was just trying to help, but I couldn't take any more of these deep conversations.

He stared at me. "I keep telling your mom that you just need some space to breathe. That you'll figure it all out, but I'm scared for you. I feel like you're slipping away, and I don't know what to do. We might not be a perfect family, but we are your family. You can trust us."

"I do trust you."

"Really? So why didn't you tell me about the sponsorship letter?"

My chin snapped up. "How do you know? Were you digging through my stuff?"

"Do you really think that?" He shook his head and his shoulders slumped. "Actually, don't answer, because I don't want to know." He laced his fingers together, looking lost and uncertain. The expression didn't fit on a man so big and gruff-looking. "You're a minor. When you didn't respond to their letter, they reached out to me. I got the email a few days ago."

I pulled my good leg up to my chest, feeling trapped. This was a conversation I never planned to have. I wanted to get up and walk away, but instead I stared down at the quilt.

"You can't ignore this, Mer. Why didn't you say anything? This is what you wanted. Your ankle will be healed in no time. You can start practicing. There's still time."

"Dad, stop! Please." I rubbed the heel of my hand across my forehead, but the throbbing in my head remained. "I didn't tell you because I'm turning it down. I can't do it, because I'm not windsurfing anymore."

"Mer, honey, I'm trying to understand. Maybe it feels like the ocean is the source of all your problems, but it's not. You belong out there. It made you happy, and it could make you happy again, if you just tried."

"You sound just like—" My mouth snapped shut.

"Like who?"

Like Ben. I sucked in a breath. "Like the therapist you guys made me see."

"Maybe we stopped your sessions too soon."

"No." I met his worried gaze. "Why does everybody think I need to be fixed? What's wrong with the way I am? People give up sports all the time. They pick up new hobbies. Why does my giving up windsurfing have to be this big tragedy?"

"Because it made you happy, and I haven't seen you happy since Ben—"

"I'll find something else that makes me happy," I said, cutting him off, because I couldn't talk to him about Ben. Dad could never know what was really happening between us. "Just give me some time. Please."

Dad stared at me for a long time. Finally, he stood, holding up both hands in surrender. "Sure, honey. Sure." He stepped closer and squeezed my shoulder. "I've got to get back to the shop, but you can talk to me about anything. I love you, and I'm not giving up on you."

"I'm fine, Dad." I covered his hand with mine, and he winced. My hands were constantly cold because of this stupid weather.

"Everything's okay."

But deep down, my reassurances felt hollow, because in addition to my lingering fear of the ocean, I'd finally accepted the truth about Wyatt and Ben: I was officially torn between two guys.

For years, Ben was one of the few people I felt truly comfortable with. I let my guard down with him and became this better, happier version of myself. With him, I felt safe and protected, and I never imagined feeling even a fraction of that with someone else.

But on Friday night, it was Wyatt who'd come to my rescue, and it wasn't just about finding me and driving me home. It was also what he said and how he made me feel, like I could count on him to be there. He'd proved I could trust him. I couldn't lower all my walls yet, not when there were secrets I still couldn't share. But Wyatt seemed to like me anyway, even if I was gruffer and pricklier with him than I'd ever been with Ben. I could be direct and honest and abrasive with him, and he seemed to . . . appreciate it.

I stared at the scabs on my palm and remembered the feel of his thumb brushing across my skin. If I liked Wyatt as just a friend, why did my palm ache from thinking about his touch, and why did guilt weigh on me?

Yup. When it came to Ben and Wyatt, there was nothing fine or okay about this situation. How could I keep them both in my life without hurting someone?

A knock on the door woke me. I must have dozed off after Dad left.

I rubbed at my eyes and sat up, glancing at my watch. Three thirty. Mom and Rachel? But why would they knock? The noise continued, and I shifted on the cushion and glanced over at my crutches. I could ignore the knocking or spend ten minutes trying to shuffle over there or . . .

"Who is it?" I shouted.

"Mer? It's me," a muffled male voice called out through the door.

Wyatt? I smoothed back my hair and wiped the back of my hand over my mouth, checking for drool. What was he doing here, and why was I suddenly grinning?

"Come in!"

The door creaked open and Wyatt appeared at the entrance, wearing his normal uniform of jeans and a T-shirt. His cheeks were a little red, and his hair was mussed from the gust of wind that followed him inside. The large paper bag in his arms looked full, and he toed off his sneakers like he intended to stay awhile.

As he dropped the bag on the coffee table, his gaze drifted over me, from the top of my head down to my bare toes sticking out from one end of the bandage wrapped around my ankle. "Good. You look better."

I snorted and looked down at my plaid pajama pants and

T-shirt. The pants were old and worn, but loose enough that it didn't hurt to pull them over my ankle or scraped knees. "I don't know about that."

Wyatt winked at me and carefully sat on the empty end of the sofa, avoiding my propped-up foot. "Well, I do, and while that probably constituted an infraction of rule number one, flirting to improve the spirits of an injured friend seems like a justifiable excuse."

I forced my face into a frown. "You're pushing your luck." But Wyatt could probably see the smile I worked to hide.

"Since the flirting apparently did not work, I've brought other surprises designed to relieve boredom and lighten the spirits."

"Really?" I leaned forward, trying to peek in the bag. "How did you know that I was literally dying of boredom?"

"Two months in the hospital, baby. Plus, a very long stint at home after the release. In the beginning, people visit. They bring you shit and try to include you in stuff, but then their lives move on without you. The visits get less and less. You can't blame them, but it still sucks."

He stopped talking, and I fumbled for the right words. "Was that part of your attempt to cheer me up or to relieve the boredom?" His eyes widened. "Because if that's how shitty your pep talks are, I'm really hoping you have something better in that bag."

His mouth fell open and he snorted. He laughed from deep

in his belly, collapsing back on the sofa. "Oh my God, you're hilarious." He wiped his eyes with the heels of his hands. "This is why I like you."

"Well, I'm happy for you. I really am, but seriously, I have the patience of a two-year-old." I nudged him with my good foot. "I need to know what you brought for me."

"Okay, okay. First, the entire *Lethal Weapon* series." He pulled out a stack of DVDs. "They blow up a lot of stuff, so you're going to love them."

"Oh, give me, give me." I reached for them, squirreling them away on my end of the sofa. "What else?"

He glared at me. "Jeez. Take a tater and wait already."

"Seriously, where do you and your mom get these expressions from? What does that even mean?"

Wyatt cocked an eyebrow. "It means 'be patient.'" He pulled out a CD. "This is to broaden your musical education when it comes to country music."

I groaned and stared at the front of the case. "*The Essential Johnny Cash?* Really?"

"Hey, Johnny Cash is the original angry, rebellious artist who bucked the establishment every chance he got. The only one who could really tame him was June, the love of his life. He was actually known as the Man in Black." He pointed to my black T-shirt. "How can you not relate to him?" I must have still looked skeptical because he reached back inside the bag. "I knew you'd be stubborn about this, so I brought a bribe. If you promise to at least give him a try, you get this." He lifted out a Yellow Rose Café pastry box from the bag.

"Yes!" I grabbed for it, but he held it over his head.

"First you have to promise."

"That's not fair." I huffed. "Does your mom know you're using her baked goods to blackmail me?"

"Maybe or maybe not."

I looked at the CD again. "Fine. I promise to try it."

"Good." He handed the box over, and I lifted the top. *Oh, snap!* A mix of Harley's sweet treats, including all my favorites. I pulled out a cookie and took a bite. *Hmmm* . . . heavenly.

"And because I wanted to make sure you forgave me for blackmailing you, I also got these." He tossed bags of Skittles at me, and I laughed, trying to catch each one without dropping my cookie. When he stopped, my lap was full.

"Wow. You certainly know your way to a girl's heart."

Wait. Why did I say that? I ducked my head and pretended to read the back of the CD, my pulse suddenly sprinting. I'd spent the last couple of weeks criticizing Wyatt for being too flirty, and now I was doing the same thing. Maybe he hadn't noticed.

But he had, because when I looked up, his gaze burned into me. He tilted his head to one side, the corners of his mouth twitching up. "Do I?"

Staring into those hazel eyes, I realized how easy it was to be tempted, to forget for a minute about the guy who waited for me on the beach every evening. "Rule number one," I choked out.

"No way, darlin'. Not this time, 'cause *you* started it."

I blinked and tore my gaze away. "And I'm choosing to stop it." God, I needed to find a way to keep things just friendly with Wyatt. It was the only way this could work. It was the only way I could have them both. "What else is in the bag?"

For a moment, Wyatt said nothing, just nodding his head slowly, like he saw and understood way too much. Finally, he reached inside and pulled out a knitting needle. "The last thing."

"Umm, okay." I frowned. "Well, first off, I don't knit. Second, I have no intention of learning to knit, and third, if I ever did knit, which I won't, I'm pretty sure you need a pair of those, not one."

"It's not for knitting."

I took it and slid two fingers down its length. "Let me guess— it's for taking care of intruders at night." I jabbed the pointy end in the air.

"That's a scary image, but no." He took the knitting needle from me. "I wasn't sure if you'd end up in a cast, and I know from experience that itchiness is a killer. This can be a lifesaver."

"Ah." I held out my hand, and he gave it back. My fingers curled around the smooth, thin surface. "Well, I didn't end up in a cast, but I have become surprisingly attached to this gift. So, I will definitely find another use for it."

He chuckled, the sound low and warm. He slouched back against the sofa, turning to face me. "Now that's an interesting thought."

Damn, he was not making this easy. Blowing out a quick breath, I found the first *Lethal Weapon* movie and held it up. "Would you do the honors?"

"Absolutely." He stood and scooped up the case on his way past. Our fingers brushed, and he shook his head. "Jeez, your hands are always as freaking cold as ice. I think you need to invest in some gloves."

I tucked my hands between my legs. "You know what they say about cold hands and warm hearts."

Wyatt squatted in front of the DVD player and glanced back at me. "No, I don't. What do 'they' say?"

I paused. "Actually, I don't know what they say, but I know it's a thing."

Wyatt laughed again, and warmth curled in my belly. "I believe you, Hall. Most wouldn't, but I do."

He popped in the DVD, and for the next two hours, we watched Mel Gibson and Danny Glover get shot at and blow things up. The late afternoon sun cast shadows across the wooden floor, and I was surprised by how easy it was to hang out with Wyatt. He didn't mind when I yelled at the screen or cracked stupid jokes. He actually laughed at them, and I liked making him laugh.

When the credits rolled up, Wyatt looked at me. "Another one?"

"Sure." I handed him the second movie. "I can't believe I haven't seen these before."

"My dad made me watch them a few years ago. He loves movies. Even built this amazing home theater in our house. Well, I guess it's his house now . . ." His voice trailed off, and I stared at him, remembering why he'd been driving when he found me.

I scraped my teeth across my lip, unsure of whether to ask and knowing I would anyway. "On Friday night, you seemed to be going through your own stuff, and instead it became all about my stuff."

He nodded at the bandage around my ankle. "I think that's understandable."

"Still . . ." I shrugged and tried to ignore the sudden heat in my cheeks. "If you wanted to talk about it, you could."

"What can I say?" Wyatt's expression turned raw, his naked pain hard to look at. "It's not easy knowing your father prefers spending time with his new girlfriend than with his kid."

I remembered my own conversation with my mom. "Have you tried . . . talking to him?"

"Gee, no. The thought never crossed my mind."

I flinched, but Wyatt was already sighing.

"I'm sorry. You didn't deserve that. It's just a touchy subject."

I nodded slowly. "Were you close?"

"Yeah." His head sagged back on the cushion. "That's the

thing. If he'd never given me the time of day, maybe this would be easier, but we used to be tight. I told him everything, and then the crash happened, and he just bailed on me."

"I'm really sorry. That's got to suck." At least my mom and I had never been close. "Is there anything I can do?"

He looked over at me. "Just hanging out here helps."

"Really?" I picked at a loose thread on my quilt. "Most people find my presence annoying."

"I can't believe that."

"Ha. Only because you don't know me well enough yet."

Wyatt's gaze drifted to the mantel. "Can I ask you something?"

I followed his stare, uncertainty pulsing in my veins. I knew where this was headed, but I nodded anyway.

"The guy in the picture? He's the one, right? The one you were meeting on the beach that night? The reason we can only be friends?"

I curled my hands into fists and squeezed until my nails dug into my scraped palms. "Yeah."

"You look really happy in that picture. Do you love him?"

"Yes." The answer came easily, without hesitation, and Wyatt's mouth tightened.

"But I never see you with him. You sprained your ankle and he's not here. Kids at school say you're single. So, what gives, Mer?"

I pulled my good leg up to my chest and hugged my knee.

"When that picture was taken, things were simpler, but I messed up. Now, we don't get to have what we once had."

Wyatt stared at me for a long time. "No one knows you've been meeting him on the beach, right? It's a secret."

Shit. What was I thinking? I'd given away too much. I'd given Wyatt the power to ruin everything. How could I be that stupid? I squeezed my eyes shut, trying to control the small wave of panic growing inside.

Wyatt touched my leg, and my eyes flew open. "Don't worry. You can trust me. I won't say anything because it's not my secret to tell."

I tried to relax, rubbing my hands against the blanket, wanting to believe him. "Thank you."

"Yeah, no problem."

I bit my lip. "Can you do me a favor?"

"Sure. If I can."

"He doesn't know about this." I pointed to my ankle. "And I don't want him worrying about me. If I write a note, can you take it to the beach and leave it for him?" I hadn't seen Ben since I was grounded. He had to be worried sick, and I missed him so much.

"I want to help, but a note? This isn't the Middle Ages, Mer. Just text him."

"I know it doesn't make sense, but I can't."

Wyatt's eyes widened and one eyebrow shot up. "But he'd get a note left on the beach?"

"He will, if you leave it at the exact spot where you first found me. Just put a rock on top so it won't blow away."

He shook his head and rolled his eyes. "Sure, Mer. I'll be your cloak-and-dagger accomplice. Write your note, and I'll deliver it."

So while he loaded the next movie and made some microwave popcorn, I wrote a note to Ben, explaining why I couldn't see him for the next few days. I just hoped Wyatt would stick to his promise, and Ben would understand when he read it. And hopefully, Ben would never ask who'd delivered the note for me.

If he did, how could I possibly explain why I'd trusted Wyatt enough to share our secret with him?

Chapter Eighteen

By the next day, my ankle still hadn't healed, but I'd rested it for three days and my parents wanted me back in school. Wyatt helped, carrying my books between classes. He confirmed that he'd left the note for Ben. I'd stuck it in a baggie, and he'd tucked the corner under a rock to keep it from blowing away. I just hoped that Ben found it.

On Friday, at the end of class, Wyatt offered to drive me to the café to visit his mom. I wasn't healed enough to work a shift, but I still jumped at the chance. The last thing I wanted was another evening at home, trapped by my own clumsiness. Wyatt carried my backpack to his truck, and I stopped at the passenger door. He took my crutches and dropped them in the back. Working in sync, I balanced myself on one foot, with a hand on his shoulder, while he opened my door.

He was in my personal space and I was in his, but somehow I was no longer protesting about the rules. I'd grown comfortable around him—the way he waited at my locker each morning with a muffin from his mom; the way his slow grin spread when he took my backpack at the end of each class; the way he matched his stride to mine, using his body to shield me from the jostling in the hall, and laughing when I grumbled at my crutches or cursed at my clumsiness. I saw the looks he gave me, the way he leaned into me when we talked, the excuses he found to casually brush my arm or the small of my back. I could see the ticking bomb waiting to explode. Slowly and steadily, it was counting down to the point when I was going to hurt someone, but I chose to ignore it.

Mom would call my behavior "self-destructive."

Ben wouldn't understand, but I liked having Wyatt around. His smiles and touches made me feel less brittle inside. Despite my stupid ankle, I felt a part of me waking up, coming alive.

Now, Wyatt's hands wrapped around my waist like they belonged there. My shirt wasn't tucked in, and his fingers landed on the bare skin of my back, his thumbs hot against my belly. His biceps flexed, and before I realized what he intended, he lifted me into the truck like I weighed nothing.

I gasped and grabbed for his shoulders, my butt landing on the seat.

His hands lingered, his fingers brushing across every nerve ending. My hands dug into the solidity of his shoulder muscles and the softness of his shirt, holding him there. I tried to inhale, but my lungs wouldn't obey.

He leaned closer, his face level with mine. "Mer?" His eyes glittered with unspoken questions.

The timer on the damn bomb ticked down faster and faster. I leaned in, when I should have pulled back. His touch made me dizzy. His closeness confused me, but I couldn't let go. My breath hitched and mingled with his. I stared at his lips, wondering how they'd feel against mine, needing to know—

A horn blared. *Kaboom!*

I sprang back and dropped my hands. My heart slammed inside my chest like a frenzied, cornered animal. I glanced out the front windshield. An impatient driver was honking at a car that was waiting for a student to get in.

My gaze flashed to Wyatt. His nostrils flared, and his hands slipped from my waist. He stepped back and slammed the door, but not before I saw the confusion and hurt in his eyes, and something else . . . It looked like determination.

The ride to the café felt like an eternity, which made no sense because we didn't see a single other car on the road, like the entire population of Ocracoke had been abducted. Wyatt's foot pressed steadily on the accelerator, as heavy as the silence in the truck. I held on to the seat belt, trying to avoid the truth, but it was impossible to ignore. If that car hadn't honked, I'd have kissed Wyatt. And it wouldn't have been his fault, because I'd have been a willing participant.

What kind of a person did that make me—*disloyal, selfish?* Ben had forgiven me for breaking my promise. By some miracle, he was back in my life. And I'd almost thrown that away on a boy I'd met a few weeks ago? Why? Was I just flattered by his attention, or was it more?

I stared down at my lap. Yeah, maybe Mom was right about the self-destructive behavior.

The second we stopped in front of the café, I yanked on the handle, pushed open the door, and swung down on my good foot. Wyatt said nothing as he came around and retrieved my crutches. I took them, not meeting his stare. I wasn't sure what I'd see there, but whatever it was, I needed to stop playing with fire. I couldn't let Wyatt distract me from the love I felt for Ben.

I slipped my crutches under my arms and hopped forward. Wyatt walked ahead and opened the door. Our eyes met as I passed him. His expression challenged me, daring me to deny what had happened earlier. Too scared to admit the truth, I focused on the ground, on maneuvering into the café without tripping over anything. I reached the counter, expecting to see Harley, but another employee was tending the cash register.

Wyatt caught up. "Mom must be in the house."

So I followed him out back, but halfway through their living room, he stopped. It was so abrupt, I almost crashed into him. Then I heard it, too: His mom was shouting on the phone.

"You agreed, Jimmy. You agreed to stay away from him. You can't just change your mind now."

There was a pause, and then came Harley's voice again, flustered and desperate: "I know it was my idea, but I can't go through that again. Dammit, Jimmy, he almost died. When you're in his life, Wyatt does dangerous things. You're reckless, and it rubs off on him. Look, maybe he is hurting right now. I know he misses you, but at least he's alive, and he'll get over this. Just promise me you'll stick to the agreement. You get your speedy divorce so you can get married, and we get to keep Wyatt safe."

There was a muttered goodbye.

Shit. Wyatt stood rock still. I hopped forward and glanced at him. His jaw was clenched. A muscle ticked under his right eye. He was pissed and I didn't blame him. He'd just found out his mother had been lying to him this whole time.

I tried to find some words—something to make it better, but there was nothing. Sometimes life sucked. The people you trusted let you down.

I debated leaving. I'd even started to swing around on my crutches, but then Harley walked out of the kitchen. She saw Wyatt and stopped short. Her face reddened, and she pressed her hand against her chest, her eyes wide. "Wyatt. How long—"

"Long enough, Mom." He rocked forward on his toes, his voice strangled with pain. "Long enough to know you've been lying this entire time. You've been keeping Dad away from me, using your divorce to blackmail him."

"Wyatt." The color drained from her face. "It's not like that. I'm trying to keep you safe."

"By making me believe Dad doesn't love me anymore," he snapped at her. "By blaming him for a collision I had on my bike when he wasn't even close to the track that day. What kind of warped logic is that?"

She stepped closer. "Just let me explain."

"Don't!" His hands flew up and he stepped back. "Don't come closer. Don't try to explain. I think you've said more than enough for today."

She retreated, one hand twisting around the cloth of her apron. "Wyatt, please." Her voice held a quiet desperation, but Wyatt's stance never softened.

"I can't even look at you right now. You're the one person I always trusted to be honest and on my side." He swung around to me. "I have to get out of here."

Harley's gaze followed Wyatt's, and for the first time, she seemed to realize they weren't alone. "Mer," she choked out.

My mouth opened, but no words emerged.

Wyatt cocked his head. "Are you coming?"

I nodded and followed Wyatt to the door, looking back at Harley once. She stood in the same position, her eyes red, her fingers twisted around her apron. She looked like my mom after Aunt Lila had confronted her in the store, both of them dazed and shattered.

Only I'd done the lying that had destroyed my mom's relationship with Aunt Lila. In Harley's case, she'd done it all on her own.

Back at the truck, Wyatt opened my door and held out a hand for my crutches. He didn't step closer, and he never tried to help me into the seat. He just dropped my crutches in the back and kept walking to the driver's side. I used the doorframe to lever my weight onto the seat.

Wyatt barely looked at me, twisting the key and shoving the truck in reverse. The tires squealed when he threw it into drive and stomped on the gas. I held on to the door to keep from getting tossed around. When we reached the end of the street, he braked for the stop sign, staring straight ahead. No cars came, but he still didn't move.

"Wyatt?"

He smacked the steering wheel with the heel of his hand. "Shit. Shit. Shit." He smacked it over and over.

I closed my eyes, but the pounding continued until I couldn't listen anymore. "Stop! Wyatt, stop!"

I grabbed his arm, and he jumped and stared at me. His pulse bounced in his neck, and tears glistened in his eyes. My fingers ran down his arm to his hand. I brought his palm closer, staring at the red and swollen skin. I shouldn't be here, but I couldn't leave him alone like this. Not now. "You're only hurting yourself."

He tugged his hand free and wrapped his fingers around the steering wheel. "I don't know what else to do with it."

"With what?"

He spun to look at me. "With all this anger burning inside. I feel like it's going to tear me apart at the seams."

"So drive instead."

"Where?"

"Where I tell you."

I rolled down my window and let the afternoon air fill the cab. The wind lifted my hair, buffeting my shirt.

I directed Wyatt to a spot on the beach. It was a spot I'd only shared with Ben before, but I was realizing that almost every spot on this island held some significance for Ben and me. That's what happened when you grew up together on a chain of tiny islands.

Wyatt parked, and we climbed out. My crutches slowed me down, but soon we stood on the sand, staring out at the endless stretch of ocean, watching the waves turn the water white and frothy.

Wyatt folded his arms. "Why did you bring me here?"

"Because if you're going to live on these islands, you have to learn that the ocean is the one thing you can always count on. You can scream at it, hurl the nastiest insults at its feet, and it'll still be there tomorrow. We can't drive it away, no matter how hard we try." It was true. As much as the ocean no longer brought me happiness and as much as I tried to avoid it, every damn fork in my life always led me back here.

Wyatt stared at me, like I was speaking in tongues.

"Go ahead. What are you waiting for? Throw all the rocks and insults at it that you want."

I carefully leaned forward, balanced on one foot. With my crutches for support, I picked up the largest rock I could find. "Dammit, I hate having a stupid sprained ankle," I screamed at the ocean, the wind whipping my angry words away. I should've yelled about the way I kept hurting the same people over and over again, but I couldn't confess that in front of Wyatt. I chucked the rock as far as I could. It disappeared in the rolling surf, and I brushed the sand off my fingers before nodding at Wyatt. "Your turn."

"You think yelling and throwing rocks at the water will take care of my anger."

"Basically, yeah."

"In Texas, we'd line up some bottles on the fence out back and shoot at them."

"Well, this is what we've got." I pointed at the ocean. "So don't knock it until you've tried it."

I pivoted on my crutches and walked back to the dune. After easing myself down on the sand, I leaned back on my hands and lifted my face to the fickle sun.

In front of me, Wyatt cursed and chucked a rock into the ocean. Soon, he was shouting and winding up, throwing his full body into each pitch. His feet came off the ground, his whole body surging forward. I lay back and sifted my fingers through the warm sand, watching the clouds drift across the sky. This was Wyatt's anger, and it wasn't for me to see. I had enough of my own problems to deal with. Finally, he collapsed next to me, leaning back on one elbow.

I squinted up at him. "Feel better?"

"No . . . yeah. I mean, maybe. I guess I no longer feel the overwhelming urge to break something."

"That's progress."

He sat up and stared at the ocean. "I can't believe she did it. She knew how I felt when he didn't come to the hospital. He barely acknowledged it when we left. She knew what that did to me, but she still said nothing."

"She thought she was protecting you."

He glared down at me. "That's no excuse for lying. Are you defending her?"

"No." I tucked my hands behind my head. "But at least your mom lied because she thought she was looking out for you. How shitty would it be if she had done it entirely for herself?" Like the reason I'd lied to Ben—because the abortion was what *I* wanted, and I didn't want him to talk me out of it.

"If you're trying to make me feel better, it's not working."

"What can I say? Life just sucks at times. Those people who think it's all a bag of Skittles are clearly kidding themselves. People lie, people get hurt, *blah, blah, blah*, the world keeps turning."

Wyatt snorted. "Okay, I take it back. I have no idea why, but your pessimistic the-sky-is-falling proclamations on life are actually making me feel better."

He faced the water again, and from my angle, it looked like

the weight of the world had taken up residence on his shoulders.

"Hey." I sat up and touched his arm, his skin warm under my fingertips. "For what it's worth, I'm sorry. You deserved the truth." Just like Ben had.

Wyatt glanced over at me, his hazel eyes catching the late afternoon sun. In their depths, I saw all the colors that had been missing from my world for a very long time now. My fingers still rested on his arm, and despite my vow to stop playing with fire, I couldn't bring myself to break that physical connection.

"Thanks, Mer."

His hand landed on top of mine, capturing my fingers in place. Only they didn't feel trapped; they felt electrified. He turned to fully face me, and I tracked his movements, my breath quickening. His hand moved, freeing me, his fingers now threading through my hair.

His thumb stroked across my jaw, an unspoken question in his eyes. I tried to remember why this was such a bad idea, why I needed to jump up and run from Wyatt as fast and as far as I could, but those thoughts couldn't keep pace with the feelings racing through my body. His hold on me was so light, I could have easily broken free, but I didn't. Instead, my gaze lowered, fastening on his mouth. His head also dipped and the wind gusted. Sand flew up, but Wyatt held me steady.

His lips brushed mine. Once, twice. Back and forth. They trailed across my skin, like my board skimming the water, teasing me, never staying in one place long enough.

My heart thumped. I wanted more.

Turning on my knees, I pulled him closer, forcing those tormenting touches into a real kiss. He groaned against my mouth. One hand slid down my back, and the other cradled my scalp. I arched into him and tasted his colors—red and orange, hot and fiery. The colors paraded past my eyes and exploded inside me. This was no familiar feeling. This was new and intense and amazing.

Clinging to his neck, I climbed into his lap. His hands slid down to my hips, and I ignored the twinge in my ankle. For the first time in weeks, I wasn't cold. God, this felt nothing like Ben.

Ben.

Ben.

I pulled my lips from Wyatt's.

Shit. Shit. Shit.

I lifted my head to the clouds and panted.

"No." My eyes widened, and I pushed at his shoulders. What the hell was I doing? I couldn't look at Wyatt's flushed face or the confusion in his eyes. "No. No. No."

I dragged the back of my hand across my swollen mouth, trying to wipe away the taste of Wyatt, the evidence of my betrayal, but I could still feel him. I scurried off his lap and buried my burning face in my hands.

"Mer?"

I lifted my head, panic churning inside me. "I can't believe we did that. It was wrong. It was so wrong." If the earlier moment in his truck had been a bomb going off, this was nuclear Armageddon. This was me destroying everything, again.

He caught my hands. "No, it wasn't. We kissed because I really like you. It wasn't some spur-of-the-moment thing. What's so wrong about that?"

I pulled my hands free. "It's wrong because I love someone else. It's wrong because I can't cheat on him." I covered my mouth. "Oh God, I think I'm going to be sick."

"Nice." Wyatt jammed a hand through his hair. "Just what I want to hear—that kissing me makes you physically sick."

"That's not fair." I glared. "I told you I had a boyfriend. I told you we couldn't be more than friends."

Wyatt's expression turned heated, his brow furrowing and his jaw clenching. "I know what you told me, but that's not the way you act. Damn, Mer, you're all over the place. How's a guy possibly supposed to know where he stands? And don't act like it was just me kissing you, because you wanted it, too. I never forced myself on you."

He was right. I'd chosen this. "I never said you did."

"But you're acting like it right now. You're acting like this was my fault."

"I'm sorry." My anger fizzled, leaving guilt behind. "I wanted it, too."

Wyatt's expression softened, his gaze searching my face. "It's not a crime, you know, to change your mind. Maybe you thought you loved that other guy. Maybe you really did love him, but things change. You're seventeen. The last time I checked, we're not supposed to be making lifetime commitments."

"You don't understand." Guilt and frustration seemed to be my constant companions lately. "I'm never going to fall out of love with him." But would he ever forgive me for betraying him again? How could I possibly tell him? "I need to go home." I struggled to my feet, leaning on my crutches. "I need you to take me home."

Wyatt slowly stood, brushing the sand from his jeans. "I'll take you home, but I can't do this anymore. My mother is more than enough to deal with right now."

"What do you mean that *you* can't do this anymore?"

"I mean that I can't sit here getting these mixed signals from you. I can't be around you every day, knowing I want more and you don't." Wyatt's expression turned grim. "I think it's best if we both keep our distance."

"Oh." I spun away on my crutches, tears pricking my eyes.

It's what I wanted. If Wyatt and I couldn't work as friends, a clean break was the best option. My focus needed to be on Ben and how I could possibly fix this.

So why did I feel like this was going to rank right up there as one of the worst moments in my life?

Chapter Nineteen

I parked Sally and walked to the lighthouse on Hatteras Island, a black-and-white-striped spiral visible from miles away. It was dusk, but still warm. Like the rest of the island, the area crawled with tourists, everyone trying to get that perfect shot of the light-house at sunset.

I loved it in winter when Ben and I had the area to ourselves. Of course, Ben and I would never have anything to ourselves anymore if I left it up to him. There'd be no Ben and Mer, but I couldn't accept that. I couldn't give up, because he'd been a part of me for too long. Losing him felt like losing a limb, like without him, I'd been forced to relearn even the simplest tasks.

In the two weeks since he'd walked out of my living room, I'd tried talking to him. I'd hoped that he just needed time, that he'd *realize I'd never meant to hurt him. I'd texted and called. I'd even shown up at his house. That had been a major mistake. Aunt Lila had told me to leave and not come back.*

Reality was slowly sinking in. Maybe Ben wasn't coming back, either.

If he never forgave me, all the dreams and plans we'd made would be wiped clean. Maybe I should have felt free, liberated. My future would be a blank slate. I could travel all I wanted and not worry whether Ben wanted to go with me. So why did that freedom feel more like a lifetime prison sentence?

I walked the road to the lighthouse, trying to ignore the love-struck couples—tourists laughing and holding hands, snapping selfies of their happiness. I had the same pictures on my phone, taken before I'd ruined everything, but they meant nothing now.

When I reached the base of the lighthouse, I tipped my head back, searching for the top. I turned in a slow circle, watching that highest point slip in and out of my vision.

After, I headed for a spot in the dunes where Ben and I once made a campfire and watched the lunar eclipse. But when I arrived, I wasn't alone. Ben sat there in cargo shorts and a T-shirt. His knees were drawn up, and his head hung in his hands.

My mouth turned dry. "Ben?"

He lifted his head. His expression snatched the air from my lungs. He looked lost and hurt and miserable.

I fell to my knees at his side. "Are you okay?"

"Yeah." He moved sideways on the sand, widening the gap between us. "Just perfect."

I ducked my chin. "I'm sorry. I didn't know you'd be here." But finding him here couldn't be a coincidence. It had to be fate finally giving me a chance to explain.

He angled his body away from me. "I needed a minute alone. I wanted some quiet to think, but it's not helping."

I sat on my butt. "I know the feeling. You were always the one I called when things were bad, and now I feel like there's no one." I spoke so softly, I wondered if he even heard.

"Don't."

I looked over at him.

"You don't get to make me feel guilty over this. You chose to go behind my back. You made it impossible for me to trust you anymore."

I swallowed. "I know."

"So, why did you have the abortion without telling me? Didn't you know what this would do to us? You could have just talked to me. I'd have listened."

I toed off my sneakers and buried my feet in the sand. I needed to do something to distract me from Ben's dark stare. As much as I wanted another chance to explain, finding the right words seemed impossible.

"No answer, Mer? Don't I at least deserve that much?"

"I was scared, okay? I was freaked-out."

He let out a long, low breath. "You used to come to me when you were scared. *You talked to me about everything, but on something this important, you decided to go solo and shut me out. Do you have any idea how much that hurts?"*

"I'm sorry," I whispered. "I am." I ran my hand back and forth over the warm sand. "I keep having these dreams. I hear a baby crying. I'm supposed to be taking care of it, but I can't find it. I'm searching my room, but it's not there." *I kept waking in a cold sweat, my heart racing. I was sure I'd made the right choice, so why did it haunt me? Was it because I'd lied to Ben?*

His expression softened. He rubbed one hand across his forehead. "I'm sorry. I know this is hard on you, too."

"But you could make it better"—I bit my lip—"if we were still together, like before." *Ben said nothing. He just stared out at the ocean, but I couldn't give up.* "You were wrong. I do know what love is. I've loved you for as long as I can remember. First, I loved you as my best friend, and now it's so much more. It's the same for you. I know you love me. We're supposed to have the rest of our lives together."

I reached for his hand, but he moved it at the same time and buried his face in his palms. When he finally lifted his head and looked at me, my throat tightened.

"I know we were, but here's the thing that keeps going around in my head: You say you're sorry, but if you were able to do it over, would you keep your promise? Be honest. Would you wait and let us make the decision together?"

I knew what he wanted me to say: Of course I regretted my

choice to break my promise; of course I'd include Ben if I could do it over. But maybe I didn't regret it. I regretted getting pregnant, I regretted hurting Ben, and I regretted hurting our families, but did I regret making the right choice for me?

Still, all I needed right now was to tell this one little lie. I could say this one thing, and maybe I'd have Ben back again.

But lying was no longer an option. I'd waited too long to answer, and my expression had betrayed my thoughts.

He reared back. "You lied to me, Mer, and you'd still do it again, even knowing what it would do to us."

"That's not fair." I straightened. "It was an impossible situation. You'd made up your mind. You even bought that... rattle. And I'd made up my mind. We couldn't have had it both ways. One of us had to lose."

"It wasn't a competition. It was a discussion we should have had together."

"Oh, really? It's your turn to be honest. Would you actually have supported my choice if I'd told you beforehand?"

"How can you even doubt that?" His expression was grim, his dark eyes glittering with unshed tears. "I bought the rattle because I wanted you to understand that it was a real choice for us, but I've been there for you our entire lives. Name a single time when I didn't have your back. If this was what you still wanted, of course, I'd have supported your decision. I'd have gone with you, but you never gave me the chance. You never trusted me even half as much as I've always trusted you."

His words were a light switch. I suddenly understood exactly how much I'd screwed up.

I allowed myself to picture another scenario, one where I told Ben about my choice, where we'd gone together, and he'd held my hand instead of my mom, where every step of the process hadn't been weighed down by the guilt I felt for lying to him. Fear had kept me from seeing it before, but Ben was right. That option had been there all along, if I'd just trusted him.

"I'm sorry," I whispered. "You're right. I should have trusted you. So tell me how to fix this. Tell me how to make you forgive me."

Ben squinted up at the setting sun. He looked as miserable as I felt. "This is not about forgiveness. It's about trust. If I can't trust you with the important things, how can I be with you? I can't be best friends with someone I don't trust anymore. I can't be your boyfriend when you don't trust me."

He stared over at me, and I saw everything I'd lost, every familiar feature, every moment together, every kiss, every memory. Tears burned my eyes. It couldn't all be over.

"Couples break up all the time, Mer. I used to think we were different, that we'd last forever, but it turns out we're just like everyone else. Now, I need to figure out how to move on. So stop calling and texting, and please don't come to my house anymore. It upsets my mom."

He stood up and my spine collapsed. I was a jellyfish, with no strength, no ability to control my life. He blocked out the sun, leaving me lost in his shadow.

"If it helps, I don't hate you, Mer. I just don't want to see you anymore."

He walked away.

Nope. It didn't help at all.

The following week, Wyatt ignored me at school. He'd only sent me a brief text asking me not to work at the café anymore. Given the circumstances, I couldn't really argue. So I was also out of a job.

On Thursday, I finally got permission to drive Sally. I was so desperate for some independence, I drove my scooter to school even though the gray sky threatened more rain. I arrived late, but not late enough to avoid Kim's ambush at my locker. I read her expression as easily as a front-page headline. She had news, and I wasn't going to like it.

"Hey, Mer." She leaned against the locker next to mine.

I pulled out my books and clanged the door shut. "What do you want?"

"You don't need to be mean. I'm just trying to talk."

"You're right." I sighed and headed toward history class. "What's going on?"

She grinned, her mood clearly recovering. "Guess who I'm going to the dance with this weekend?"

"What dance?"

She slowed and pulled a brightly colored flyer off the wall.

"The spring dance. We have it every year. How can you not know about it?"

I stared down at the paper. It didn't even look familiar, but then again, maybe it was because I hated dancing. Still, shouldn't I remember an annual dance? The letters on the flyer were streaked with water stains. Obviously, another victim of the leaking that continued around the school. I crumpled it into a ball and tossed it in a nearby trash can.

Kim frowned. "You are such a poor loser."

"Poor loser?"

"Yeah, because Wyatt is going with me to the dance." She hugged her binder to her chest and got one of those dreamy-eyed looks I figured only existed in the movies.

I froze. "He asked you?"

"No, but he said yes when I asked him. He's picking me up at my house."

Crap. Knowing Wyatt and his Texan charms, he'd even bring her stupid flowers and chocolates. "Congratulations," I bit out. "Are you expecting a parade now?"

"Wow, Mer, you can be a real bitch sometimes."

"Thanks." I rolled my eyes. "I need to get to class."

"I'm glad Ben dumped you," she said as I walked away. "You never deserved him."

I continued down the corridor, my chin in the air. Wyatt stood by his locker, and I glared at him as I stomped by. He returned

my stare, his expression giving nothing away. Then he turned
back to the group of guys he'd been hanging with.

Only one thing kept me upright: the thought of finally seeing
Ben tonight.

"Ben!" I threw myself at him. We stumbled backward, a tangle
of arms and legs and thudding hearts. "I missed you so much.
Did you get my note?"

"Yeah, but I was still going crazy." He rested his forehead
against mine, his arms locking me against him. "Are you okay
now? Is your ankle still hurting?"

"I won't be tap-dancing anytime soon, but I'll live." I stared
down at the uneven sand. "This doesn't help any."

He swung me up in his arms, and I gasped. "Better?"

"Yeah." I buried my face against his neck, breathing him in.
I'd forgotten how much I loved his smell—flannel and the faint
tanginess of the ocean. "Much better."

He crossed the beach and stopped at our little hollow between
the dunes. I slid to the ground, and he brushed the hair from my
face. "I was really worried about you. I hated that I couldn't be
there."

"You didn't have a choice," I said against his lips. "I was okay."

His large hand cupped the side of my face. "Yeah?"

"Yeah." *Because Wyatt was there for me. Because I kissed him.*

I stiffened, trying to wipe out the memory and his stupid fresh laundry smell. Fortunately, Ben didn't seem to notice. He lowered his head and kissed me. I tried to enjoy it, but the taste of guilt tainted everything. It clogged my throat, and suddenly I couldn't breathe. I pulled back, hiding my face against his chest.

"What is it, Mer? Did I do something wrong?"

"No," I mumbled. Ben had done nothing wrong. It was always me. "It's just been a tough couple of weeks."

He tucked one hand under my chin and lifted my face. "Tell me."

I shrugged, staring beyond him at the cloudy night sky, still not able to meet his gaze. "Mom and Rachel and I were in Buxton, and we ran into your parents."

"Oh." His expression darkened. "Let me guess—it didn't go well."

"Your mom hates me." The words spilled out. I should have tempered them so he wouldn't feel bad, but it was too late now. "She still won't talk to my mom."

Ben sighed and rubbed his thumb across the spot on my forehead that always creased when I frowned. "My mom hangs on to things and won't let go. I'm sorry."

"It was awful. She looked at me with so much hate."

"Hey, don't let her get to you. I forgive you. That's the important part, right?"

"Are you sure you've forgiven me?" I caught the front of his shirt in my fists. "You said you'd never trust me again. I don't even know why you changed your mind. I don't know why you showed up that night on the beach, the night I . . . cut my hair." Why was I pressing this point? Even if he truly did trust me again, I didn't deserve it. Not after I'd kissed Wyatt. Maybe I was just trying to reassure myself that he had the capacity to forgive me again.

The wind gusted, but it wasn't strong enough to carry away the honesty in his words. "I forgave you because when I tried living without you, I only felt empty and miserable. I'd convinced myself that I couldn't trust you again, but then I realized—the only things standing in the way of our second chance were my own pride and stubbornness."

"I don't deserve you." A bitter taste filled my mouth. "I never have."

"Stop saying that, Mer. I love you." He hugged me. "Hey, isn't the spring dance this weekend?"

I slowly pulled back. "How does everyone know about this stupid dance but me?" I muttered. "And you know I hate dancing."

"I know." He swayed back and forth, and I swayed with him. "One lousy middle school dance was all I got, and that was back when we were just friends. One of these days, I'm going to trick you into it. You won't know it's happening, and suddenly you'll be dancing."

Despite everything, I laughed and kept my body still. "That's a challenge you'll never win."

He swept me off the ground and set me back on his feet. I gasped and curled my arms around his neck. He rocked back and forth, and I had no choice but to follow his lead.

"You should know better," he whispered in my ear. "You know I like challenges."

My head fell back, and I lost myself in the cool breeze and night sky. Why did these moments have to keep ending? Why did I keep doing things to destroy them?

But not yet. I buried my guilt in the sand under Ben's feet and closed my eyes. He hummed and swayed, accompanied by the waves, and I hung on. He found my lips, and this time, I kissed him back. Once I told him the truth, I'd no idea how much longer we'd have. So I'd steal his kisses, his love, and his trust for just a few more minutes.

He caught my hand in his, crooking his arm and bringing our joined hands to his chest. His thumb skirted across my wrist, leaving tiny goosebumps in its wake. I arched into him, his other arm at the small of my back. God, I loved him. How had I let Wyatt's charm and touch confuse me? How could I forget what this felt like? This is what I wanted, and now because of Wyatt, I might lose it.

Anger stiffened my spine. Our kiss ended, and I bit my lip.

"What is it, Mer?"

I looked up at him.

"I know there's something else you're not telling me."

I stepped back, and he let me go. I sank down on the sand, my knees weak from just thinking about my confession and what it would do to us.

"Whatever it is, we can deal with it together. It's the one thing I've learned—we are stronger together than apart."

"I know," I mumbled, staring at the ground. A drop of water hit my nose, and I glanced up at the rain starting to fall. *Seriously?*

"It's like a bandage. Just rip it off. Just do it. Just tell—"

"I kissed him!"

My words exploded out and then faded into the painful silence. Ben's expression hid in the darkness, but I knew. Disbelief and disappointment radiated from him.

"I kissed Wyatt Quinn and it's killing me. I love you, but then Wyatt came along, and he makes me feel things I don't want to feel. When I'm with you, I can forget all about them. But when I'm with him, I wonder about all kinds of things. I feel excited and reckless and curious, and I . . . I like feeling that way."

More silence. More darkness. The rain turned from a sprinkle to a steady drizzle, and the drowning feeling was back.

"But it was only once, and it's over now. We don't even talk at school." Of course, that was Wyatt's choice, not mine. "Say something, Ben. Please say something."

"Do you really want me to?" he asked, his voice rasping. Rain clung to his hair and the shoulders of his jacket.

I swallowed and nodded, but uncertainty weighed down my limbs.

"I gave you a second chance." His expression twisted in pain, his dark eyes blending with the night. "I let myself trust you again because I love you, and you kiss another guy. You betray me again." He shook his head and rain droplets landed on my upturned face. "I can't even look at you right now. You're not the same girl I fell in love with. I don't know who you are."

No. I sobbed and struggled to my feet, my ankle slowing my progress. By the time I was standing, he'd already walked away.

"Wait! Ben!"

I tried to run after him, but my foot twisted on a dip in the sand. I landed on the ground, my ankle throbbing and my heart thudding. Sitting on the sand in the rain, I watched Ben's back disappear into the night.

Wetness stained my cheeks, but it was from rain and not tears. I couldn't cry yet, because that would mean it was truly over. I still had a chance to make it up to Ben, to earn his trust back.

I had to believe that.

Chapter Twenty

Saturday dragged on. My ankle supported walking, but running was still out of the question—the one thing I really needed. I wanted to run until I couldn't feel or think anymore.

I obsessed over the clock, waiting for evening and the chance to apologize to Ben. I planned to plant my butt on the beach until he showed up. If he was too stubborn or angry or hurt to come tonight, I'd wait tomorrow night and the next night, until he finally appeared. There was no justification for my actions with Wyatt, but I trusted in the goodness in Ben's heart. He'd forgiven me once before, and I had to believe he'd do it again.

Supper was a quiet affair. These days, my whole family walked on eggshells around me. They'd sensed my frustration with everything since I kissed Wyatt. Mom and Dad had both asked me what happened, but this was one life crisis I'd no intention of sharing with anyone.

On the other side of the table, Rachel and Mom sat talking about the spring dance. My sister wanted to go with some friends, and Mom offered to drive her. Rachel looked at me. "Can Mer take me instead? You're going, right?"

"Yeah, sure." I popped some mashed potatoes in my mouth. I'd drop Rachel at the dance, go to the beach to wait for Ben, and be back to pick her up when it ended—the perfect excuse to be gone all evening without Mom and Dad prodding me with more questions.

Later, I waited for Rachel on the front porch. She came outside, wearing a sweet little dress and ballet flats, with her hair curled and gold studs shining in her ears. I did a double take when I recognized the blue satin. "Hey, is that my dress?"

She twirled once. "It was your dress, but now it's mine."

It looked beautiful on her. I tried to remember how I'd felt in that same satin, but all I remembered about that night was Ben—how he'd made me feel perfect the way I was. My resolve strengthened. I'd find a way to make it right between us.

Rachel gave my jeans and black top a once-over and laughed. "I love that some things never change."

She hooked her arm through mine, and we headed to Mom's car. We drove to school with Taylor Swift songs blasting on the radio. Once we were in the school parking lot, I stopped in front of the main door.

Rachel frowned at me. "Why aren't you parking?"

I squeezed the steering wheel. "I'm dropping you off, but I can't come in. There's something I need to do."

"What do you mean? Do Mom and Dad know about this?"

"No, but I'll be here when the dance is over. I promise."

"Mer—"

"Look, this is really important. So please just go in and have a good time." I tapped my thumb against the steering wheel, waiting for her to hop out, but she didn't move. "Rachel?"

I glanced over at her. In the glow from the school lights, she looked small and pale. She chewed on her lip, a habit we'd both gotten from my mom.

"Come in with me, Mer. Whatever you were planning to do tonight, don't. Just come inside instead. I know you don't like to dance. So we can stand on the sidelines and make fun of people. I don't care. Just come with me."

There was something desperate in her voice, something I didn't understand. My gut twisted. "What's going on? Are you okay?"

She grabbed my hand and squeezed my fingers so tight, I hissed. "For a while there, I thought you were better, but I see it happening again and . . . I'm scared."

"Of what?"

She looked me in the eye, and I shivered, because I saw bleakness there and utter helplessness. "I'm scared this is the last time I'll ever see you. I feel it every day now, whenever I leave the house or you go out. Everyone thinks I don't know what happened the night you cut your hair, but I do. It feels the same now. So don't go." Her words tumbled together. "Please. Just come in with me. I never ask anything of you. Just come in with me so I don't have to worry for one night."

Tears welled in her eyes and spilled over. Her shoulders shook and I pulled her into my arms. "Shhh. Stop, Rachel. It'll be okay."

But my reassurances were a lie because her words echoed the feeling I'd had while sitting on the side of the road when I sprained my ankle, and while watching the deer take its last breath. I didn't believe in premonitions, but somehow I also knew something bad was coming, something out of my control. Maybe the bad part had been my fight on the beach with Ben, but instinct told me there was more.

Rachel circled her arms around my neck and clung to me. "You'll come in with me?"

Despite how badly I needed to see Ben, I nodded. I'd do this for Rachel, even if it meant seeing Wyatt dance with Kim and even if it meant one more night of not knowing if Ben had for-given me. I'd do this for Rachel because she obviously saw so much more than I gave her credit for. I'd do this for her because she never asked me for anything and I loved her, and mostly because I was suddenly scared, too.

So I parked and we both climbed out. We paid our entrance fee and made our way to the gym. Under the dim lights, balloons and streamers hung from the ceiling. A DJ table blasted music from the corner. I stood in the doorway, disoriented. The gym seemed larger than usual, crowded with kids I barely recognized. Were they even from Ocracoke?

Rachel grinned at me, like everything was normal. She spotted some of her friends and ran over to them, hugging and squealing with the enthusiasm of middle schoolers, which left me to wander along the edge of the dance floor.

In the dark, I skirted past dancing couples and excited girls in their dresses and high heels. I ignored their disapproving looks and the fact that the guys barely gave me a second glance—that part I was used to.

Besides, there was only one guy here I did care about. I wasn't supposed to, but he drew my attention like a shiny lure. He stood with his back to me, talking to a group of kids from our class. I stopped and stared. I'd have recognized him anywhere—bronze hair brushing the collar of his button-down shirt, strong forearms exposed by his rolled-up sleeves, jeans hugging his . . .

He spun around. Our gazes brushed, caught, mingled. My hands curled into fists. He was done with me. I was done with him. So why could I remember the exact feel of his kiss, the heat of his mouth on mine, the fiery colors he brought to me?

Someone bumped into me, and someone else crossed our paths, but when they moved, our gazes found each other again, like those eels that travel an entire ocean to find their way back to one sea—back to their home.

I stepped forward. What was I doing?

He strode toward me, determination on his face, stopping a foot away. "You came?"

I nodded.

"But you don't dance."

"I know. Look, about that day, on the beach——"

"Don't." His word cut me off, firm and insistent. "If we talk, it'll mess everything up. If we talk, we'll end up walking away in different directions, and I don't want to do that. Not now."

I bit my lip. The fast, pulsing music slowed to something soft and sexy.

My heart was being torn in two. I couldn't pretend this connection with Wyatt wasn't real. The air between us buzzed with it—a living, breathing thing. Maybe I was a terrible person, but I was tired of the constant push and pull warring inside me. I was even more tired of the guilt and regret. Letting Ben's image slip away, I focused on the curve of Wyatt's mouth. It didn't matter that I didn't dance. I wanted Wyatt's arms around me. I wanted to match my steps to his and bury my face in his neck and feel alive. He stepped closer, and my mouth turned dry.

I gave in and walked into his arms.

His hand slid under my shirt, resting on the bare skin right above my jeans. His other hand caught and lifted mine, trapping it between his chest and my heart.

His gaze swept across my face, warm and possessive. But it didn't feel controlling, because I understood it. He wanted us to belong together, to challenge and inspire each other. Did I want the same thing? His stare landed on my mouth and my breath quivered in and out, forgetting its natural tempo. We swayed to the music. The lyrics curled around us, filled with longing.

At one point, I saw Kim's face; it was flushed red with anger. I saw her turn and storm from the gym, but she was a part of reality. This was my fantasy. I closed my eyes and laid my head on Wyatt's shoulder, my lips brushing his neck on the way past. He stiffened and missed a step, but then his hand squeezed my back, and his head lowered. His breath whispered across my ear, promising me all the things I couldn't have—a chance to be happy, to not be crushed by the weight of a choice I didn't know how to make.

I breathed him in, the scent of sweat on his neck mingling with his fresh laundry smell. We stayed like that—lost in the music; hidden in a crowd of sweaty couples; aware of every spot our bodies touched, the pad of his thumb circling the base of my spine, our joined hands pressed against his chest, my thigh brushing his, the scrape of his jaw against my cheek, my heart thudding next to his.

While I was in his arms, I could forget everything else, but eventually the music stopped.

Our swaying slowed and Wyatt lifted his head. I kept my face buried. Couples around us broke apart, and the music picked up pace, but I ignored it all.

"Mer?" His single word said too much. It was a statement and a question. It held hope, confusion, temptation.

Reality crashed down on me. My head snapped up, and I stepped back, but his fingers dug into my shoulder.

"Don't leave." He leaned closer. "I need to find Kim. I might act like a jerk sometimes, but I can't lead her on. And then you and I are going to talk."

I swallowed, trying to find the words to make him understand how impossible everything still was, but he was already gone. I spun around and watched as he wove his way through the crowd, searching for Kim. Hugging myself, I pushed my way across the gym floor, the same gym where I'd been attending school assemblies and concerts since kindergarten; only tonight it didn't look right. Everything felt . . . off.

I found my way to the bathroom. I stared in the mirror at my flushed cheeks and wide eyes. Ben said that he didn't know who I was anymore, that I wasn't the girl he'd fallen in love with. So who was I? Would I like myself any better if I gave up on everything Ben and I had together and started something new? Was it time to finally accept the limitations of our relationship and let each other go? Could I find a way to be happy without him?

Rubbing my palms against my burning eyes, I cursed the universe. It never gave me a break these days, not even for a moment. I yanked the bathroom door open and strode out.

Later, had I thought back on it, I'd have known that what happened next was always meant to happen. Secrets find their way out of the darkness and into the light, no matter how many people get hurt in the process.

I wasn't sure where I was headed, but I never made it there. Instead, I found Wyatt pacing in front of the school office. He pulled both hands through his hair, talking to himself. He looked nothing like the cocky, self-assured guy I knew. He seemed off-balance, on the edge of something I couldn't understand.

I glanced around the hall, looking for an explanation, but it was empty. I must have made a noise or maybe he sensed my presence. His head whipped up.

"Mer?" His hazel eyes widened, disbelief in his expression, but then something hard and determined swept over his features. He marched toward me. I backed up, but he kept coming. He planted himself a foot away. "Just the person I wanted to see," he ground out. "For a moment, I thought I'd conjured you out of thin air." His fingers wrapped around my arm. "But, no. You're real. At least that much is true."

I swallowed. Fear danced up my spine. "What are you talking about?"

"Good question." He spun around, pulling me behind him. He stopped right in front of the bulletin board, and I crashed into his back.

He ripped a piece of paper off the wall and pushed it into my hands. My heart sank.

No.

I didn't need to look at it, because I already knew what he'd found. I'd forgotten it was posted there—a photocopy of the original newspaper article, including a picture and a reprint of the eulogy his dad had written.

Wyatt knew the truth. Was this what I'd sensed coming, what I'd feared?

"I found Kim. She informed me I was wasting my time with you because you were still so screwed up from your last boyfriend. She told me to check out this article if I wanted details." He shook his head. "I don't know how I missed it earlier." His words exploded at me. "What the hell, Mer? If you didn't want to go out with me, you should've said so. Don't make up stories about a guy who . . ." He swallowed and his nostrils flared.

"Say it." I met his gaze, and my fingers twisted around the paper. My heart stuttered and my knees shook, but I held my head high. "Finish your sentence."

Wyatt's jaw clenched. He slapped his hand flat against the bulletin board.

It shook, and I jerked like it was me he'd slapped.

"You want me to say it out loud? Jesus, Mer, fine. Ben Collins is dead. He died. You're pretending to date a dead guy."

Three weeks after my meeting with Ben at the lighthouse, I ran up on my porch, jogging in position, waiting for my heart to slow and my body to cool. I ran almost every day now—longer and faster. It

was the only time I stopped obsessing over Ben and wondering what I could possibly do to make him trust me again—or even talk to me.

The door swung open, and I looked up. Dad stood there, his face pale under his beard, his eyes red and darting around. He reached out his hand and said something, but I couldn't hear.

"Dad!" I yanked out my earbuds. "What happened?"

He stepped closer. He folded me in his arms, and his body trembled like an earthquake around me.

I pulled back. "You're scaring me, Dad."

"I'm so sorry, Mer. It's Ben."

I frowned. "What about Ben?"

He gripped my shoulders, but I looked past him. Mom stood in the doorway, pressing a balled-up tissue against her mouth. She looked devastated. I stumbled, but Dad held me up. Something deep inside me told me to run—a protective instinct. I didn't want to hear what he was about to say. His words were going to change everything.

But he was talking, and I couldn't shut him up. " . . . An accident . . . his dad's boat." I couldn't find the strength to make him stop. " . . . still looking . . . unconscious when he hit the water . . . recovery now . . . so sorry."

No. I shook my head. No.

No!

Ben was not lost somewhere in the water. Not in my ocean. Not in the ocean we'd played in since we were kids. Not in the place that understood me. It wouldn't turn on us like that. It couldn't be that cruel. Ben hadn't forgiven me yet. He had to still be alive. His smile. He was the only one who understood . . . everything. He was the one . . .

"Mer!" *Strong hands shook me.* "You need to breathe."

But my knees collapsed, and the world crumbled around me, and the whole time, Mom watched. Tears spilled down her cheeks, and she watched me break into little shards of myself while Dad desperately tried to catch them all. I didn't blame her. She was only accepting the inevitable truth: There was nothing anybody could do to stop this.

Ben was gone. The only source of light in my world had been snuffed out, and now there would just be darkness.

"Jesus, Mer, you even had me deliver a note to him, just to avoid going out with me. This is so fucked up!"

Wyatt threw the words at me, each one so much worse because it was Wyatt who was saying them, pointing out the things I could never explain. They landed with precision, slicing into my skin, puncturing my lungs, making it painful to breathe.

I stared down at the page in my hand. Ben smiled up at me, wearing his football uniform, his helmet tucked under one arm. The headline read, "Local Football Star Lost at Sea." Ben had been lost, but then I'd found him, or maybe he'd found me. How could I explain that to Wyatt? But then I realized. Wyatt didn't have to believe me. I knew the truth, and it was all that mattered.

"It's him, right?" Wyatt pointed to the picture. "It's the guy from the photo on your mantel. You told me he's the guy you've been meeting at the beach, the reason why you're not free to be with me."

I shook my head, my stomach knotting. "You don't understand."

"That's right, because you never trusted me with the truth. Your boyfriend died, and you're still mourning him. You go to the beach because maybe it's a special place for you. Do you really think I'm such a jerk I couldn't understand that?"

"No." I stepped back. He was too close and loud, and I couldn't think. "That's not right."

"What part do I have wrong?"

"I . . . I don't . . ." The words wouldn't come. I glanced down the hall. I needed to leave.

His voice lowered, and his expression softened. "I know that I can act cocky and maybe insensitive, but I liked you. I like you. I'm not going to hold your grief against you. But you need to tell me."

He stepped closer, backing me against the bulletin board. Heat radiated from his body, his warm breath fanning me. I looked at his chest and swallowed.

"Why did I bring that note to the beach, Mer?"

Chapter Twenty-One

Dad stood at the door of my bedroom. I lay curled on my bed, the giraffe rattle twisted in my hands. "You need to come, kiddo. As painful as this is, you need to say goodbye."

But that was just it. I couldn't say goodbye, because Ben was already gone. He'd never get to forgive me now. I'd never earn his trust back. He'd never love me again. When I closed my eyes, I saw him drifting alone in the dark ocean. So I didn't sleep. I didn't eat. I was a ghost now, just like him. I just needed to figure out a way to stop feeling.

Dad sat on the edge of my bed and placed his hand on my shoulder. "I know it hurts now, but it will get better. Not today, not tomorrow, but one day you'll wake up and realize that it doesn't *hurt as much. You just have to hang in until then."*

I didn't know if I could.

But I didn't speak these words out loud. Instead, I climbed out of bed and pulled on the black dress Mom had dug out of her closet for me to wear. It was loose, and it made my skin look even paler, especially when I scraped my hair back into a ponytail.

We drove to Hatteras Island. During the ferry ride, we sat quietly together, a sad little group dressed in black. The bright sunny day mocked me. Henry stopped to offer his condolences. "Ben was a good kid." He looked at me. "I'm so sorry. He was too young to go. He still had too much of his life ahead of him."

I nodded and swallowed. Dad thanked him, and then we climbed back in the car at the Hatteras terminal. We drove to the church in Buxton. We parked two streets over because the parking lot was full. It looked like the entire population of the Outer Banks was here. Even the people who didn't know Ben very well knew his mom and dad. Their family was a fixture on the island. Ben was an only child, but there were aunts and uncles and cousins.

We walked to the church. Halfway there, Rachel caught my hand in hers. I looked down at her, and she shot me an encouraging smile. I was jealous. Everything was so black and white for her. She just felt sadness. She missed Ben, but she wasn't burdened with the same sense of helplessness or regret. She didn't have to constantly wonder like I did about how things might have been different if I'd only chosen to be honest with him.

I tripped, but Rachel caught me. "I'm right here, Mer. I won't leave you."

I nodded, my throat clogging.

People lined up, waiting to enter the church. Sun beat down on my shoulders, and sweat beaded on my forehead. We joined the end of the line, and I tried not to look at anyone, but eventually I heard the whispers. Students from Ben's school stared at me, shooting daggers. When Ben broke up with me, everyone assumed I'd cheated on him. I guess they figured it was the most likely reason for Ben to dump me like he had.

Rachel squeezed my hand. "Ignore them."

We got closer to the big double doors. Aunt Lila and Uncle Al stood in the shaded vestibule. They both wore black—shadows of the people they'd been, both grayer and thinner. Uncle Al and I made eye contact, his expression unreadable. He looked away. Mom and Dad stepped in front of Aunt Lila and her eyes widened.

Mom reached for her hands and her nostrils flared. "We're so sorry, Lila."

Aunt Lila's eyes flashed to me, and her expression tightened. "I don't want you here. Please leave."

"Lila!" Mom gasped.

Aunt Lila leaned forward, her breath hissing out. "Ben died with a broken heart because of what she did. Do you think I can forgive you all for that? How dare you show up here?" Her voice broke. "How dare you?" Tears glistened in her eyes, and she pulled in a ragged breath.

"Lila…" Mom reached for her, but Uncle Al stepped between them.

"I'm sorry, Jess. I'm not saying she's right, but we're saying goodbye to our son today. So I need you to respect her wishes."

Dad put his arm around Mom's shoulder. "Come on, sweetheart. Let's just go."

She slowly nodded, and Dad led her away. For a few seconds, I just stood there. I hadn't wanted to come. It wasn't even a proper funeral because there was no body to bury. Ben wasn't lying inside, waiting to be lowered into the ground. But standing outside that door with Uncle Al blocking the entrance, I wanted to go in.

I wanted to hear the minister explain how this all somehow made sense, how it was all part of God's plan, that Ben was in a better place now, that he wasn't still out there drifting, lost beneath the waves. I wanted to hear people remember all the good things about Ben. It should have been me talking about those things because I'd known him best. I'd known all his hopes and fears and dreams because he'd shared them with me.

We'd been perfect, and I'd broken everything.

Someone tugged on my hand. I looked down at Rachel. "Let's just go. Ben knows how much you loved him."

Did he? Uncle Al met my gaze, and I finally understood what I'd seen there earlier: shared guilt, shared regrets.

He nodded. "Listen to your sister. You need to leave."

So I turned and let Rachel lead me away.

No one talked on the ride home. When we got back to the house,
I tugged off the black dress and threw it on the floor. I pulled on my
pajamas, jammed in my earbuds, and climbed into bed.

Maybe I'd fallen asleep, because when I opened my eyes again,
the room was dark. A tray was on my desk—supper sat on a plate.
It was probably cold, but I didn't care. I wasn't hungry.

I found the giraffe and held it to my chest.

The hard frame of the bulletin board pressed against my back,
but Wyatt was still too close. "He died," I whispered, "but then
he . . ."

"He what, Mer?"

I glanced around the empty hallway. God, I couldn't believe
I was about to say this out loud. Wyatt wouldn't believe me, but
deep down I wanted him to. I wanted to share this secret with
someone and know that they didn't think I'd gone off the deep
end. "I know how this sounds, but he came back."

Wyatt's chest expanded, and he rocked back on his heels.
"What are you saying? He's still alive?"

"No." I rubbed the heel of my hand against my forehead. "I
mean, I don't think he is, but every night he comes to the beach,
and I can see him . . . I can talk to him."

Wyatt's eyebrows lowered. "Like a ghost?"

"Maybe." Only it was more than that. I could touch him.

He could hold me, kiss me, forgive me.

Wyatt shook his head and gave me a small, sad smile. "Darlin', I don't know what you think you're seeing, but it's not real. That article tells the whole story in black and white. He was on his dad's boat. He got hit by some equipment and dragged overboard. He never came up."

"Don't believe me." I straightened and pushed him away. I didn't need Wyatt's pity. "I don't care, because I know the truth. When I go to the beach, Ben will be there waiting for me."

At least, I hoped he'd be there, because it wasn't like I could go and find him if he decided to stay away. I had to believe he wouldn't stay angry forever, but even the possibility of that turned my legs to mush.

"Mer..." Wyatt reached for my hand, but I ducked around him.

I needed to leave, but my limbs froze when I saw Rachel a few feet away. From the fear on her face, I knew she'd heard.

Damn. This was all Wyatt's fault.

Rachel would tell Mom and Dad, and they'd freak out. They wouldn't believe me, and everything would be ruined.

God, I couldn't do this anymore. I'd tried. I'd tried for weeks and weeks now. Months had passed. Dad kept saying it would get better, but it didn't. I didn't want to live in this world without Ben. I couldn't sleep. I couldn't forget our last words, that he'd died angry at me.

Ben's death was punishment. I'd destroyed our love, and in return, they'd taken Ben from me. I couldn't . . .

I leaned against the bathroom mirror, so close my breath fogged my reflection. I stared at my limp strands of hair. Ben used to curl his hands around them. He used to tug me closer and tease me into a kiss.

I yanked open a drawer and dug through it.

Damn. I slammed it shut and pulled open the next one.

Where were they?

Yes. The scissors. I held them up in front of my face, grabbed a hunk of hair, and sawed at it. It fell from my hand and slithered into the sink. I glared at it for a long moment, waiting for something to change inside me, waiting to feel something, even regret, but there was nothing. I picked up the next strand and attacked it with the blades. I kept hacking, and it kept falling.

Tears dripped into the sink, disappearing among a sea of long black hair. I dropped the scissors, and they clattered to the counter. I rubbed one hand over the remaining jagged strands.

Wiping my cheeks with my sleeve, I faced the mirror. I looked nothing like the girl Ben had fallen in love with, but inside, I still felt the same. The pain and regret were still there.

No!

I understood then—there was nothing I could do to make it stop. My throat ached with the need to scream. I grabbed a towel and slid to the floor. I pressed my face into it. Agony ripped across my throat and buried itself in the towel, but it still wasn't enough.

I needed to get out of the house. I needed to hurtle down the highway into the night. So I snuck out and started my scooter. I pulled up my hood on the ferry so Henry wouldn't see. I stood by the railing, oblivious to everything around me, and stared into the dark ocean, wondering how Ben had felt at the very end.

Then I drove to the beach and walked to the edge of the water. I pulled out the packet of cold medicine I'd grabbed from the cabinet. One by one, I pushed them out of their foil homes and swallowed them.

My fingers shook as I tugged the giraffe from my pocket and then pressed it against my face. "I'm sorry," I whispered, but there was no one around to hear.

I dropped it on the sand and walked into the rolling surf.

"Rachel!" I caught my sister's hand. "I know how that sounded, but I'm not lying. The night I went to the beach, the night I cut my hair, I thought everything was over. I didn't want to go on, but suddenly Ben was there. He stopped me. He saved me. I know it's impossible, but he's real."

I watched her expressions change, like one of those flip-books. She wanted to believe me, but she didn't. I couldn't blame her. If I hadn't been meeting Ben on the beach for months, I wouldn't have believed it, either.

"Mer," she said softly, like she was talking to a stray dog that was cornered and afraid. "We need to tell Mom and Dad. They'll know what to do. They can help."

They can get me help. That's what she meant.

Wyatt appeared at my side and wrapped his arm around my waist. Damn. Even now, I couldn't stop myself from leaning into him, just a little. "Your sister's right." I let him lead me to a bench. "Just sit here while we call your dad. Okay, Rachel?"

She nodded, already digging her phone out of her purse. Could I stop her from calling? But how?

Wyatt squatted in front of me, his presence too distracting. I needed to think. Under the fluorescent lights, his eyes looked greener against his pale skin. "Are you okay?"

I would be, if you just believed me.

"Mer?"

If they refused to take my word, maybe I needed to show them. If I went to the beach and found Ben, I could prove he was real. I just needed to get away. "It's so dry," I lied, ducking my head and pressing my hand against my throat. "I can barely swallow."

"I'll get you something to drink. Would that help?"

"Yeah." I gripped the edge of the bench, fighting the urge to run.

He looked over at Rachel. "Your sister's right there, and I'll be right back." He met my stare. "We're going to figure this out, Mer. Everything's going to be fine."

I huddled on the bench and nodded.

Wyatt strode away. I waited until he disappeared around the corner, making his way toward the vending machines in the lunchroom. Rachel stood with her back to me, talking into her phone.

I did not imagine Ben and I'd prove it.

Easing off the bench, I slowly backed away from her. When I was ten feet away, I turned and ran. Rachel yelled out my name, but I didn't stop. Seconds later, I heard Wyatt's voice in the distance, but I was already bursting out of the front doors and racing toward Mom's car. I jammed the key in the ignition and peeled out of the parking lot. I drove with the pedal to the floor, just rolling onto the ferry before they pulled the ramp clear.

I needed to reach Ben and tell him our secret was exposed. I needed to find a way to convince my family he was real before they locked me up and threw away the key. But would he be there? He was angry. I'd let him down, but he'd always been there for me. After all the nights we'd shared together on the beach, I had to believe he wouldn't let one kiss get in the way of his being there when I needed him the most.

Chapter Twenty-Two

"**B**en!" I ran the remaining distance to the dunes. "Ben! Where are you?"

But the beach didn't respond. I searched the shoreline and stared at my watch. He should have been here. He always came—rain or shine. After he'd stopped me that night on the beach, after he'd forgiven me and said he still loved me, we'd been so happy and confused and scared.

We didn't know why he'd been allowed to come back. Was it God or magic or fate? Was he a ghost, or were we somehow being given a second chance?

We'd tested the limits of his existence. He'd tried coming

home with me, but he couldn't leave the beach, like some invisible wall limited his presence to that area. And he didn't have all day, only the evening and only a few hours. We tried to understand the significance of it all, but somewhere along the way, we'd stopped questioning and started accepting.

The "why" and "how" didn't matter, because Ben fought off the desperation gnawing at my heart. For the first time in a long while, I could sleep and eat. I started to feel again. It wasn't perfect. I'd never been perfect, but at least I'd felt like me again.

On some level, I'd known our meetings couldn't last forever, but I'd always hoped there was a loophole. The universe couldn't give us this time together without having some kind of plan. That's the way it happened in the books and the movies: There was always a happy ending.

It's why I'd fought so hard against Wyatt. He represented my deepest fear—that my time with Ben was meant to be temporary, that we'd only been given this time to find some kind of closure. But if I was meant to move on from Ben and find someone else, how come Wyatt's kiss hurt him so much? Why hadn't Ben understood when I'd told him? Instead, he'd looked like I'd broken him all over again.

Now, I just needed to find him. Everything was messed up, and I needed him to explain what I was supposed to do next.

"Ben!" I screamed his name into the wind and the night. I cupped my mouth and shouted louder: "Where are you?"

"Meredith!"

"Ben!"

I spun around in the direction of the road, and there he was: tall and solid and searching for me. I squeezed my eyes shut. Thank God. He was real.

I ran toward him but skidded to a stop.

No!

It wasn't Ben. It was Uncle Al. Disappointment filled my lungs.

Uncle Al looked like he'd been yanked from his bed, his hair messy and his jaw dark with whiskers. His shirt wasn't tucked in, and his boots weren't tied. Even in the dark, I could make out his somber expression. Staring at him was like looking into a time machine. This is what Ben would have looked like in thirty years if things had been different.

"What are you doing here?"

He held up both hands in front of him. "Your parents called."

"They called you?" I shook my head. "You don't even talk anymore."

"I know, so that tells you how worried they are. They're stuck waiting for the next ferry, but they asked me to come here, to check on you."

I spun around and faced the ocean, inhaling its salty, pungent scent. Nothing was going right. I just needed Ben to show up. *Where are you?* The air had turned cold again, way too cold for spring on Hatteras. Something brushed my arm and I jumped.

Uncle Al stood at my side. He rubbed one hand over his jaw and shifted his weight. "What's going on, Meredith?" Like my dad, Ben's dad was a man of few words. He wore his discomfort like a flak jacket.

"What did my parents say?"

"That you've been coming here because you believe you're seeing Ben."

His words confirmed what I already knew. My secret was no longer a secret. My chin lifted. "I don't believe it. I know it."

His jaw tightened, and he stared at the ocean. "When your mom called, I didn't tell Lila. She thinks I've gone to check on the boat. I didn't want to cause her more pain."

And I didn't ask you to come. I rubbed my palms against my thighs. "I didn't ask for any of this."

"So tell me how it started." He stood with his legs slightly apart, braced against the wind, like he was ready to confront my problems head-on.

I bit my lip, reaching up to smooth down my hair, remembering the feel of those jagged ends. Uncle Al wanted me to bare my soul and expose the darkest night of my life, but could I trust him? Before he'd sided with Aunt Lila, I'd always felt close to him. Maybe because he reminded me of my dad. My mom and Aunt Lila had fallen in love with the same kind of man.

"Please. He was my son. Just tell me."

His expression cracked, revealing all the pain hiding just under the surface. That pain connected us, and my words flooded out.

"It was a few months after he died. Nothing was getting any better—the guilt, the way I missed him, the way I couldn't sleep, the constant ache in my chest. Ben was more than my boyfriend. He was my best friend. Before I destroyed his trust, he loved me. He made everything bearable."

Uncle Al stood ramrod straight, not moving.

"Without him, it felt like I was suffocating, and I just wanted it all to end. I came here to the beach to join him out there." I stared at the dark, rolling waves, and Uncle Al flinched. "But before I could, Ben appeared. He was as real as you are. He held me and told me that he still loved me, that he'd forgiven me."

Uncle Al pulled in a deep, shuddering breath, like he was in physical pain. "This is my fault."

"No. I was the one who lied to Ben."

"And I killed him!" The words burst out of him. They flew through the silence of the night like a flock of hungry, squawking gulls.

I shook my head. My eyes burned, and I shook my head again.

"It's true." Uncle Al's shoulders curled over. He held his sides like he'd been running for years. "You hurt Ben's feelings, but I'm personally responsible for his death. He was on my boat. I should have secured that equipment myself. It was a dangerous job, and Ben was still a kid, my kid. Worse yet, he was distracted, and I knew it." His voice was so sharp, so full of regret that it hurt to even listen. He looked up at the night sky, where the stars were lost behind the clouds that clung to my life. "If I'd just switched places with him, no one would have been hurt. My son would still be sleeping in his bed at night, and Lila's heart wouldn't be filled with anger and pain."

He stepped closer and gripped my shoulders. "If you'd suc-ceeded that night in ending things, that would have been on me, too. Ever since Ben's death, I saw the weight of your guilt. I understood it, because I share it. I should have said something to Lila when she shut you out, but I didn't, because I was trying to protect her. She needed someone to blame, and it was easier if it was you. She doesn't have to see you every day. But if she directed her anger where it truly belonged—at me, at the person she lies next to every night—I figured there was no way our marriage could survive. I thought her feelings toward you would soften, but I was so wrong. You're just a kid, and you and Ben loved each other. Even more than that, you were like a daughter to me. Instead of trying to protect you, I threw you on the track and watched the train race right for you."

Tears streaked down my cheeks. At some point during Uncle Al's speech, I'd stopped trying to blink them away.

"I'm sorry. I'm so sorry." These words were gruff and so thick with emotion, I almost missed them, losing them to the wind and the waves. I gripped his hands, and he pulled me against his chest. It felt like being in Ben's arms again; it felt safe and secure.

After a moment, we pulled apart, an awkward silence descending around us, because despite his confession, I still didn't know. I looked up at him, afraid of the answer, but knowing I'd ask anyway. "Do you believe me . . . about Ben? Do you think I'm imagining all this?"

He said nothing, staring out at the ocean.

"It's okay if you don't believe me." I dug my foot into the sand. "I'm not going to do anything stupid."

He chuckled, but it was a low, serious sound. "God, I wish I had an answer. Most people only trust in what they can see, but we mariners are a superstitious lot, and I've spent most of my life on the ocean." He jammed his hand through his hair. "Here's what I do know: You're still a kid. You have your whole life in front of you. You're supposed to be out there exploring and discovering and pushing the limits. You can't do that if you're spending all your time on this beach living in the past. Even if you are somehow seeing Ben, he's gone. He died. I watched the ocean take him. So, the only thing we can do now is try to live without him. I know it's hard. I struggle every day. Parents are not supposed to outlive their kids."

I swallowed past the lump in my throat. His words made sense. They did. But it didn't explain why Ben and I were special.

The wind gusted, and he glanced around the deserted beach. "Is Ben here now?"

"No."

"Are you expecting him to come?"

I squeezed my hands into fists and hid them behind my back. "We had a fight. I don't know if he'll come back."

Uncle Al took this in, nodding slowly. "But you're planning on waiting here for him?"

"Yeah."

"Then if you don't mind, I'll wait with you."

I suspected my response didn't matter. Uncle Al wouldn't leave me alone until my parents arrived and he knew I was okay. So, we sat together on the sand. I hugged my knees, shivering in the night air. "How can you still go out on the ocean every day?"

Uncle Al stretched his legs out, picking up a small piece of driftwood. "Why wouldn't I?"

I rested my chin on my knees. "I feel like the ocean betrayed me. I spent so much of my life on it. I thought I could trust it."

"Aw, Mer, it doesn't work like that. The ocean has always been a fickle creature. You can love her, you can hate her, but you always have to respect her. She holds all the power. On the day of Ben's accident, I was careless. I forgot, but it's still my life and my livelihood."

I stared at the surf and thought about his words. Maybe the answers were there in the waves if I just let them in.

We sat in silence for a while. Eventually, two sets of head-lights illuminated the beach. Vehicle doors opened and slammed shut, and I tensed.

"They love you." Uncle Al awkwardly patted my shoulder. "They only want to help."

"They won't believe me."

He shrugged one shoulder. "Maybe. Maybe not. I only know that Ben would hate to come between you and your family. He loved them, too."

"Mer!" Mom's voice reached us, tinged with panic.

"Over here," Uncle Al called out.

Mom appeared in front of me, kneeling in the sand, hugging me. "Meredith." Her hands shook when she touched my cheek. "We were so worried."

Dad and Rachel arrived. Rachel fell to her knees next to me, and Dad exchanged handshakes with Uncle Al.

A few feet away, Wyatt stood on the sand, his hands jammed in his pockets. Our gazes met. Something passed between us, something intense that I didn't want to feel. Not here, not while I was still searching for Ben, not when I needed to convince my family he was real. So I looked away. I pulled free from my mom and climbed to my feet. "I'm fine."

Mom followed me and gripped my arms. "No, you're not. We know what you've been doing here, and it's not okay. It's serious. Honey, you need help again."

And there it was—their total inability to even consider that Ben might be real. "I knew you'd react this way. Why do you think I kept it from you?"

"Mer." Mom shook me. "Ben's gone. We loved him and we miss him, too, but he died. I know what you think you saw on this beach, but it wasn't Ben. You created him to deal with the grief, and we should have seen this earlier. We should have gotten you the help you needed."

Bitterness filled my mouth. As usual, she didn't even try to listen to me. "You don't understand."

I pulled free and strode toward the ocean, but Wyatt blocked my path. "Then explain it to me. I'll listen. I promise."

Mom stiffened. She probably didn't like Wyatt's interference in a family matter.

"Mer?" Wyatt's voice tugged my attention back.

I straightened and met his gaze. I saw the tension around his mouth, the stiffness in his shoulders, and the concern in his eyes. I knew he just wanted to help. The fact that he drove all this way proved he cared, that our connection was real, but he shouldn't be here. "I know what you're thinking—that I'm depressed and hallucinating Ben—but it's not true. He comes here because we need each other."

Wyatt blew out a breath. "The night we met—was he here then?"

I nodded.

He scanned the beach, his gaze coming back to me. "But I didn't see him."

"He'd just left."

"To go where?"

My chin dropped. "I don't know. We don't have all the answers. I just know that he comes here as the sun goes down and stays for a few hours. Then he gets pulled away."

"So where is he now?"

Frustration curled inside me. "I told him about you and me." I lowered my voice. "Now he's angry. I ruined things again."

"Again?" He raised an eyebrow, waiting for answers I didn't want to give.

"Yeah. It's not something I'm proud of, but I hurt him once before. I lied to him about something really important."

"The abortion?" My gaze snapped up, and Wyatt frowned. "Rachel told me." My lips pressed together, a low buzz in my ears. When did Rachel find out? But Wyatt was still talking, and I forced my attention back to his words. "I can't know exactly how you feel, but I can try. You felt guilty for hurting Ben, and then he died before you could make things right. Maybe Ben's presence was your mind's way of giving him a chance to forgive you."

"No!" I shook my head and crossed my arms, afraid of the tiny insidious whispers inside me: *Maybe they're right. Maybe he's not real.* "The night we met, right before you showed up, Ben and I sat together on the blanket and talked. He hugged me, kissed me, joked with me. Do you really think I was sitting here the whole time by myself, imagining Ben was here? That doesn't make sense." I swung around to stare at my family. "Maybe there are things in this universe we can't explain. Maybe our connection was so strong, it could last even after death. Did you ever think of that?"

Mom and Dad looked heartbroken. Dad had his arm around her shoulders. Mom leaned into his waist, but I couldn't tell who was holding up whom. Dad was my pillar, and he always seemed so strong, but now his face was pale under his beard, and he frowned at me, disbelief in his eyes. It was worse than the look on his face when he'd found out I was pregnant. My gaze flicked to Rachel. She hugged herself, the wind pulling at her satin dress and messing her hair. She shook her head and sniffed. Rachel always took my side, but not now. None of them believed me.

"Mer?" Wyatt called out and I swung back to him. "What if I can prove he's not real?"

"That's impossible." My eyes narrowed. The tiny doubts in my head grew louder, but I ignored them. I couldn't let any of them shake my faith, not even Wyatt, but the question still slipped from my lips. "How?"

"I delivered that note to Ben, right?"

I nodded.

"Did he get it?"

"Yeah." He'd told me that he'd gotten it.

Wyatt reached for my hand and used his phone as a flashlight. He strode across the beach, taking me with him. In the dark, he searched the sand and the grass but came up with nothing.

"See." I was right. I pushed my doubts aside and remembered the feel of Ben's strong arms around me, the way I'd thrown myself at him, and he'd caught me and held me and made everything bearable. *He's real.* "You can't find it, because Ben got it."

Wyatt frowned and tugged me farther down the beach. He walked right to a little nook at the base of our dune and released my hand. I froze. A bag fluttered in the wind, still weighed down on one corner with a rock. *No.* Wyatt plucked it from the sand and held it up to the light. *No.* The blood rushed from my head. The plastic bag was covered in sand, but the paper I'd folded neatly and placed inside was still there.

"Ben got that note," I whispered. "He told me he did." I tried to remember our exact conversation, but it blurred in my mind. I clenched my jaw, trying to force the memory to sharpen, but the voice inside my head wouldn't shut up. *Ben's dead. He can't be real.*

No! I spun away from Wyatt and that damn note and ran to the ocean. "Ben!" Cold water frothed around my feet, soaking through my sneakers. Hot tears burned my eyes. The pull of the waves terrified me, but the thought of never seeing Ben again scared me even more. "I need you. I'm sorry. Please. *Please.*" *Don't do this. Come back. Please be real.*

Wind buffeted my body. I waded farther out. Cold water seeped into the bottom of my jeans, and I couldn't stop shaking.

"Mer!"

I looked over my shoulder. Wyatt ran toward me, with my dad close behind. Wyatt skidded into the waves, fear on his face. It took me a second to realize that he wasn't afraid of the ocean; he was afraid for me.

Water soaked his jeans and sneakers, but he kept coming. "Do you remember the night I found you on the side of the road?"

A wave pulled at me, trying to knock me down. I stared out at the ocean. Was Ben still out there, lost? That wasn't right. He'd made fun of my harmonica playing.

Wyatt's voice cut through the night, low and determined. "Mer, look at me."

I dragged my gaze back to him.

"Remember that night. You said you felt like you were drowning, and I promised I wouldn't let you." He reached out his hand, his expression so intense it made my chest hurt. "I'm going to keep that promise, but I need you to trust me. Just take my hand."

Ben isn't real? The waves roared and the current tugged at me. The cold numbed my toes. I stumbled farther out and shook my head. "He wouldn't just leave me," I whispered. Our very last words couldn't be angry ones. It was history repeating itself, like some cruel time loop—me betraying him and then losing him.

"He didn't have a choice, Mer. He didn't plan to die. But I'm not leaving. Look around at all the people you still have. We all care about you. We all . . . love you. None of us are leaving."

I rubbed at my eyes with the heels of my hands. None of this was right. *Wyatt. Ben. What was real?*

"Mer?" Suddenly Wyatt was right in front of me. I looked up at his flushed cheeks and glittering eyes, and a small sob escaped from my lips. *Wyatt was real.* He wrapped his arms around me, and I collapsed against him, hanging on as tight as I could. "*Shh.* It's going to be okay, Mer. I promise. We'll figure this out."

I desperately wanted to believe him. *Don't let me drown. Save me.* I pressed my face against his warm neck like I had at the dance. A tired, broken feeling threatened to consume me. I recognized it from back when Ben first died. But Wyatt's arms around me felt real, and I clung to that. His cheek brushed my hair, and his breath felt warm against my temple, so different from the cold water soaking my jeans.

"Am *I* real?" I whispered, tears clogging my throat.

He held me tighter.

Dad appeared next to us. "Come on, sweetheart. We need to go home. You're shaking."

I lifted my head, and Wyatt slowly released me. Dad swung me up into his arms like I was still his little girl. I should have been embarrassed, but all I felt was numbing tiredness. I hid my face against his shoulder, his beard scratching at my cheek, and avoided looking at Uncle Al or my mom or even Rachel. Dad set me down next to the car, and I crawled in the back. Rachel climbed in with me.

I didn't want to face it—the pain of losing Ben all over again. But the voice in my head was screaming now, blocking out everything else. I scrubbed at my forehead with my fists, trying to make it stop. But it just kept yelling: *Ben never came back. I imagined him. I'm hallucinating my dead ex-boyfriend.*

I heard Wyatt asking my dad before the door slammed shut: "What happens now?"

Yeah. What the hell happened to me now?

Rachel wrapped her arms around me. "It's going to be okay," she promised. "You're going to be okay."

But I didn't believe her, just like I hadn't believed Wyatt.

How could any of this possibly be okay?

Chapter Twenty-Three

My eyes snapped open. I lay in my bed and my heart thundered. It was night. Cold wind whipped through my open window, swirling my curtains and messing with the papers on my desk. A smattering of rain hit the glass.

Ben.

Everything came back to me in a hot rush. I'd let Wyatt convince me he wasn't real. My parents thought I was hallucinating. In the morning, they were taking me to a shrink. Who knows? Maybe they'd have me committed.

But it couldn't have been in my head because I remembered exactly how it felt when I curled against Ben's chest and stared up at the stars. We'd argued about windsurfing, and he'd held me in the rain. God, we'd even played beach bowling. I did not imagine all of that, and without the scared and disappointed looks from Wyatt, Rachel, and my parents to confuse me, it was easier to think and remember.

The note didn't mean anything. Ben could have read it and put it back. My memories were proof enough. I could go through each night I'd spent with Ben and recall everything we'd done and said.

Ben is real.

It was the only explanation that truly fit. He had to be, which also meant something else. He'd chosen to stay away when I needed him the most. He'd been so upset by a kiss that he'd refused to show up, even if his absence meant my sanity would be questioned.

I yanked back the covers and slid from my bed. In the dark, I pulled on sweatpants and my warmest sweater. I crept downstairs. Dad lay asleep on the sofa. He was clearly standing watch, not trusting that I wouldn't do anything stupid. But confronting Ben and proving what I knew in my heart was the opposite of stupid. For the first time in a long time, I knew exactly what I needed to do. I didn't feel fragile and afraid; I felt strong and determined.

I cracked open the door and slipped outside. Wind tugged at my hair. I lifted my face to the rain and let it wash away any lingering doubts.

My parents had probably hidden the keys to Sally, but I didn't need her this time. I pivoted in the driveway and jogged in the direction of the windsurf shop, my breath coming out in small puffs of mist between the raindrops. The glow from the security lights illuminated our motorboat where it sat rocking against the dock. I jumped in and lowered the motor, my knees shaking. When I had everything ready, I untied the painter and started the engine. I tried not to think about the rippling black surface and everything the ocean was hiding beneath it. The boat sprang forward, and I guided the bow toward the southern tip of the island.

Ben wouldn't come to me, so I'd go to him. I'd search in the one place I'd been too scared to look: the ocean. This time, I wouldn't let history repeat itself, not when it was within my power to change it. Last time, Ben had left me, and the unspoken words between us had suffocated me. I'd almost drowned in them. I wiped my face with the sleeve of my sweater. This time, I'd force Ben to hear me out. Maybe he couldn't forgive me for kissing Wyatt, but he didn't get to leave without listening to what I had to say.

The boat hit deeper water, and I opened the throttle, attacking the waves head-on. The wind gusted and the water grew choppier. It would be worse when I reached open ocean. Salt spray covered me, mingling with the rain, seeping through my sweater, and coating my hair. I licked the salt from my lips and shivered. Uncle Al told me to always respect the ocean, but maybe he was wrong. The ocean had taken Ben from me, and I'd let myself be cowered by it.

It was time to challenge it.

The wind picked up, whipping past me. The motor strained under each oncoming wave. Water sloshed in the bottom of the boat, but I kept going, keeping the light from the shore at my back. I didn't know exactly where the accident had happened, but I had a general idea.

I should have been scared—plowing into the ocean, alone in a small boat on a rainy night—but instead I felt like I was finally doing what I was supposed to do, like I was coming home.

My confidence lasted right until the wave appeared directly in my path. A small wall of water surged up from the ocean. It slammed into the boat and washed me over the side. One moment, I was in control of everything and the next I was in the water, struggling to the surface, coughing up the ocean and fighting the cold shock. Salt burned my throat and my eyes.

I searched for the boat, just catching a glimpse of it; it was overturned and drifting away. I needed to reach it. I crawled through the waves, my wet clothes dragging me down, but the boat drifted faster than I could swim.

"No—" Salt water filled my mouth, and I gagged, coughing it up. I treaded water and looked for the lights from the island. They were visible, but barely. How the hell had I gotten so far out so quickly?

"Ben!"

I swallowed back panic and twisted in the water. *"Ben!"* He had to come. He couldn't desert me now. I was out here because of him, because he'd refused to come to the beach.

For the next long minutes, I yelled for him, swimming in the direction of shore. I fought against the currents and the wind, but doubt wormed its way inside with the cold. The voice whispered again: *Ben died and never came back.* If he wasn't real, I was in real trouble. Was this the true source of the bad feeling that had haunted me for days? Rachel's worst fears were coming true, but I didn't want this to be the end. I didn't want to die.

My strength, like my hope, was slipping away. "Ben," I screamed.

"Mer!"

I spun around.

Ben treaded water a few feet away and relief flooded through me. I reached for him, still worried I might be imagining him. But even though he was obscured by the dark and the rain, my hands found his solid form. *Ben is real.* Why had I ever doubted him? "Ben, thank God."

"Mer." Our fingers linked. "Why are you here?"

I clung to him. "To find you. I looked for you on the beach. My family thought I made you up. Why didn't you come? I know you're angry, but I needed you!" I yelled above the wind.

Ben's dark hair stuck to his scalp, rain dripping down his face, but he didn't struggle to stay above the waves like I did. "I'm sorry."

I frowned and gripped his shoulder, my soaked clothes

encasing my limbs like cement. "For staying away?" *Damn*. It was too cold. "I hurt you when I kissed Wyatt. I shouldn't have, but the truth is . . . I'm being torn apart—" A wave hit my face, and I gasped, sucking in water. Coughing, I struggled to catch my breath. God, I was getting tired, but I needed to say this. "I love you, but I feel something for Wyatt. I don't know how. You've always filled every part of me. So how could there be room left for Wyatt?" I lifted my chin and dug my fingers into him. I had to finish this. My heart was being pulled in two, and Ben deserved the truth. "I don't know how to let you go. It hurts too much."

"But you already made your choice."

I swiped at the wet hair in my eyes. My legs churned below the surface, but I was slowly sinking, losing energy. "When I kissed Wyatt? It was once!" I yelled. I found his hand again and squeezed his fingers. "It doesn't mean I'm ready to say goodbye."

Ben gave me a small, sad smile. "Of course it doesn't, because the kiss never happened. It wasn't real."

What? A wave hit us and dragged me under. I thrashed, caught in the ocean's pull. Fighting panic and exhaustion, I clawed my way to the surface. My eyes and throat burned, the salt water mingling with my tears. "Ben?" I panted, but I was alone. "Ben!"

His dark head popped up a few feet away. "Over here."

"Don't leave . . . me," I gulped out, grabbing his arm. "I'm scared."

He shook his head, the droplets on his face a mixture of rain and ocean. Why did he look so calm? "That's because you're supposed to be scared, baby. You've gotten yourself into one hell of a situation."

"Why are you saying this?" My teeth chattered, the cold working its way deep into my core. "I came . . . out here . . . for you."

"I know you did. You cut your hair off, and you came to the beach because you couldn't handle the regret and the sadness anymore. You wanted it all to end." His cold fingers trailed down my cheek. "I don't blame you, Mer, but you left it all behind. You never thought about Rachel or your parents or the life you could have had."

"No." I sank down a little, my legs slowing under the surface. "I came to find you . . . to prove you're real . . . to explain about Wyatt."

He frowned, his forehead creasing. "But you can't prove I'm real because you were never seeing me. You couldn't, because I died."

My legs faltered, the cold winning the fight. "No. You're here now." I gripped his fingers, my jaw locking, my words slurring. "How can I touch you . . . if you're not real?"

He pulled me close, so close I could make out every familiar angle and line of his face. He leaned down. His lips brushed my cheek. "Because none of this is real," he whispered. "It never was."

"What—" A wave crashed over me, driving me under. I gasped in cold water, and it burned on its way down.

No. I was drowning. And it felt familiar. Like I'd already been here, under the waves . . .

I dropped the rattle on the beach and stepped into the surf. The ocean was cold, but maybe it was just the numbness in my body. I kept stumbling forward. My fingers dragged through the waves. I thought about all the other times I'd run into the ocean—warm, sunny days when the waves had made me happy. But I'd never feel that way again.

The ocean had stolen Ben. It had stolen all the goodness from my life and left me with nothing but this numbing darkness.

Water rushed past my waist. The waves slowed my progress, yanking at my limbs, trying to knock me over, but I held my ground. I was determined, because if I kept walking, the pain and the guilt would end. If I kept going, I'd be wherever Ben was.

The ocean seeped through my clothes. My heart raced, but my breathing slowed. The water reached my chest.

Someone called to me. A voice. Ben?

I took a final look at the stars. "I'm here," I whispered. "I'm coming." I pulled in a deep breath and dove deep under the waves.

It was dark and cold here. Ben was close. I could feel him. I just needed to open my mouth and breathe in the ocean.

So, I opened my mouth . . .

Under the waves, I found him. His body hung lifeless, his limbs pulled by the currents. His face was deathly white against the blackness of the ocean, his floating hair a dark wreath around his head.

No.

But then his eyes snapped open, and he swam toward me. His pale fingers tangled with mine, like wet seaweed. He pulled me to the surface.

I gasped, my lungs struggling to gulp in air and cough out water at the same time. My nose burned and my throat ached. "Save me," I cried, clinging to him. "I can't hang on . . . much longer."

He nodded, his expression too peaceful, his voice too soft. "It's because you're tired of fighting now. Your brain is accepting what your body already knows."

I shook my head, choking back sobs. "I . . . don't understand." Hysteria fought its way to the surface. "Help me."

Ben swept the hair back from my face and tapped my temple. "It's all in here, Mer. You just have to remember. You cut off all your hair. You came to the beach to end it all."

"Months ago. You stopped me . . . forgave me."

"No, I didn't."

I couldn't control the sobbing or the shaking. It took over my body. I didn't want to die. The fear tasted metallic in my mouth, because I remembered walking in the water now. I remembered diving deep, letting the ocean in. But Ben had stopped me. *Hadn't he?*

"I couldn't stop you, because I was never there. You walked into the ocean, and you never came out."

"No." That was months ago, but that memory of walking into

the ocean, of sucking in the cold water, suddenly felt too fresh, too immediate.

He touched my face, his hand as icy as the water. "It's only been minutes," he said, like he could read my thoughts. "Time only matters to the living."

"No," I said, forcing the word past my chattering teeth. "It's real . . . Wyatt . . . my life."

"This was the life you could have had if you hadn't ended yours, a fantasy in the final seconds between life and death. But it couldn't last. You were always going to end up back here—drowning in the ocean. Some part of your mind accepted the inevitability of this. It brought you back here."

"No." My muscles seized. I was tired, my limbs heavy and my body shutting down. "You're wrong."

"Stop fighting it, Mer." He looked so sad—but not sad for him or for us. He looked sad for me, and then I knew.

The last months flashed through my mind—the constant cold and rain, my fear of the ocean, the deserted town streets, the fact that nothing seemed quite right.

Ben died. He drowned in the ocean, and his body was never found. I recalled every moment we'd spent together on the beach—a perfect collage of beautiful memories—but I couldn't have held him, touched his hand, or kissed him. He didn't exist anymore in the land of the living. Neither did I.

"You've been fighting for so long, but it's time to let go," Ben said over the roar of the waves and the rain. "Let go of the guilt and the sadness. I love you. I just want you to find peace."

My breathing grew shallow, the cold deadening my limbs, my chest, my heart. But then I pictured them—my dad, Rachel, my mom. I couldn't leave them alone. I couldn't break their hearts like this. A spark of defiance flashed through me. *Fight.* I had to see them again. It wasn't over yet. *Fight.*

I twisted toward shore. Ben wouldn't save me, so I'd save myself. This wasn't the end. I couldn't give up. My limbs felt weighted down with bricks, but I kicked and stroked, gasping for air.

"Mer, what are you doing?" Ben kept pace with me.

"Saving myself." I turned away from his grim expression and focused on the shore, but it wouldn't get any closer. I swam until my muscles were on fire, until they seized and refused to work anymore. "No!" I gasped into the night. *I don't want this anymore.* I reached for Ben, yanking on his arm, my fingers clawing at him. "If you love me . . . even a little . . . help me."

"Ah, Mer." His dark eyes glistened with unshed tears. "I loved you until the very end. Deep down, you know that. Deep down, you know I would have forgiven you if I'd just had a little more time, but I can't help you now." He caught both my hands. "This is the choice you made."

The choice I made.

I looked down through the dark nothingness below. This is why I felt betrayed by the ocean, why I couldn't feel joy in it anymore. Because it had taken me like it took Ben. This was my real fear—that I'd be lost down there with him, that no one would ever find me. But unlike Ben, I couldn't blame this on anyone else. I could only blame it on me. I'd chosen this.

It didn't matter that it wasn't what I wanted anymore. I wanted to live, even if it meant finally saying goodbye to Ben. I wanted to see my family. I wanted a chance to live my future, even if it wasn't the one I'd dreamed of sharing with Ben, even if it was uncertain and a little scary.

But it wasn't my choice now. I'd done something I couldn't take back. I looked up at Ben, lifting my face to the rain. The shaking suddenly stopped. My muscles relaxed. "Don't leave me."

He squeezed my hands and pulled me close. "I'll always be with you. Don't you remember—I promised to always like you best."

"I'm afraid," I whispered, wrapping my arms around his neck. "I'm not ready."

Our foreheads touched. "You'll never be ready, but you're out of time now."

No.

His cold lips covered mine.

I inhaled his salty taste. His kiss filled my lungs with icy water, but somehow I wasn't afraid now. Instead, peace flowed through me.

I let go.

My body floated under the waves, carried by the current, but I didn't care. Because I no longer needed it.

Chapter
Twenty-Four

Chapter Twenty-Five

"Come on."

Cold.

"Come on. Breathe."

So cold. Leave me alone.

"What did you say?"

Nothing. I said nothing. I am nothing.

Chapter Twenty-Six

"Mer?"

Light. Pain in my throat. Can't swallow.

"Mer? Open your eyes, sweetie."

No. Too much work. Not now. Leave me alone.

Darkness.

Why won't she wake up?"

Too much noise.

"She will, Mr. and Mrs. Hall. I know this is hard on you both, but you need to be patient. Your daughter came as close to drowning as you possibly can and still come back. Just hang on to that."

Hands squeezing mine. Kisses on cheek. The ocean. The cold. The vast emptiness. I wasn't alive. Ben died, and I died with him.

Chapter Twenty-Eight

I cracked open my eyes, even that small movement making my head pound, and licked my dry lips. I tried to swallow but couldn't. Too dry.

My hand flailed, or I thought it did. Maybe it only moved an inch.

"Meredith." A face leaned over me—a stranger with a friendly smile and red hair pulled back in a bun. Something tugged my eyelids further open. Bright light flashed in them. I moaned at an incessant beeping that wouldn't stop. *Too loud.*

"It's okay, sweetie. You're safe. You're in the hospital."

I tried to swallow, but my throat refused to cooperate.

The face left and reappeared, offering a straw. "I'm going to sit you up a bit so you can take a sip."

Something whirred and my body shifted. The straw landed between my lips, and I sucked in cold water. It eased past my dry throat, and I almost cried because it felt so good.

"That's enough for now." The straw disappeared, and the face was back. "Just try to rest. I'm going to tell everyone you're awake."

The face started to leave, but I grabbed her arm.

"What is it? Do you need something? Are you in pain?"

My mouth struggled to form the words. "Am I dead?"

She frowned and leaned closer. I could smell the mint mouthwash on her breath. "You are very much alive, and you're going to stay that way."

"How do I know?" My gaze darted around the room. It looked real, but it had looked real once before. Panic swelled in my chest.

"Know what?"

"That it's real. That I'm not dead. That I'm not dreaming," I rasped. I still remembered slipping below the surface, letting go, Ben's lips on mine.

She grasped my hand in hers. "I can't prove it. I can only tell you that it is. Every day you'll feel more and more like it is, okay, honey?" Tears slipped down my cheeks, and she wiped them away. "You are going to be okay."

I pulled in a shaky breath. She didn't have any proof. I didn't feel okay, but I believed her anyway, because more than anything, I wanted it to be true.

"Mer?"

I opened my eyes. Sunlight streamed into the room. Mom and Dad leaned over me. Rachel stood a few feet away. They all shared the same expression: a combination of weariness, hope, and concern. I'd done this to them. Guilt surged inside me, the emotion that seemed to occupy most of my heart since Ben died. I lowered my head.

Mom stroked my hair, and I raised my eyes to hers. Above the dark circles marring her pale skin, they glistened with tears. Pain was etched in the tightness around her mouth. "I'm so sorry. We should have known. We should have been there." Her hand jerked back, and she pressed it against her chest.

She looked so uncertain, so unlike my mom, but it wasn't her fault. She hadn't done this to me. I'd chosen this for myself.

Dad leaned in to kiss my forehead, touching me gently, like I was made of glass. I remembered feeling the same way the first time I held Rachel. The truth was that Ben's death had turned me into a brittle person, ready to shatter at the slightest touch, but did everything I'd just experienced change that? I felt stronger, but was that also an illusion?

"We love you so much." Dad's breath caught. The hand that touched my shoulder shook a little. "We need you here with us. Nothing would ever be the same without you."

But I'd chosen to keep them out. I'd let the numbing darkness take over because I didn't know how to start living again. I felt it even now, hovering over me, ready to take up residence again if I let it in. It was strange—I'd walked into the ocean only . . . hours ago, but it felt like a lifetime had passed. In the end, I wanted to live and have a second chance, but now that I was here, the pain still lingered. The work of learning to live again remained.

Rachel stood with her arms wrapped around her belly, her head lowered.

"Rachel?" My throat still hurt.

She looked up at me. Her eyes were red and puffy, and I knew she'd been crying. She was too young to deal with all of this. I'd forced her to grow up too quickly.

"I'm sorry." My voice cracked. "I shouldn't have . . . I didn't know how . . ."

She didn't move, and I understood the pain I'd caused her. It was time now for me to take the first steps in rebuilding the things I'd broken. I shifted over in the hospital bed and lifted the edge of my blanket.

"I promise, Rachel. I won't leave again."

Her stiff expression melted, and she stumbled closer, collapsing on the bed. I pulled her into my arms and held her while she sobbed. I smoothed the hair from her face and kissed her forehead. "Shhh. It's okay. I'm not going anywhere. You don't need to be scared for me anymore."

She pressed her face against my chest, her tears wetting my hospital gown. Mom and Dad leaned closer, and we were suddenly in a big family hug.

I squeezed my eyes shut. I could do this. I'd been given a second chance—not with Ben, but with my life, with my family. I could fix things. I could make us whole again.

After the hug ended, an awkward silence descended. I watched my parents searching for the right things to say. Every choice had consequences. When I'd come back from the brink of death, I hadn't come back alone. Our new family dynamics included a giant elephant in the room, and it would be a long time before that elephant went away.

Rachel played with my hacked-off hair.

"It's bad, isn't it?"

She swallowed. "It's kind of badass."

"Rachel!" Mom said, but there was no anger in her tone. She looked more relieved to have something she could actually fix. "Don't worry, honey. We'll get it evened out. You still look beautiful."

I smoothed one hand down my scalp, trying to remember the exact feeling of desperation that had gripped me when I'd held the scissors, but now it felt like I was looking at that moment through frosted glass. I could vaguely make out the shape and size of it—big and dark and overwhelming—but the details were blurred. "I still don't understand what happened. I mean . . .

I know what I did." My fingers shook, and I clasped them together. "But how did I end up here?"

Dad's grip on my shoulder tightened. "It was kind of a miracle. There was someone else on the beach. He saw you . . ." His voice trailed off, and he cleared his throat. "He went in after you."

"He?"

"Yes," Mom said. "He's new to the island. He just moved here with his mom, and by some miracle, he was there on the beach at the same time."

I shivered. *Wyatt?* But Ben told me none of it was real.

"What's his name?" I held my breath, my fingers curled around the bedcover.

Mom's brow furrowed, questions in her eyes. "Wyatt. Wyatt Quinn."

In an instant, everything changed, and every moment I'd spent with Wyatt replayed in my mind. Our talks, our fights, our jokes, my rules, his persistence . . . our kiss.

I slowly released my breath.

Wyatt was real.

Five days later, I sat in my mom's car, staring out at a familiar house with faded wood siding. Uncle Al's pickup sat in the driveway. All the blinds were drawn, and the display of pumpkins Aunt Lila had set up on the large front deck was the only splash of color. A year ago, Ben and I had dressed as a pirate and his wench and handed out Halloween candies. I'd been the pirate, and Ben had been the wench.

"Are you sure you want to do this?" Mom asked.

I turned to her. Her fingers gripped the steering wheel, her face pale. I laid my hand on the armrest between our seats, and she released the wheel and tangled her fingers with mine. I didn't pull away even though it felt strange. I was working on this: letting her in. Maybe we'd never have the perfect mother-daughter relationship, but it could be better than it was. I'd been so sure I'd never meet her standards that I'd gone looking for her disappointment in every conversation. I'd found it, even when it wasn't there.

"Yeah. I should have done this earlier. I need to make things right . . . for you, too."

"Ah, honey, I don't care about me. I can live with the way things are. I just don't want to put you through anything else. It's so soon. Your doctor said not to rush things."

My doctor was the very nice psychiatrist I'd started to see in the hospital before they'd discharged me. She'd asked a lot of questions. I liked her, so I'd given a lot of answers. Honest ones. She must have been happy with them because she'd agreed to let me go home. But I'd be seeing her twice a week for the foreseeable future. I was okay with that. I felt like I'd changed, that the dark thoughts were under control, and the pain of Ben's death was finally manageable, but I never wanted to be back in that same spot again.

"I can do this, Mom. I need to, or I'll always feel like it's hanging over my head. I need to start facing things instead of burying them."

She nodded and I climbed out of the car, lifting my face to the autumn sun and welcoming its warmth on my skin. I pulled back my shoulders and climbed the steps to the front door. I'd spent so many hours in this house. Ben had lived his whole life here.

I knocked on the door and glanced back at Mom. She gave me a worried look. The door swung open, and I turned back to find Aunt Lila standing there. The welcoming smile that had started to take shape on her face died the second she focused on me.

"Meredith." Her gaze continued past me to where Mom sat in the car.

"Can I come in, please? I'd really like to talk to you and Uncle Al."

Her fingers tightened on the door, and for a second, I worried she'd slam it in my face. But then she gave a small nod and let it swing fully open. I looked back at my mom and shot her a quick smile. Then I walked into Ben's house, shutting the door behind me.

The house smelled faintly of fried fish, probably Uncle Al's latest catch. Uncle Al was already in the living room, sitting in his plaid recliner. In front of him, the television was on, but the sound was muted. Except for the new television, nothing in this living room had changed for as long as I could remember. An open book and a cup of tea sat on the pine coffee table next to the overstuffed sofa. Aunt Lila had obviously been sitting there with him, but instead of the coziness I remembered, there was something stiff and solemn about the atmosphere.

Uncle Al looked at my new extreme haircut. He popped in the foot of his recliner and turned off the television. "Mer. How are you? Are you okay?"

"You heard?"

He nodded. "We heard there was an accident at the beach, that you almost drowned."

I shifted my weight and pointed to one end of the sofa. "Can I sit for a moment?"

Uncle Al and Aunt Lila exchanged looks, and finally, she nodded.

I lowered myself into the cushion, remembering all the evenings Ben and I had curled up on the same sofa watching movies, me making fun of them and Ben laughing. Then, the house had smelled of popcorn and Ben. It had felt full and alive.

I rubbed my sweaty palms on my jeans and searched for tactful words to start the conversation, but couldn't find any. So I stuck to the truth. "I didn't almost drown by accident. It was deliberate." Aunt Lila froze. Uncle Al sat up straighter, but I didn't stop. I had to keep going, before I lost my nerve. "When Ben died, I thought it was my fault, because I hurt him. I know it doesn't make sense, but it felt like the universe was hurting me back by taking Ben away."

I glanced at Aunt Lila. Tears glistened in her eyes as she sat with her hands clasped together.

"Mom and Dad kept telling me it would get better with time, that I'd stop missing him so much, that I'd finally be able to sleep and eat and feel like myself again, but it didn't. It got worse. It was like a giant sucking hole in the middle of my chest, and it hurt so much that I just needed it to end—the pain, the regret, the guilt. So, I walked into the ocean. I wanted to be with Ben, even if it meant leaving everything and everyone else behind."

I stopped and took a breath. Uncle Al's head hung in his hands. Tears dripped off Aunt Lila's chin.

"By some miracle, I lived and I get a second chance. Look, I should have been honest with Ben about my decision to have an abortion, but I know now that his death was not my fault." I looked at Uncle Al, remembering our conversation on the beach. "It wasn't your fault, either. It was an accident. Ben wouldn't want this for us. If he'd lived, he would have forgiven me. I have to believe that, because Ben had the kindest, most generous heart of anyone I knew. He wouldn't want this for you, Aunt Lila."

She flinched, a small sob escaping.

"You blame me. I get it. You need somewhere to direct your anger, but anger and blame are dark, draining feelings when you hold on to them for too long. I can't make you forgive me, but we used to be family. You and my mom were best friends, like sisters. So I need to try to make it better. I need to do my part by saying I'm sorry that I lied to Ben. I am so sorry that I hurt him, but I am not responsible for him dying."

I paused, waiting for someone to fill the silence, but it remained. So I stood up.

I stared at the framed pictures of Ben on the walls: baby pictures taken at the local portrait studio; school pictures of him growing from a gap-toothed, grinning kid to an awkward, lanky middle schooler to a high school athlete with his handsome dark looks; team pictures; even a photo of him holding a ribbon for the only science fair he ever won. It was a tribute wall, but these posed pictures couldn't capture even half of the Ben I loved. That Ben filled a room with his warmth and spirit and his good heart. God, I missed him. I would always miss him, and that was okay. I could live with that, because I was still alive.

I'd almost reached the door when Uncle Al touched my arm. I swung around. His eyes were red, and he pulled me into his arms. I hugged him like I had that night on the beach. "It's not your fault," I whispered into his chest. "It's not your fault."

He squeezed me tighter and kissed the top of my forehead. "Thank you."

Behind him, Aunt Lila still sat on the sofa. Her shoulders sagged and she quietly cried. She wasn't ready to let go of her anger yet. I understood that, but I'd done my part. I'd no longer carry the responsibility of the split between her and Mom. Now, she'd shoulder it on her own.

The next day, I stood in front of the café in my running clothes. A black truck sat in the driveway. I'd started out running, but my stamina wasn't back yet, so I'd walked at least half of the distance. It was a perfect fall day—warm, but not too hot. The scattered clouds had gradually thickened, but even if it showered, I knew it wouldn't last long. Tonight, we'd planned a family bonfire on the beach under the stars.

Now, I glanced around, nervous anticipation tightening my stomach. The café wasn't open yet. So, how did I go about meeting these people?

I squatted down to adjust my shoelaces and debate my options.

"You're Meredith Hall, right? But everyone calls you Mer."

My head snapped up, and my eyes widened. Wyatt's mom stood a few feet away, holding a carved pumpkin and looking just like I'd known she would. How the heck did she know my name?

She chuckled, like she could read my mind. "It's the cropped hair. I figure there aren't too many teenage girls on this island with 'badass hair and amazing blue eyes,' as Wyatt put it."

"Oh." At a loss for words, I stood there with my mouth open.

"You must be looking for Wyatt. He's not much of an early riser, unless I boot his sorry ass out of the bunk. But I'm sure I can get him up, if he knows you're here."

Wow. Déjà vu.

She adjusted the pumpkin in her arms and stepped closer, sticking out one hand. "I'm Harley Wilson, by the way." We shook hands and then she grunted. "I'd better put this down before I drop it. It already looks like I carved it with a spoon and only one eye open, but I figure the kids will be too hyped up on sugar to care, right?"

I sprang forward. "Do you need help?"

"Nah, I've got it." She set it down with a group of other pumpkins next to the door. Then she turned back to me. "So what can I do for you today? Are you here to see Wyatt?"

My gaze drifted up to the second floor. "I heard what he did for me. I just wanted to come by and . . . thank him."

"Of course, sugar. Thank God he was there at the right time." Her hazel eyes met mine, and I saw the unspoken questions there. How much had Wyatt seen? How much did he know about why I almost drowned? "It was nothing short of a miracle."

Maybe it was a miracle or fate or maybe just the universe deciding that I deserved a second chance. In the end, it didn't matter. It only mattered that I still got to wake up tomorrow and find Rachel in my bed in her pink flannel pajamas talking my ear off. I still got to argue with my mom while she tried to control my life, and I still got long evenings of floating on my board on the sound with my dad.

I looked at the storefront. "So, this is your café. Does it have a name yet?"

She glanced at the front window, her hands on her hip. "Well, I'm not sure, but I've got a couple of ideas bouncing around."

"The Yellow Rose Café," I said under my breath.

"What?" Her head whipped around. "What did you say?"

"Um . . ." *Crap.* Why was she staring at me like that? "I was just thinking that the Yellow Rose Café would be a pretty name."

"Follow me." She marched toward the door and disappeared inside.

I followed, but on the other side of the doorway, I stopped short. It was like being in a time machine. The floors were the same wood I remembered, and the walls were painted with the same pastel shades, but there were no tables or chairs yet. The chalkboard wall behind the counter didn't exist.

Harley reached under the counter and pulled out a spiral ring binder. She flipped through the pages and stopped at one, then stuck the book under my nose. On the page, someone had doodled the words *Yellow Rose Café* with flowers all around. "I did that last night. I never even had time to share it with Wyatt yet. So how did you know?"

I pointed at the yellow walls and tried to calm my thumping heart. *How did I know?* "I saw those through the window, and it gave me the idea."

"Oh." She shot me a long look, like she was searching for something. "That's an amazing coincidence. It's like we were on the exact same wavelength." She shook herself. "Let me get

Wyatt for you."

I glanced around the half-finished café. It already felt like a place I wanted to hang out in. "Hey, before you go, I was wondering if you happened to need any employees when you get this place up and running—just for the winter months." I brushed the bangs from my eyes. They were going to take some getting used to. "During the summer, I work at my dad's shop."

She cocked her head to one side. "Well, I'm not sure. Do you have any experience as a barista?"

I paused. *Did I?* "Not really, and I'm pretty sure I'd be lousy at it anyway, but I'm a hard worker, and I can serve, handle the cash, and clear tables."

"Well, honey," she said, laughing, "that's quite the proposition. Tell you what, let me think about it. I'll let you know."

She turned again, presumably to get Wyatt, but I grabbed her arm.

"One more thing." I swallowed hard. *What was I doing?* "I know this is going to sound strange, but my near-death experience taught me something." I released her arm and stared down at my sneakers. "Keeping secrets from the people we love and blaming other people for the bad things that happen in our lives never solves anything." I lifted my head and met her gaze straight on. "Wyatt deserves to know the truth about his dad."

Her mouth fell open. Her cheeks flushed, and her gaze darted to the floor. "I—I don't understand," she stammered. "What are you talking about?"

Until that moment, I wasn't sure how I could possibly know these things. My time with Wyatt hadn't been real, but maybe my future with him could be. That possibility blossomed inside me, but along with that realization came another one. I'd be okay no matter what happened with Wyatt after today. I didn't need him to make me happy or whole. I could do that for myself, with the support of my family.

"Look, I nearly died, and somehow in all that, I saw your son. Maybe it's not true, but if it is, you need to tell him, because Wyatt feels abandoned by his dad. That hurt is worse than anything the bike accident did to him. You need to tell him before he finds out on his own."

Tears welled in her eyes, and she slowly nodded.

But I'd stopped watching her because Wyatt appeared through the door in a faded gray T-shirt and sweatpants. He looked exactly like I remembered—lean, with bronze hair curling around his neck and hazel eyes that made my knees shake a little.

I released the breath I'd been holding and smiled, a spark of excitement and anticipation burning low in my belly. He grinned back, but there was uncertainty in his expression. I tried not to read too much into that. The last time he'd seen me, I'd been mostly dead.

I bit my lip and reached into the pocket of my hoodie, pulling out two bags of Skittles. "I brought you these."

He stepped closer, his feet bare and his hair damp. He must have showered recently. He smelled amazing and real. I swallowed back a smile—he smelled like fresh laundry. He took the bags from me and frowned. "Is this an early Halloween gift, or are you thanking me for saving your life with Skittles?"

I shifted in my sneakers, staring at the faded Texas flag on his T-shirt. "The second one, but if that's too weird, I'll go with the first."

He laughed, a warm, cocky, infectious sound. "Are you kidding? That's the best 'thank you for saving my life' gift ever. I also love the haircut."

I reached for my hair. We'd stopped at the salon on the way home from the hospital to even it out. It was basically a pixie cut now. "It'll grow out in a couple of months."

"I like it, especially the purple streaks. They're new, right?"

I looked up at him and nodded. Butterflies took flight in my belly.

"Oh, I also have something for you. I found it on the beach after . . . you know . . ." He swallowed, and meeting his stare, I realized that he knew. He knew what I'd done, but he wanted to talk to me anyway. "Just wait here. I'll be right back."

"Yeah, sure."

Wyatt disappeared and Harley looked at me. "I haven't seen my son look that happy or excited about anything in a while."

I swallowed. "I was in a very dark place, but when Wyatt

saved me, he gave me a second chance. I intend to make the most of it, and I'm hoping Wyatt might be a part of it."

Harley hugged herself, her gaze intense and her expression questioning. "I've got to be honest, meeting you and hearing what you said to me earlier is freaking me out a little. I feel like I know you, and I don't know why." She opened her mouth and closed it, clearly struggling to find more words.

Fortunately, Wyatt reappeared. He looked at his mom. "Can you give us a minute?"

"Sure, honey." She squeezed her son's arm and slipped into the kitchen.

Wyatt stepped closer, holding up a baby giraffe. My heart surged. "I wasn't sure if it was yours or not. It's kind of dirty, but I kept it anyway."

"Yeah." I took it from him and pushed it in my pocket. I'd put it back in my closet, packed away with all my other memories of Ben and the life we could have had together. But right now, the only thing I could do was live this life, without him.

"Do you remember me?"

Wyatt's question made my head snap up. Wait. Did he somehow know? "What?"

"That night on the ferry . . . we met."

I frowned.

"We were both on the ferry to Hatteras. You looked really upset. I tried to talk to you, but you seemed really out of it."

His words jogged a memory—Wyatt and I standing together on the ferry at night—but was the memory real or just a part of the life I'd imagined? Heat filled my cheeks. "I was in a bad place. A few months ago, I lost someone I really loved, and I wasn't dealing with it very well. I don't remember much about that night."

"I'm sorry. That's got to be rough." Wyatt stuffed his hands in his pockets. "I knew something wasn't right, because after you drove off on your scooter, I couldn't get the look on your face out of my head. It sounds kind of stalkerish now, but I followed you."

I stiffened. My world had suddenly come full circle. "That's why you were there . . . to save me."

He stared at me, his eyes more green than brown. "I didn't know what you were planning. I called out to you. I was almost too late . . ." His voice cracked.

I reached for him but stopped myself just in time. We were still strangers, even though it felt like we were so much more. But the knowledge didn't make me sad. We had time now to start over, to discover each other again.

"You did everything right. You saved me."

He smiled—a small, tentative expression that promised more. "Yup. So I guess you owe me now."

I laughed, my heart racing a little. "I already paid you back in Skittles."

He cocked an eyebrow and looked over at the bags of candy he'd left on the counter. "So you did, but I'm thinking your life's worth a whole lot more than a few bags of candy, darlin', 'cause you're clearly sweeter than a whole candy store."

I sighed and shook my head. "Hey, Wyatt."

"Yeah?"

"You don't need to do that with me. You can be yourself, and I promise that I'll still find that Wyatt just as interesting."

His grin faded. *Damn.* I'd probably just overstepped and totally weirded him out. *Great. Nice work, Hall.*

For a long moment, he said nothing. Then he nodded, rubbing one hand through his damp hair and stepping closer. My palms tingled. "I know this is an odd question, Mer, but you don't happen to play the harmonica?"

My heart stuttered. "Why?"

He shook his head, frowning. "I don't know. For some reason, when I look at you, I think about bad harmonica playing."

I slowly reached into my back pocket and pulled out the instrument. "I bought it yesterday. I'm going to learn how to play."

His eyes widened. Neither of us spoke, but something passed between us, something real that defied logic or explanation. It warmed me all the way down to my toes. Finally, I cleared my throat and pulled my gaze away from his. Outside the window, the wind gusted and a smattering of rain hit the glass. *Right on time.*

Wyatt's gaze followed mine. "Looks like we're in for some rain."

"Yeah, you'll get used to it."

"Along with all the sand. So much sand . . . everywhere." He paused. "I could give you a ride home if you wanted."

My stomach somersaulted. Maybe I hadn't weirded him out. I chewed on the inside of my cheek, trying not to smile too much. "Yeah. I'd really like that."

His grin slowly returned, and he bounced once on his bare toes. "Awesome. Just wait right here."

"Hey, Wyatt."

He stopped halfway across the café and turned. "Yeah?"

"Just for future reference, I'd be really offended if you compared me to a horse."

One corner of his lips twitched, and he cocked his head to one side. "Any horse or a specific horse, 'cause I was thinking of you as more of a wild filly with a lot of spirit."

"Yeah . . . no."

His mouth clamped shut and he nodded. "Okay, then. No horse comparisons, for future reference."

I hugged myself. "Perfect."

"You're an odd one, Meredith Hall." Wyatt backed up, not taking his eyes off me. "But you have definitely piqued my curiosity. I'm looking forward to this 'future' you just mentioned."

It was my turn to grin, the expression feeling like a long-lost friend. "So am I."

Wyatt winked and disappeared through the doorway into his house.

I stayed and watched the rain running down the front

window. Tomorrow, I'd go back to school. I'd continue to heal and work on myself. I'd get the chance to know Wyatt. I'd be there for my sister when she needed me, and I'd help heal my family. When spring came, I'd windsurf with my dad.

I'd never forget Ben or stop loving him. He'd always be the boy who promised to like me best. He'd always be the first boy to love me, but I knew now.

He wouldn't be the last.

Author's Note

I've only been fortunate enough to visit the Outer Banks once, but I fell in love with these islands and their beaches. I knew they would make a great setting for a book, especially a love story where the characters were separated by a ferry ride. When using a real location for a novel, an author must decide between staying true to the details of that location or creating specifics that suit the requirements of the story. While I've spent many hours researching both Ocracoke Island and Hatteras Island, the names, characters, schools, businesses, places, events, locales, and incidents in this book are either fictional or used in a fictitious manner. Any resemblance to actual persons, living or dead, or actual events is purely coincidental (but I'd love to believe that Henry really does work the ferry between Ocracoke and Hatteras).

Acknowledgments

Let me tell you a secret. For many authors, writing acknowledgments is more intimidating than writing the novel. There are so many people to thank, and there's so little space to convey how much everyone's support and encouragement has meant.

First, I want to thank Page Street for sharing my vision for this book. From my first conversation with them, I knew I'd landed in the perfect place. Working with Ashley Hearn has been a dream. From the beginning, she's loved Mer, Ben, and Wyatt as much as I do. She's respected the story I wanted to tell, and she's helped to make it so much stronger. The whole Page Street team has created a wonderful new YA line, and I am so proud and happy to be a part of it.

I also want to thank Prospect Agency and my agents there

(first Carrie Pestritto and now Emily Sylvan Kim). The publishing industry can be tough, and it's wonderful knowing you have someone in your corner, someone who advocates for you and gives you that much-needed advice and support.

Though writing itself is a solitary endeavor, I've been so lucky to be surrounded by fellow authors, critique partners, and beta readers who understand how important it is to support and lift each other up. This includes all my writing friends at YARWA, OIRWA, and RWAC, and the whole Pitch Wars community. There are too many of you to mention by name, but I'd like to give a quick shout-out to the people who always respond to my "Ah, I need advice" messages: Shelly Alexander, Anne O'Brien Carelli, Beth Ellyn Summer, Rebekah Ganiere, Brenda Drake, Kacey Vanderkarr, Christine Webb, Moriah Chavis, Pintip Dunn, and Donna Alward. Double thanks to fellow authors Anne, Kacey, Christine, and Moriah, as well as Sarah Ribeiro for beta reading various versions of this book. Thanks also to my bestie, Sharon Andrews, my daughter, Liz, and my sister, Laurel Lively, for continuing to read all my messy drafts, and to my IRONMAN-conquering friend, Anita Jain, for answering all my fictional medical questions! Thanks also to Gail Johnson for the awesome new author photos.

The Sound of Drowning, like most of my books, was written during National Novel Writing Month. I am so grateful to the organizers of NaNoWriMo for creating a program that encourages writers of all experience levels and ages to explore and challenge their creative side. Special thanks to Nakhari Alberto, who participated in NaNoWriMo's Young Writers Program with me and gave me the idea for the baby rattle! Thank you also to all the YA book bloggers/vloggers out there who volunteer their time and share their passion for reading by reviewing books and helping get them in the hands of readers.

I also want to acknowledge my family for being my biggest fans and supporters. I couldn't do this without you! Mom and Dad, thank you for listening to all my long-winded publishing trials and for always having helpful advice. Love to Sunshine and her lunch ladies (you know who you are). Thank you for bringing fun and adventure to my life. You keep me from being too serious.

If you are reading this acknowledgment, I'm so grateful you took a chance on this book. I know I put you through an emotional roller coaster, but I really hope you loved the ride. If you still need help with processing all your feelings right now, feel free to reach out to me. I *love* hearing from readers!

And finally, thank you to Skittles and Twizzlers for your sheer awesomeness. If you are reading this and thinking *Huh?*, go back and read the book!

About the Author

After a decade of living in the sunny Caribbean with her pilot husband and three amazing kids, Katherine Fleet moved back to her hometown of St. John's, Newfoundland, the easternmost point in North America. She loves to read, write, travel, and embarrass her kids on social media. She is an active member of RWA and loves NaNoWriMo. *The Secret to Letting Go* (Entangled Teen, 2016) was her contemporary YA debut. You can connect with her at www.KatherineFleet.com.